THE GREEN KANGAROOS

JESSICA MCHUGH

PMMP

Perpetual Motion Machine Publishing
Cibolo, Texas

The Green Kangaroos
Copyright © Jessica McHugh 2014

All Rights Reserved

ISBN: 978-1-943720-42-2

Second Edition 2019

www.PerpetualPublishing.com

Cover Art by Lori Michelle

ALSO BY JESSICA MCHUGH

Rabbits in the Garden

PINS

The Darla Decker Diaries (Books 1-5)

The Train Derails in Boston

Home Birth

The Maiden Voyage & Other Departures

Nightly Owl, Fatal Raven

PRAISE FOR JESSICA MCHUGH'S
THE GREEN KANGAROOS

"I write junkie fiction. I read and watch junkie fiction. Call it a lifestyle choice. I honestly didn't think I'd discover anything new under the sun when it came to the genre. I was wrong. *Green Kangaroos* is the freshest, most wholly original work I've come across concerning the subject of addiction. Think *Requiem for a Dream* meets *Cabin in the Woods*, only funnier, fresher, and more harrowing. Potsticking makes krokodil seem like a good time. Jessica McHugh has crafted one mindfuck of a novel."

—Joe Clifford,
author of *Junkie Love* and *Lamentation*

"[A] sci-fi mind-melting experience of Philip K. Dick proportions."

—Sean Leonard, Horror News.net

"In *The Green Kangaroos*, Jessica McHugh gives us the bastard love-baby of William Burroughs and *The Matrix*, thankfully devoid of Keanu Reeves. Its needle-sickness-meets-dopesick *Blade Runner* world is horrifying. Even the likeable characters are shitbags, but they are so richly drawn and the story is so wonkily brilliant you just keep your hands and feet inside the car and enjoy the ride."

—John Boden, *Shock Totem Magazine*

TABLE OF CONTENTS

Introduction i

The Green Kangaroos 1

Bonus Short Story: "The Fix" 253

INTRODUCTION:

A VIVID AND VICIOUS SHADE OF GREEN

THE BEST WAY to read *The Green Kangaroos* is to know it will inject itself into your testicles. From the first sentence, this book grabs you, a powerful, short jab into your most sensitive areas, as if mutating your reproductive systems, the very part of you that creates life. What follows is an onslaught of visceral moments that pummel your senses and take you inside a dystopian world where a heroin-like substance is the preferred method of escape.

Just when your mind is blown, the story twists into something much more intense.

The Green Kangaroos is a complex tale with socio-economic messages, a vivid portrayal of a family in crisis, and behind all of that, the most powerful piece of 'junkie fiction' I have every read—and I've read a ton of junkie fiction. The writing here is unique, sharp and crisp. Incredible sentences that made me grin in admiration come one after another. The big picture is a fantastic piece of 'world-building'. A place where addicts sell their body parts for their daily fix, and the metaphors in this imaginary land only serve to make the story all too real. Transgressive, dystopian, horrific, yet also pulled from today's newspaper headlines of an opioid epidemic.

As happens with all great works, while reading I kept wondering how it would end, and *The Green Kangaroos* stuck the landing with a creative and ingenious '10'. I am thrilled this book is getting a second edition, a second cover, and comes with a short story added on. "The Fix" is a revisit to the Green Kangaroo universe and is a gift that I've been aching for. It would have been a shame if the world that McHugh created was not blessed with more fiction. It begs for backstories of every character who walks these pages.

I discovered *The Green Kangaroos* researching addiction-themed books with a horror content. *Addiction horror* has been my jam, and as I was putting together a collection of addiction-themed stories for an anthology, I read this with slacked jaw. Had I seen *Kangaroos* earlier, I might have canceled the whole anthology, for when I read this book, I realized everything I hoped to capture, in content and tone, was sitting right there before me.

As one who is recovering from addiction, this book resonates particularly powerful, clawing inside me. It was the phantom limb that was removed but I could still feel it in every chapter. The descriptions sung to the addiction still dormant inside me. Like a lawyer watching a court room drama, inaccuracies burn my eyes when I read about drug use, but this story rings true. McHugh takes the reader into the soul of an addict—how they think, their daily

INTRODUCTION

torments, their lies and manipulations, the visceral cravings that demand to be fed.

But it would be a mistake to think *Green Kangaroos* is just about addiction, and that its content only accessible and enjoyable by those who've had heroin coursing through their veins. The deep hurt, the desperation, and the tragic powerlessness of the addict's family, and the socio-economic messages of the dystopian land, are two things that resonate. A few more words about them both.

The title itself tells you this is a story about family, siblings, and what it is like to be *the one in the middle*. The concept of the green kangaroo was made famous by Judy Blume and the story of a middle child who feels emotionally squashed between his older brother and his younger sister. He doesn't seem to get much attention, until he lands a role in a school play as a *green kangaroo*. Well, McHugh certainly paints her main character, Perry, in the most vivid and vicious shades of green, and like any family unit, the insanity and despair revolves around how to handle their colorful family member.

I was the green member of my family, but by the grace of the old Gods and the new, I learned how to stay clean. I then went back to school to get a Masters in counseling, and since this time, I've worked for years in treatment centers. I've seen the look on family's faces who have been through wars with their loved one. They come in with battle scars, exhausted, lost, looking like the mother in *The Exorcist*, with a *you-don't-know-what-I've-been-through* look on their face. I don't know, but I feel the hurt, the despair, the desperation of living with a loved one committing suicide by degrees. Addicts certainly suffer, but in order to subsist and feed their sickness, they become grossly self-centered and masterful cons. As *Kangaroos* states, "when you live with an addict you learn to recognize the lies behind the theatrics," because they suck out your soul and sanity while you sleep.

Every addict puts their family through a war, and as in any war, there's always a 'last woman standing.' *Woman*, I say, because it usually is a woman, because addicts manipulate their nurturing nature.

Perry's sister, Nadine, is the last woman standing, and when she says, "I'm just trying to make sure you're happy. If you're happy, I'm happy," the molten core of the cliché-ridden codependency erupts from the page. Especially when Perry begs his sister, "stop trying to free me from a prison I love."

You can feel McHugh's empathy for these characters, no matter how insidious their actions. In that way, Nadine is who this story is about.

The family exists, to a degree, in a dystopian, virtual world that would make Philip K. Dick proud. The dark but incredibly vivid Patterson Park is unforgettable. It's a place where Neovision dominates the internet, where access to the web is no longer free, it is only for the elite to dominate and control, including places where it is blocked entirely. Nonstop broadcast of rehashed sitcoms, where scenes from *The Wire* are cut. The constant onslaught that makes the poor just as trapped in their universe as an addict trapped in the body of eternal cravings.

This is where *Kangaroos* becomes not just micro, but macro, where the rich feed off addicts who will do anything to find moments of joy.

INTRODUCTION

And to find that joy? All you have to do is sell your most precious body parts at the Kum Den Smokehouse where the dream is raw Liquid Atlys.

While this book may aim to strike you in the heart, it will certainly not miss your stomach.

Green Kangaroos is deliciously visceral, which it needs to be to capture addiction. Addiction is a spiritual malady—there is a reason we scream for God during orgasms and drug use, and there is a reason that Perry's drug use and sexual appetites are rolled into one—but like some sort of misguided Siddhartha, addicts use the physical to ascend to the spiritual, constantly monitoring how their body responds to the intake of substances. Will our veins take in any more dope? How much more can we ingest before our heart explodes? Is it worth trading parts of our body for the one glorious high?

Every demon wants his pound of flesh, and addicts give of it willingly for that brief bit of high. Of course, they are forever scarred. There is not an addict who reads this who hasn't thought to themselves that they might Potstick for the brief ecstasy some raw Atlys. I did. I would have. And after reading this book, part of me still wants to.

Thus is the beast of addiction, and I've often felt that addicts in the throes of a craving become monstrous, a monster that evokes empathy, yes, but monstrous, and *Green Kangaroos* nails this, with its depiction of addicts who "creep out of the shadows like parched lizards, their jaws slack and veins aching."

Is there hope in this kangaroo world? Well, sometimes the cure is worse than the curse.

MARK MATTHEWS

"Sunny Daye Institute" is the name of a fictional treatment center, which is the perfect name for such a place with its shiny bright promises that boasts a ridiculous 100-percent success rate. Once again, this is where the science fiction of *Kangaroos* just entrenches itself in more fact.

Not long ago, Google stopped accepting ads from treatment centers due to their scandalous natures and outrageous claims. Far-away 'destination rehabs' advertised just like Sunny Daye, taking advantage of desperate families googling options for help. If you can find a cure, I'll do anything to find my *sunny daye*, but they were nothing more than body-laundering, rainmakers. (For more on this, just internet search: "Florida rehab center scams".)

Google has started accepting ads again, but audited by an outside entity. You can trust places like Sunny Daye will adapt to reach their audience.

I've spoken too long, but I'm grateful for this chance to be heard, because I have already been telling others to read this book quite often. Pointing to it. *You see that one? Yes, that one,* The Green Kangaroos. *You've got to read that.*

I envy you, dear reader, who gets to discover this for the first time.

—Mark Matthews,
Author of *Milk-Blood*

FOR THOSE WHO INSPIRED
(BUT ARE THANKFULLY
NOTHING LIKE) THESE
CHARACTERS.

PROLOGUE

"**MAMA THREW MY** junk out in the cold."

The words can't travel further than Mia's mind. Try as she might, her lips won't work right. Then again, they're often out of order when she doesn't get her atlys. Thoughts get lost somewhere between brain and tongue as if devoured by that beast with a bottomless belly. The doctors call it "addiction," but Mia calls it "playtime with a deadline."

Based on the frigid temperature assaulting her body, she figures her deadline is close.

"Why'd you hafta throw it out, Mama? Why'd you hafta hurt me like that? I can't see it, Mama, and it's so cold. It shouldn't be so damn cold. It's September. You should be at the ranch, and I should be high. Why'd you hafta ruin my high, Mama?"

The last time she saw her mother, the woman had looked too old. Mia knows it's her fault her mother has aged so fast, but she doesn't even remember how old Mama is supposed to be. Time doesn't move normally with atlys pumping its own ticks and tocks into her brain. Hell, she can't even remember her *own* age. Mia's pains are no indication—she ached with the same sickness in her twenties, in her thirties, and now, well into her sixties. Her pain is a constant reminder of Mama's. Each pang screams, "Don't you know what this does to me, Mia? Can't you see how this hurts your poor mother?"

"Yes, Mama, but being separated from my junk hurts too."

In the irrational cold, Mia thinks nothing could compare to having her atlys taken away. But the sudden thud of her face hitting what feels like a brick wall hurts so much worse.

Fighting against vicious wind, her eyes open to a whitewashed world. Through frigid tears, it appears more theater than reality, but the cold is too intense to be fake.

She peers across the tundra, her teeth chattering so hard she's convinced they've broken. When she sees a metallic dome peek through the snowy gale, she automatically thinks it's a mirage, but there's something about the way the doorless structure shimmers that Mia finds familiar. She tries walking toward it, but her legs icily refuse. Her brain screams, bashing against her skull for escape while her veins splinter beneath her skin. As her other organs join the violent dance, Mia's thoughts become garbled in her gazpacho mind—except for one:

GET WARM NOW.

Her hands tunnel through the snow, tossing it aside as she digs the hole she believes will save her life. Without a scrap of lucidity remaining, she digs for warmth like a zombie who believes human brains comprise the Earth's core.

She hits something solid and combs back the

snow, her brain spending its last moment of clarity on the most painful sight of Mia's life.

Mama's face is blue-gray. Scales of frozen skin chip away when Mia wipes off the frost, giving her a glimpse of her imminent future. She wants to help Mama, to push warm air into her, but she has none to give. There is no helping Mama. There is no helping Mia.

When the second body in the tundra is still, the dome's exterior shimmers again. A rectangular panel illuminates, and a woman's face appears on the metallic skin. The eyes fix on the corpse, and the lips part, her voice ringing across the frozen dark.

"Time of death: 1600 hours, March 18th, 2099."

No one regards the words with any importance. When the door opens, the face disappears, and two people emerge dressed in silver insulated suits. They grab the corpsicles and pull them through the drifts like sledges without riders. When the door closes behind them, the dome is a secret again.

For the time being, there is no more junk left out in the cold.

ONE

THE BEST WAY to take atlys is to inject it straight into the testicles. Your balls feel like they're made of iron, and sure, they hurt for a few minutes, but afterwards you wonder how you ever lived without iron balls.

In the thick of withdrawal, splayed across my rotten couch in the corner of former-Highlandtown High, delicious atlys-memories engage my mind. Not just with fantasies of shooting my own junk. I think of drugged up women, too—Serena, in particular. She told me shooting into her nethers made her clit feel like a cannonball. She called it "The Head," back when I still called her "wife." The Head had its own voice, its own thoughts, and its own desires—namely the "Iron Men" between my legs.

And who could blame it? The Iron Men were good boys back then. When life got too heavy for me to handle, they were always heavier, swinging around my knees. "It's better down here," they'd sing. "Just shoot some more atlys, Perry, and you'll see."

Life was sweet in those days. That's how it is in the beginning. Even slathered in shit, a beginning always has some gold beneath. It's more than anyone can say

4

THE GREEN KANGAROOS

for the middle. Endings are uncertain—they can be good or bad—but the middle is an excremental obstacle course. The best you can hope for is fool's gold, but you'll have to sift through a lot of shit just for a glittering lie.

That's where I am now: the middle, where the Iron Men aren't so good. They can still be heavy, but they don't swing. They hang. They sink. They grunt, "What happened to The Head? She was such a doll. She used to make us tuna sandwiches and massage us when we were sore. Now we just wallow, waiting for the next pinprick as we slam against Perry Samson's little pin-prick. Come on, man. Look up The Head and see what she's doing these days."

But I already know. The binoculars I found in the dumpster behind the Kum Den Smokehouse leave a slimy film around my eyes, but they also leave me more informed about my ex-wife's activities. The truth is, I don't have the heart to tell the Iron Men that their old friend The Head is long dead.

But Serena is still alive, and goddamn her for it. She's still living, still smiling, still screwing the piece of shit lawyer who made sure I couldn't come within five hundred feet of her. Luckily I don't need to get that close. The binoculars may reek of mildewed meat, but at least they let me see her: in her apartment, at her job, even at the Inner Harbor where she walks hand-in-hand with a man who knows the horrible person she was and loves her anyway. The lawyer does for Serena what Serena can't do for me. She can never say, "I love you despite your faults, Perry. In fact, I love you *because* of them. I love how devoted you are to atlys. It takes a long time to build up a relationship like that, and I admire you for it. I was too weak to hold on to my devotion."

Yes, you were, Rennie. You were so weak you fell into the arms of the first man who pouted his lip and told you you were too good for junk. Now you're safe and warm in the arms of the law; the same law that beat you black and blue just three years ago, the same law that put you in a tin can with rapists and cuntcutters when you were twenty-four. How quickly recovery makes people forget, and how nice it must feel to be empty-headed with the law between your legs.

I'll be the first to admit the binoculars aren't enough. I miss feeling her. Hell, I miss feeling every woman who isn't a bag of bones with a lipless snatch. I miss giggling women with butterfly tattoos above their asses and cosmos spilled on their breasts. I miss women who would fawn over and praise me for being a tortured soul hanging on a needle and a prayer.

But you have to take what you can get, right? Patterson Park has a lot to offer in the way of women, but there's not much variety in the dog-eared bunch. The only differences lie in their flavors of poison, or how much meat remains on their diseased bones.

I've gotten laid since Serena left, but none of those women were more than rough, gray holes leading to tunnels that had been banged too often to constrict. I don't claim to have the biggest dick, but I shouldn't feel drafts between my thrusts. I shouldn't hear the ghosts of thrusters past wailing at my short-lived libido. I haven't needed a woman in a while anyway. The only time I get hard anymore is when raw atlys calls the Iron Men to active duty. With liquid junk, I can fuck for hours—as long as I don't focus on the fact that I'm banging a desperate crank whore missing her labia.

Since potsticking became a fad in the early 2080s, a complete chick's been hard to find in the park. When I first joined the ranks of Patterson trash, I fought to overlook the meat a girl had sold from her arms and legs because I knew fresh compensation from the Kum Den Smokehouse would fill the empty spaces. Now I have to block out the fact that they're no more useful than my fist, and rarely as warm. People pay a lot for a regular addict's meat, but cuntcutter meat is filet mignon to Baltimore Fatcats. They'll pay a hefty sum, and the girl will be in lipless hog-heaven. But the money comes and goes fast, and I, pumping away at the resulting ravine, don't cum at all.

It doesn't matter anyway. I can't screw when I'm atlys-sick.

The lingering ghosts of schoolgirls who once walked the halls don't help me accept my frigid fate. Even with the rot and ruin of Highlandtown High, I picture those perfect girls, their hopes as high as their tits. I bet they thought neither could ever drop. Hell, I sure didn't when I was that age. Youth ensures that bodies are firm and futures flexible. At twenty-seven years-old, I'm still a young man, but there is no youth to be found.

When I shamble through the crumbling halls, I'm reminded of girls I can no longer have. Even the warped, rusted lockers remind me of them, my favorite kind: women who are difficult to open.

Serena was like that in the beginning. With legs

like stubborn pickle jars, she required the right type of pressure to pop her open. If I'd known atlys's powers of persuasion when we were seventeen, it wouldn't have been hard for me to get inside.

We were a couple for four years before we ever did atlys together. I enjoyed doing it alone, but like sex, it was way more fun with a partner. After the first taste, her lips parted. After the first snort, her thighs followed. After her first shot, she was up for anything. We did things no one in their right mind would think of as pleasurable. But we weren't in our right minds, and that's what she liked about it . . . for a while.

Jail changed everything. After three years of carefree atlys use, we slipped up and bought from an undercover cop. The only options were to sink or swim. I always saw myself as a swimmer, but unfortunately, Serena's family saw me as the captain of Team Sink. Even when I was clean they never warmed to me. So, after she was bailed out of jail, they begged Rennie to swim away from me, as fast as possible. Our marriage was over soon after that. I tried to convince her that our wrongs had felt right because they *were* right, that if she let go of sober definitions, we could be happy again. Unfortunately, she wised up—or dumbed down, depending on how high I am when I evaluate her abandonment. She sold our apartment, moved to Eastern Avenue, and never asked where I would go. After she got clean, she put all of her dirty deeds behind her, and I was the dirtiest of them all.

It broke me. She was my wife for Christ's sake. We were married for three years, in love since we were seventeen. It sounds cliché, but Serena took a piece of me with her when she left. Not in a sappy she'll-own-my-heart-forever kind of way. No, it was more of a that-bitch-whore-stole-my-manhood kind of way. She killed the man she married: the master of the Iron Men, the lover of The Head.

That man had hope. He had a family. Even though my parents and sister are just a cab ride away, it feels like they live on another planet. The way they talk, the way they think. They assume they're better than me because they live in the sun. Well, I see the sun from my atlys-shadows, and you know what? Fuck the sun.

I'll make the best of life in the shadows, without a family. Who needs a family when you have a potsticker roommate who still gets free shit from his?

Loshi is an atlys addict, too, but if he wants to leave our wallow in the school he has a place to go. If he wants, he can get warm, get full, get money to get high, and start the process all over. I often encourage him to do these things, because it's one of the easiest ways I can touch them. Even if I only get crumbs from Loshi, they're better than nothing. It's why I've stayed friends with him all this time.

Maybe "friends" is going a little far. If he couldn't help me, I doubt I'd hang around him. Loneliness isn't an issue for me. Sure, a shooting partner is preferred, but Loshi's no Serena. If I had easy access to atlys, I'd need his company like Loshi needs another potsticking hole in his belly. I could be buried alive and still be happy as long as I could shoot atlys in the dark.

Loshi doesn't get a lot from Mommy and Daddy these days, but it's enough to maintain his addiction . . . and mine, when he nods out. My thievery causes him to blow through his parents' money faster, but Loshi has another income that keeps withdrawal at bay for a few days. Thanks to the handouts and long free lunches with his family, Loshi has been able to stay pretty plump. It made potsticking a lucrative option. When his parents take him out to eat, knowing he'd use their money on drugs rather than food, he eats as much as possible. The fatter he gets, the more flesh he can sell to the Kum Den Smokehouse, and the more atlys he'll bring home to me. It's our own fucked-up version of bringing home the bacon. I guess that makes me the bitch in this relationship.

Fuck it. As long as he gets me high, I'll be the bitch.

My uselessness is never more obvious than right now: moldering in withdrawal, waiting for Loshi to return with a bag. I don't have any money, and even if I did, I'm too sick to cross the park. In fact, walking upright is difficult most days. When I'm atlys-sick my legs don't hold on any better than my stomach. I puke as I fall along the park, taking forty-five minutes to cross what should take ten.

Instead, I've stumbled around North Highlandtown for the past few days, hoping to find a lost Primetimer or easily duped dealer. But it's tough to score near home. These snakes are varied in their grit, as many coming from posh streets as filthy ones. But education doesn't show in transactions. Just because you're smarter than your nineteen year-old toothless, gouged-up dealer, it doesn't get you a bag any easier. You're only as fast as your slowest man. I'm happy to dumb myself down for the greater good.

THE GREEN KANGAROOS

Loshi enters holding onto a bag. I can tell, and I'm not the only one. Addicts creep out of the shadows like parched lizards, their jaws slack and veins aching. I doubt I look much different. Scooting to the edge of the couch, I claw my thighs, my mind screaming for Loshi to hurry the fuck up. I know the powder isn't meant for me, but I also know I'll find a way to make it mine.

Loshi sits down, his hand still in his pocket. He probably doesn't want me to know how much he has, but he has to break out the bag eventually. And when he does, I'll be on him like bloodstains on a hooker's mattress.

"You were gone a while. Your parents give you anything?"

"Took me out to eat, yeah. I didn't think my mom was going to give me any cash—my dad said no way. But before they dropped me off, she slipped me a fifty."

I wheeze. "Mama's boy."

"I bet you wish you were one right now."

He's not wrong. I'd be anyone's boy if it meant I could score a bag.

"You go to the pond?"

He smirks, and my mouth waters.

"The good side?"

His silence is telling. If he doesn't want me to know his quantity, he sure as hell doesn't want me to know the quality.

"I heard the Vagina Bake's having a free night," he says.

I roll my eyes. "I'm fine with my hand until the right girl comes along."

Loshi laughs. "I think we already met her. Atlys be thy name. Hey, didya get anything from that fat bitch last night?" He scratches an itchy divot in his forearm.

I'd forgotten about it 'til then. I'd jumped a whore in the alley, hoping she had enough cash to get a hit or two, but she was just as dry.

I shake my head, unable to speak for the salivation when he pours out his bag.

"Don't mind sharing her, do ya?"

"Actually, I do." I laugh this time, but Loshi doesn't crack. "I'm serious, Perry. I know you've been swiping my shit when I nod out."

I've been waiting for this. My natural impulse is to lie, to accuse one of the other snakes in our nest, but lying to a fellow liar is hard work and I'm too sick to try.

I bow my head. "I don't know what to say."

"But you know what you gotta do." He pops his switchblade and points it at my minimal gut. "You have to contribute, man. Say you will, and I'll give you a bump."

The thought of potsticking disgusts me. I'll get a free hit of liquid before surgery, but that alters my attitude only slightly. I swore I'd never fall that far. Even then, with Loshi's bag begging to disappear up my nose, my body revolts against the thought. I've already deemed myself worthless, but I still believe a tiny shred remains, buried deep in my flesh. If the knife slices in, I'm afraid all worth will slide out.

I'd just tell him what he wants to hear today and tell him to fuck off about potsticking tomorrow, but I've played that game too many times before. I'm afraid he might actually listen this time. Although it doesn't bug me to imagine Loshi abandoning me for a better friend, imagining that new guy gorging himself on what should've been *my* jacked atlys makes my blood itch.

Loshi scoops a bump of powder with his filthy blade, and my nostril gets wet with anticipation. Cackling, the Iron Men say, "Go on, Perry. What's a lump of flesh compared to free junk?"

He prods me again, and my craving answers, "I'll do it."

Leaning in for the snort, I accept my disgrace. But atlys says, "Forget it," and I obey with a grin.

TWO

PATTERSON PARK BELONGS to the lowlifes. I once heard certain parts of Florida are hit by storms at the same time every day. Patterson Park is much the same. At six o'clock every day, when the sun hunkers down on the hill and the Netvision TVs scattered throughout the park brighten, it's time for the night children to emerge from their slums and taste the high life. Some people walk the dark paths untouched, but that's because their hands are firmly clamped to half-concealed weapons. It isn't a guarantee of safety, but it's better than walking the park with a rape whistle.

Most people don't like walking the park at all, but it's a necessary evil if someone wants to get high, fucked, or potstuck. The second option is the farthest away from the Snake Hill slum. What used to be the "Virginia S. Baker" rec center has deteriorated so bad, it's the "Vgna Bake" now, the cheapest whorehouse in Baltimore.

The cops are around, and they'll respond quickly if called, but they don't usually give offenders more than a punt to the nuts. I don't know the politics, and I don't want to know, but the cops don't seem to care about the play-for-pay as long as they're getting paid. Hell, they probably get their share of play, too.

Dealers populate the perimeter of the pond. It's prime real estate, and because the higher-class dealers hang out on the northwest side, they can pander to the cooler parents and filthier kids at the ice rink. Most of the park is surrounded by Primetimers and walkers. The walkers aren't so bad— all they do is stroll by the aching veins in their way. It's the Primetimers who poke fun. They also poke literally. They kick and slap and throw garbage, waddling away when a snake shows the nerve to bite back.

Patterson Park has only a few good sections, protected from the snakes and rats of the outlying swamp. Those places, and the nicer homes that line Patterson, are hard to avoid looking at. So, it's hard to avoid the self-loathing they inspire. Those neighborhoods remind me that I wasn't always the kind of cockscum who would live in a Snake Hill slum. I used to belong in the good places, or was at least tolerated there. My life pales in comparison to those people now. Literally. The constant flicker of neon and Netvision from the Primetimer side fades the surroundings. Nature is dull. People, too. Any luster you see is manufactured, either coated or injected into entities to generate a false sense of health. Much of the plant life has been replaced with composite plastic, but it has to be redone twice a year, or the city starts to look like a McDonald's PlayPlace. It makes it hard to see the brilliance of life when everything's chapped and pale. But if things were different, I'm not sure I would feel it.

I doubt the Primetimers and Fatcats would ever allow a change. They're too in love with their routines, like stopping eighteen times to watch Netvision while stumbling home from the bar. The only way to interrupt the constant sitcom broadcasts is to jump on the internet, but you can't just browse as you please. The internet access on the street is reserved for purchases only. If you want real internet, you have to be in a residence or a building that provides WiFi in exchange for sales. After too many texting and walking deaths, the mayor had several streets blocked from internet usage. No one surfs for free, and since I can't buy atlys online, I have little use of it. Besides, if there's one thing Primetimers hate more than looking away from their beloved screens, it's sharing anything with someone from Snake Hill. It makes us lowlifes want to fuck with them even more. Even when they call the cops.

I guess it's a good thing snakes are faster than pigs. The fuckers look like sweaty potatoes on roller skates, gasping for air as we laugh our asses off. But our bodies are no better. As soon as we're home free, we gasp too, our veins crying out for comfort. *If* we get home free. Being chased by an unmarried cop could be a different story. But the park isn't a fit cop's usual beat. They're needed to represent the beauty of authority—to convince the world outside that Baltimore is healthy when it's anything but. They're a different breed, but they're all assholes in my book.

The mark of a true Primetimer is in the weight. The middle-class neighborhoods around Patterson Park are flooded with fat husbands and thin wives, looking like the familiar duos of primetime comedies.

THE GREEN KANGAROOS

They say the trend started in the early 2000s, but I think it really began when the city started its nonstop broadcasts of rehashed sitcoms and reality shows about putting on—rather than losing—weight.

The few posh communities clinging to the edge of Baltimore have different transmissions; I don't know the specifics, but I've heard they get to choose what nonsense bombards them, and their options are wider. Primetimers are stuck with cartoon families and happy slobs while people in slums like Snake Hill get reruns of some ancient show called *The Wire* and hardcore porn. It's no surprise for a guy to see his crankwhore mother in a golden shower skin flick showing on Eaton Street. You'd think the Fatcats wouldn't want to show so much porn for fear of driving us to reproduce. They must know how hard it is to fuck when you're a junkie. No atlys, dick can't get hard. Hard from atlys, no worthwhile pussy in sight. Sometimes I settle for whatever floppity fish I can get, but I usually opt for my hand and a happy memory.

It seems like the broadcasts want us all to think happy memories don't exist anymore. When they show episodes of *The Wire*, scenes are obviously cut. Just when the show appears to be going in an uplifting direction, the broadcast jumps to scenes of the slums. They're played on a loop, making me think they want us to see our whoring forebears and know, in decades of technological advancement, our breed hasn't evolved. We're the same useless puddles of ooze desperately clinging to whatever crutches we can.

All it takes are a few lumps of meat sold to the Kum Den Smokehouse to keep us in powder. But I dream of liquid. Raw liquid. Cooking powder doesn't match the intensity of raw atlys. The proprietor, Ling Sugarman, has liquid in stock, but he saves most of it for the cuntcutters. Their meat goes for a much higher price on the Smokehouse menu, I assume because each chick can only be cut twice. However, since most cuntcutters are also hookers, they usually go for both lips at once. Saving one wrinkled flap doesn't change the truth about who they are and what they've done to themselves.

That's why Loshi keeps digging in. After you have one potsticker hole, you might as well have two—or ten. And once they're on your arms or shoulders, visible to the whole world, what's the harm in digging out a cheek or a chin? Hell, who needs a chin?

Fatcats and Primetimers, apparently. They're the ones who pay to eat the flesh of their lessers. I assume it's for the feeling of superiority, but it's also for the buzz that tags along. In addition to being paid in powder, Ling Sugarman also gives potstickers a free hit of liquid atlys. That way, his flesh is dosed when the surgeon cuts out a lump. The diners won't get as high as Loshi, but the drug supposedly tickles the tongue in a wonderful, addiction-free way.

I swore to myself I'd never get into potsticking. Even when Serena kicked me out, and I was forced to accept that the rundown school was my new home. Even when I spent the last dollar to my name and the atlys sickness felt like it was going to tear a hole comparable to potsticking, I refused to twist a knife into my flesh. That conviction felt like the last thing I had. I used to have so much more. When I was clean. When I was a good person. When I was like my parents, my sister, my brot—

THE GREEN KANGAROOS

No, not like Trevor. At least, not toward the end. He was worthless then, too.

I forget about it sometimes: what happened to him. I wish I could forget about it forever, but a family member's death always sticks with you, especially since he was supposed to be too smart to die young.

My older brother Trevor wasn't an addict like me. He was more of a dabbler, one who had a really bad luck day when it came to sobriety. But that's all it takes: one bad luck day to kill you and dub you an eternal junkie.

As my sister Nadine says, "You have to live so you can restore a broken reputation. There is no redemption in death."

She never said it to Trevor, though. I guess she wasn't clever enough yet. I'm the one who has to hear it over and over. Every time I OD, it spews out with her sobs. Luckily, it's been a while since I've ODed—it's been a while since I've seen Nadine, too. I guess she got tired of being threatened every time she visited me in Snake Hill. Honestly, I'm glad. I'm tired of protecting her from guys who want to rape, kill, or turn her out. I'm tired of explaining why Loshi has a new divot in his gut and why we're so happy about it. Most of all, I'm tired of seeing how hurt she was by my refusals to go to rehab. Like I've told her a thousand times, rehab only changes someone if he wants it. Me, I just want atlys. I want the feeling of being able to lift the world above my head and, should the mood strike, smash it to pieces. With the world in shards, I wouldn't have to see Nadine hurt. She'd be dead. We'd all be dead, like Trevor. Dead, and free from annoying helping hands, in a place where wants have been obliterated by the last blink. Maybe Nadine is right: there is no redemption in death because no one can want redemption once they're dead. Once you're dead, maybe life is a long memory of rights and wrongs and seeing no difference. You can only feel happiness. And for me, that's feeling atlys.

I might be jumping to conclusions about the afterlife, but who the hell isn't?

THREE

THE KUM DEN SMOKEHOUSE occupies a brass pagoda overlooking Patterson Park: a beacon for the Haves and Have-Nots alike. Loshi must know how nervous I am about the upcoming surgery because he says, "It ain't so bad, Perry. You can't even feel it until the next day."

"So, how does it feel the next day?" I ask.

"What do ya think? Like someone tore a goddamn chunk outta your stomach."

I picture a hole in my belly and think, *Jesus fuck, how can I do this to myself?* But when my mind answers by filling the hole with a bag of atlys, it makes sense. Through the sweaty sickness of withdrawal, I can rationalize almost anything.

From the pagoda, Serena's apartment is just a short hike to the other side of the park. I see the tip of her building beyond the Kum Den—it makes me wish I'd brought my binoculars. There's nothing sweeter than having a raw atlys buzz as I watch Serena's tits escape her bra. She drops it to the floor and massages the underwire creases. She sighs, and I sigh. She smiles, and I smile. She kisses her boyfriend and I shoot atlys into my sack. Getting hard, I watch them,

21

pretending his hands are mine. Cupping, pinching, turning fingers into lips that suck away the problems of the day.

After those visits I carry my dirty thoughts back to the school. Loshi doesn't mind when I jerk off in front of him as long as I don't fuck up the couch. Honestly, I've stained those cushions more times than I can count on sticky fingers, but considering we stole it from an Eaton Street whorehouse, I doubt Loshi notices the extra crust.

My fantasy of Serena is so thick I don't see how close we are to the Kum Den until a clotted voice calls me back to reality.

"Hey pretty boys . . ."

Loshi and I turn to see Shankara wave at us. She nearly topples as she flashes a brown grin. Speaking of eaten whores . . .

Her face is drawn bone, her arms are twigs freckled with gouges and injection sites, and I can tell by the way her shirt hangs that her tits are gone. They probably made some Primetimer a hefty meal long ago.

"Off to Kum Den?" she asks.

"What's it to you?" Loshi replies, giving her a shove that nearly knocks her to the ground.

She runs her hands over her misshapen body. "I got what you want right here. I got what you need."

"You got atlys?"

"Nah, what I got is better than that. Atlys might make you feel like God for an hour, but an hour inside me will make God wanna feel like you." She strokes her inner thighs as if the ravine has never known a man. She must not remember I had her two years ago.

THE GREEN KANGAROOS

"Not interested," I say, but she throws her indented chest in my way.

"Wait, I know what you like, Perry. I know what all Samson men like."

"What the fuck is that supposed to mean?"

"Your brother Trevor. He liked it rough. He liked to be choked." She draws her putrid grin so close I can smell her colon. It's no surprise, considering how full of shit she is. I tell her so, and she laughs. "Fuckin' snakes. You wouldn't know good snatch if it bit your dick off."

"I know good snatch doesn't bite my dick off," I reply.

"And your lipless twat can't even kiss," Loshi spits. "You're not getting one sniff of our junk."

"I don't want your junk," she says. Her face shakes, but none of her features move. The skin is stretched too thin over her skull to risk a tear. For a moment, I think she's about to scream at us, but what shoots between her shrunken lips is more bawl than yell.

"I need food," she weeps. "Please God, I need to eat!"

Hookers aren't well known for tugging heartstrings, but I feel the slightest yank in my chest. My sympathy makes me nod and reach out in consolation until she cries, "I need to feel the knife again!"

"You what?"

"You don't understand what it's like, watching people go in and out of the Kum Den, bleeding from their bellies, their thighs—oh God, I'd do anything for someone to open up a love handle."

She moans, sliding her fingers around the mutilated bowls in her body.

Her shirt is pulled aside by the desperate clawing, revealing her crude surgical scars, black with rot. The men at the Kum Den are more careful than that; Shankara must have done the extractions herself.

"A twenty, that's all," she says. "Just one twenty, and I'll never bother you again. I need the food. I need the fat. I'll fuck you better than I ever fucked Trevor."

I hate the way she says his name, but I don't expect my hands to jump to her throat. Frankly, I don't think I have the strength.

I knock her to the ground, ordering her to shut up. But she doesn't. She screams Trevor's name, over and over, while faking an orgasm. She hikes her skirt to her waist and fingers her withered tunnel. We've drawn several eyes by this point, including some from the Primetime side of the park. Loshi pulls her up and hoists her twiggy body onto his shoulder, but she doesn't stop shrieking until he throws her under a tangle of nearby elms.

"Do you want your pot stuck or not?" he says. She nods, causing several strings of drool to abandon her lips. "Look, you still got a profitable piece of meat to sell, and Ling'll pay a shitload for it. Then you'll have the money you need to plump up and start over."

"What meat? Where?"

Loshi pulls out his switchblade and grabs her bony face, forcing her yellow tongue to flop out of her mouth. The moment Shankara gets his intention, her eyes light up like a kid staring at her first Christmas tree. She curls her tongue, staring at the quivering tip. I can't tell if she's warring with the decision or saying goodbye, until her eyes snap to Loshi's and, with her tongue still extended, she says, "Do it."

Loshi's knife isn't one I'd want slicing me. He uses it to cut food and atlys, but he uses it just as often to sift through garbage when we dumpster dive. When he doesn't want to touch a rancid mixture of chowder and slaw to reach the discarded pizza beneath, the knife goes to work. It doesn't look sharp, either. Or maybe there's too much trash caked on the blade for the sharpness to shine through.

It takes nearly two minutes for Loshi to saw off Shankara's tongue, but through every crimson spurt, every "accidental" nick of her skeletal chin, the pathetic twat sings in joy. Blood pools in the back of her throat, intensifying the glottal aria. She reaches out, clutching at nothing. But the look on her face makes me think she sees something beautiful. Cash, food, maybe a dozen razorblades turning her fingers into happy hotdog slivers for some wealthy Primetimer's mac-n-cheese.

Her tongue falls into a puddle of scarlet mud. She looks down at it in glee, the bottom half of her face so thick with blood it looks like a cavernous hole. She spits up a tiny piece of tongue and frantically searches for it on the ground. Waste not, want not.

Loshi wipes his knife on the plastic grass, but it doesn't come clean. I tell myself to remember how it was employed today so I can stop him before he uses it on our next meal. But once atlys steamrolls my logic, I doubt I'll remember. I might even lick the blade.

Shankara appears to pray as we walk away. The only word I recognize in her clotted rambling is "god."

I can't tell if it's "Dear God, what have I done" or "Thank you God for this wonderful gift," but the way she cradles her limp tongue, like it's the baby Jesus, makes me think the latter.

The Kum Den Smokehouse has two entrances: one for customers and one for trash like me. To prevent patrons from running into the disgusting origins of their meals, the restaurant entrance is situated several yards away from the pagoda, in the Casino. While the pagoda's exterior is ornate, the Casino is as plain as it gets. I've heard rumors about the inside, that gold and diamonds encrust every surface. I've heard it's draped in velvet, and singing servants bring you hot towels in the foyer before you're led downstairs to the restaurant stretching beneath Patterson Park. I've heard that every Smokehouse appetizer comes with a free blowjob from the server of your choosing, but that claim came from a cracked-out bum with egg-beaters for legs, so I don't know if I should trust it.

It makes some sense, though. The most desperate addicts, yearning to get their rocks off, have begged Ling Sugarman to cut off their rocks in exchange for atlys. And while the Primetmes and Fatcats suck down our dosed genitalia, a hired mouth sucks on them. It's Baltimore's own little Circle of Life.

In reality, it's probably no different from a T.G.I. Friday's—a bunch of kitschy shit stuck to the walls, memorabilia from when we used to have popular sports teams, art, and culture. Hell, maybe we still do. Maybe I've just been in the park so long I don't see anything but the junk: drugs, TVs, and people included.

THE GREEN KANGAROOS

Whatever happens on the inside, it's special enough for four armed guards to protect it. The entrance to the pagoda is guarded too, but not as well. While the casino guards look like military men, the pagoda guards are obvious ex-potstickers, who gave up the practice for Sugarman's professional compensation, whether with cash or drugs. They're no one to be fucked with, but I'd rather tangle with them than the beefy assholes in front of the Casino. The closest I get is in strolling across the park. At any moment, I'm walking on the heads of rich people eating pieces of Loshi—and after today, pieces of me.

I tried to convince Nadine to go down there once. Not for a meal—just to satisfy my curiosity. She wouldn't even consider it.

"Clean up, get a job, and go down there yourself," she'd said.

I wish she could be as devoted as she was when we were kids. Next to Trevor, I was her biggest hero. She would've done anything for me back then, and after Hero Numero Uno was out of the picture, she was more inclined. But she didn't love me as much as she'd loved Trevor. My parents, either. No matter what I did, I wasn't good enough to step into his role. They'd rather it remain empty, which further emptied me.

I have to admit I saw a bit of hope in Trevor's death. With him gone and my family devastated, I thought I'd finally have room to shine. But there's nothing people hate more than someone who tries to shine through grief. My hope mocked their mourning. It was unintentional, but it helped me realize the truth about my station in the Samson family. Even with the death of my older brother, I would never become the coveted eldest child. I would always be in the middle—always invisible.

Maybe I'll have a more useful transparency once I have a few potsticking holes. Maybe my family will see the real me, the one in pain, when they see what I've given up to feel whole. And if they don't, at least I'll be high.

I try to summon my courage about the surgery ahead, but I keep thinking about what Shankara said. Did she really sleep with my brother, or was she just trying to get a rise out of me? A lot of scum in my circle know about Trevor; some of them knew him back when he was just a stoner. He'd score bags from the Snake Hill residents, never thinking he'd get into anything harder, until the day a particularly pushy pusher convinced him to buy a few hits of liquid atlys.

"Hey, Earth to Perry."

Loshi tries to snap his fingers in front of my face, but they're too sticky with Shankara's blood to snap.

"Do you think she was telling the truth about my brother?"

"That twat is a few syrup pouches shy of a waffle. You shouldn't trust anything she says. I guess you can't anymore." He snickers, elbowing my ribs. I swear I hear them crack, but it's just a syringe breaking under Loshi's shoe.

The guards at the pagoda recognize him immediately, but this is my first time getting so close to the Kum Den. They look me up and down a few times. I don't know what disqualifications they look for, since a person would have to be a dirtbag to want into this part of the Smokehouse.

"Whatsyer name?" one of the guards asks. I start

to answer, but he continues. "You look like a Gerald. That's my brother's name. You look like my brother. Is your name Gerald? Maybe Gerry?"

"No, it's Perry." The big lug stares me down, silent. "Uh, it rhymes with Gerry, though."

He smiles. "Yeah, yeah, that must be why. Come on in, boys. Line starts to the left."

When we enter the pagoda, ten addicts look up at us and glare. We're not stealing anything from them, yet they all look like we raped their dogs for half a line of coke. The looks might not be undeserved; I don't always remember what I do when I'm high.

A redhead with a meth-scratched face sitting two chairs away from Ling's office used to be a girl I knew named Becca. She's probably still named Becca, but she isn't the girl I knew. The girl I knew was pretty. She had nice legs and a serviceable rack, and her face was a gorgeous bit of strawberry tart. Ivory skin accented with delicate freckles and soft petals of lips were your reward if you could get her high enough. I thought she was a bad methhead when I knew her, but she's worse now. Either that or her last potstick-surgeon used a rake on her face instead of a knife.

As Loshi talks to a chalky black guy with eight gold chains and no teeth, my eyes make the journey up the spiral staircase to my right. Cutting stations are situated on each level, except for the observatory at the top, which is gated and guarded. It makes me want to go to the top even more, but rumor has it the gilded balcony's freedom belongs to Ling alone. Selfish prick. All I want are a few moments up there, to look out and see Serena on her own porch, joyful that I can finally look back at her. She's waited so long . . .

It's easy to slip into false fantasies about Serena, especially when I'm starving and atlys sick. And why the fuck shouldn't I? They're my memories to warp, aren't they? I don't think she would ever come back to me, but it makes me happy to lie to myself. Even if that cuntrag lawyer weren't in the picture, I think she'd be happy just being free of me.

Like she's so fucking great.

It's hard to keep my eyes open. Each time the line shortens, Loshi has to tug me into the next chair. I faintly hear him ask his new friend why he would potstick if he has gold, but I know the answer before the man says it.

"A man's gotta look his best, don't he?" he says, slapping a divoted hand on Loshi's thigh. I hadn't expected the man to have such a high-pitched voice squeak through his floppy lips. It's less a voice and more an educated fart.

Screams from the cutting rooms shock me alert. We're only a few people away from the door, only a few people away from having a chunk torn out of my flesh. It's easy to tell the first timers from the newbies, even without seeing their potstuck bodies. The newbies don't stop looking scared about the knife, but there's a confidence in them—they know the worth in what they're doing. Just a little piece to get some peace. Just a little shame, and the places drained of worth are filled with something else, something sober folks would never understand. Newbies are enlightened. Delusional, but enlightened. If I weren't so nauseated by withdrawal, I might think it was pathetic.

What's really pathetic is how easy it is for a place

like the Kum Den Smokehouse to operate. Here we are, fiends of the streets, selling our poisoned meat to the richest, fattest Primetimers in Baltimore and, wouldn't you know, the richest and fattest are the folks in charge. Politicians don't frequent the Kum Den; what kind of message would that send to the voters? I guess that's why ol' Ling started offering delivery. As long as he gives enough money back to the city, the city has no problem with him slicing and dicing the drug addicts. They never say it outright, but allowing the restaurant to broadcast commercials on the street screens trumpets their support. The Smokehouse even sponsors the WiFi in some of the kiosks, and if you mention that fact at the restaurant, you receive a free basket of "chicken" tenders.

The toothless guy enters Ling's office, and Loshi slides into his seat. I'm about to move into his when someone belches my name. I'm don't want to turn because I don't want to see Becca's tapioca face, but I turn anyway. I feel bad about wincing, but she doesn't seem offended. She must be used to it.

"You look good," she says. I assume she doesn't expect me to say the same about her, so I don't. "How's Selena?"

I say "Serena," realizing it's the first time I've said her name aloud in weeks. It feels strange on my tongue. Maybe it *is* "Selena."

"You guys still over on Linwood?"

"We broke up a while ago. Shit, I've seen you more recently than that."

"You have?" she asks, looking up at the ceiling in a daze.

She's as high as a fucking kite, smiling as blood

blooms on her stomach. I want to be where she is. I want to be high. Sobriety is like being forced to read your little sister's diary, rife with the longing thoughts of an immature mind. If I have to suffer one more sappy memory digging in its spurs and riding me deeper into withdrawal, so help me God, I will—

The door opens, and Loshi turns to me in glee before dashing into Ling's office. I shake in an eager terror that makes Becca giggle.

"What's so funny?"

"I don't know," she says. "I guess I feel like I won something today."

"What do you mean?"

"It's just funny who you see here. People you never thought . . ."

She smiles as she stumbles out of the pagoda. I stand to see her trip down the stairs and crash into one of the cannons. She recovers, straightening her ratty coat before she throws her head back with a boisterous laugh.

The office door opens, and I yelp. As I scramble for it, I swear I hear the potstickers behind me cheer. That, and Becca's comment, ups my anxiety, but once I see the bottles of atlys lined up on Sugarman's desk, the cheers from starving brain sound loudest. I leap inside, and the door closes behind me.

Ling Sugarman has the face of a Chinese baby and the body of a wrestler turned truck driver. His black hair is plastered so flush to his skull that I assume there's a ponytail at the nape. I soon realize the hair is tattooed onto his head, flecks of white granting a fake sheen. Despite his strong Asian appearance, his voice is a robust muddle of Eastern European accents.

THE GREEN KANGAROOS

"Have a seat."

I look for a chair, but there aren't any. He nods to the floor, so I shakily lower myself as he nestles down in the plush seat behind the desk. Leaning forward, he menaces over me like the pagoda over Patterson Park. His lips curl back, revealing large white teeth, perfectly squared and spaced.

"First time, yes?" he grunts. "I never forget a client."

"Even if their faces get fucked up by potsticking?"

"With as many holes you people dig in your skin, you're still the same on the inside. That's what I recognize: the excremental remains of the life that done you wrong. Everyone has a different sob story, a different list of people to blame—hardly ever themselves. So, what's your story, son? 'Cuz you're a new shade of shit."

"Just a normal guy, I guess."

"No one who enters my office is normal."

"Not even you?"

"I love a newbie. Still so much piss and vinegar. We'll drain that out in no time."

"You're just trying to scare me."

Ling snorts. "And you're just trying to be brave, to convince yourself that this is nothing to you. What is one lump of flesh compared to an entire body in ecstasy?" His teeth gleam as he nods. "This may be the first time you've met me, but I've met you thousands of times. So cut the crap and give me a vein."

Ling grabs a bottle of atlys and pierces the top with a needle.

"Does it hurt?" I ask.

As he draws up the gorgeous elixir, he says, "It hurts more than you can imagine," but I hear, *"Of course not. Butterflies and unicorns from here on out, Perry."*

I stand up, unzipping my pants.

"Zip that shit up, kid. I don't shoot sacks here."

"But I don't get much liquid. I wanna get the most out of it."

He tosses me a length of tubing. "The liquid isn't for you, it's for my customers. The arm or nothing."

It's no contest. I wrap the rubber around my arm and tie it off. It's been too long since rubber constricted my flesh. It pinches at first but quickly settles into its usual spot. My arm is an easy chair for tourniquets.

I'm sweating as the syringe nears, but I feel like crying in joy. As much as I fear what will follow the hit, as much as my desperation disgusts me, as much as it will hurt my family to see the clefted evidence of how low I've sunk, I look Ling Sugarman in his slanted eyes and say, "Thank you."

The initial prick is nice, but the flood feeds the craving. Ling snaps the tourniquet from my arm, and the drug rushes into my veins. They become golden railways, with atlys the rainbow train hauling visions of sugarplums and high-class trim throughout my body. The charge hardens every part of me, making me feel like the Incredible Hulk with more craving to fuck than smash.

Both are out of the question. The nod is minutes away from embrace. Soon, its soft thighs will clamp around my head and I'll sleep without sickness, buried in the gorgeous muff of intoxication.

THE GREEN KANGAROOS

Deliciously dazed, I'm led through a back door in Ling's office by a man with a word tattooed on his jaw. At first, I think it says "balls," but after he turns his head I realize it says "ballistic."

Mr. Ballistic pulls me up several flights of stairs, ignoring every question I ask, and I can't blame him. My questions are jumbled and meaningless, especially when I ask if he also hears the girl's voice calling the word "bear" from the distance. I stop talking. The surgeon in my cutting room appears to be in no mood for an emotional addict. His black, rubber apron hides the blood of past patients, but one look at his operation table makes no mistake about the brutality of the procedure. Sterilization liquids are untouched, still blue in their vats. One would think the liquid would have turned purple from all of the bloody instruments dipped inside.

I'm thrown into a slippery leather chair that squeaks as I try to find a comfortable position. The surgeon doesn't care about my comfort, proved by the way he clamps his gloved hand to my forehead and pins me to the headrest. The rumor is that the Kum Den surgeons are pre-med, practicing for the time when they can do reputable work, but this guy looks post-med, forced into the Kum Den because he can't perform reputable work. It doesn't matter to me. With a bag of atlys and a wad of cash in hand, who could care about a few crude cuts?

"Where do you want it from?" he asks gruffly.

My voice is trapped somewhere behind my fear, but I'm able to point to my thigh. He nods, bending over me with the scalpel. Before he's able to dig in, my voice emerges. "Is that clean?"

35

He sneers. "Are *you*? If it was my choice, I'd wear an iron suit while touching you filthy rats. All the rubbers in the world ain't enough to make this transaction safe."

"But the blue stuff—"

"Jesus titty-fuckin' Christ, fine!" He dips the scalpel into the antiseptic liquid, shakes it out, and holds it two inches from my eyes.

"There. You happy?"

"No." I exhale, more of a sob than a breath. "Just do it."

The initial scalpel slice is similar to a needle, but it lacks the glorious result. Instead of the Midas touch of intoxication filling my body with glittering wealth, the scalpel drags. It tears and twists and scrapes at bone until my entire leg is a rock-hard hurt. I close my eyes and allow the atlys to take my mind's reins.

"Please steer me away from the pain. Please take me home."

My mind goes blank. Even atlys doesn't know where my home is.

The surgeon's fingers are inside of me. One hand digs, one tugs—like an impatient kid who wants at the pumpkin guts before fully removing the top. I imagine him making a jack-o-lantern of me, popping out triangular Perry pieces and setting me on a porch for teenagers to terrorize. There's no need for a candle; atlys has already illuminated me. My insides crackle as they burn, but the drug makes me glow too deliciously for pain. Plus, how can I feel pain when Nadine's there, holding my hand?

"It will be over soon, Bear," she says. "I'm going to get you out of here. I'll do whatever it takes." I shake my head at her and she laughs. "Silly Bear, you don't get to say no."

My body screams when the surgeon cinches the last stitch. He breaks the trance. The liquid he sprays across the wound stings before it cools, but the relief is gone when I see a piece of me sitting in a pan. It's the size of a baseball, fraught with its own red stitching. It sickens me to think it'll be inside some Primetimer's belly soon. I'm really one of them now. I'm a potsticker.

My head spins when the surgeon pulls me out of the chair. He opens a safe and removes a pouch he shoves into my hand.

"Twenty grams of powder. One hundred bucks cash," he says. "Now get out."

I hadn't considered how hard it would be to walk out of the Smokehouse after being stuck. The combination of raw atlys and a carved-up leg does me no favors as I descend the spiral staircase. I can't tell if the people in the waiting room look at me with fear of what awaits them, or excitement. I had longed to be Becca in her bloody high, so there are probably a few addicts who think I'm the luckiest fuck in the world.

I ooze down the stairs, caressing the railing as if its cold metal skin will slick the pain away, leaving the sweet pulse of raw atlys. But it doesn't. It barely catches me when I stumble down the stairs.

My first step out of the Kum Den is like the cold slap of a bitch in heat. Reality is so beautiful when she's angry. I'd give up another chunk of thigh to fuck the fury out of her.

Dusk has fallen over the park and Loshi is nowhere to be found. I want to collapse, half because I want something to rub my dick against. At this point, a gopher hole would do. I have to get home, back to my binoculars. I have to see Serena and pound my pain into pleasure.

I feel like I'm walking, taking large, slow steps, but I make no progress through the park. I realize I must look like a mental patient on the moon, but I can't help it. Some asshole stops to take a video of me with his phone. I try to tell him to fuck off, but my tongue has gone numb. It lounges in my mouth, sticking to my lips like sluggish honey. I give him the finger instead, but it's the wrong one. My pinkie pops up, giving the kid more pathetic gold for his blog.

The asshole suddenly retreats. I'm able to bark, "Yeah, you better run," but his exit has nothing to do with me. It's because of the burly, suited man stomping toward me with a baseball bat in hand.

I recognize him. I should run away, but my brain moves too slow to process the command. Robert Rackman is too fast for me anyway. I hold up my hands in surrender, but he doesn't want surrender. He wants to hit a homerun with my head.

I stumble backward as he swings the bat. I'm grateful for my loss of balance until I realize it's laid me out on the ground, no stumbles left to save me. Robert's face is solid stone as he looks down, but when he sees the blood seeping through my pants, it twists into a grin.

"You stupid piece of trash," he says. "I knew it would come to this. I told Serena a hundred times."

"Now you can tell her 'I told you so.' You're welcome for that," I say. I try to crawl backward, but he stays on top of me.

THE GREEN KANGAROOS

"I don't need to say it. She knows the bullets she's dodged since leaving you. And I know," Robert says, pointing the bat at my head, "that you've been watching her."

"I don't know what you're talking about."

"You've been spying on her from the park. I'm a lawyer, you fuck. You can't lie to me."

"Bullshit. Serena lies to you every time she says she doesn't miss me or atlys. I'm sure she's glad for the bullets she's dodged, but that doesn't change the fact that she will always miss my big, fat needle."

He kicks me in the side, knocking the wind from my lungs. There's no point in trying to scream for help. Help would only come if the tables were turned.

Crouching beside me, his voice lowers to a hostile whisper.

"She made her choice, and it was the right one. You're dead to her, you got it? You're less than dead. You're abortion slime, Perry. It's as if you never existed."

I know it's stupid to piss off a man with a baseball bat and a vendetta, but I'm too high to hold my tongue. And honestly, what damage could Robert do that I haven't already done to myself?

"She might say she doesn't think of me when you're around, but it's not true. When she's alone, when her fingers slide between her legs, she still pretends they're mine."

The bat swings, smashing against the weeping wound in my thigh. Pain whips me from head to toe. As I writhe on the ground, a broken bottle cuts my arm. I wrap my hand around the jagged bottleneck and try to propel a wad of phlegm in Robert's direction. When the loogie lands on my own face instead, he doubles over in laughter. While his eyes are averted, my hand flies up, slashing at him with the brown shard. Unfortunately, my aim is also under the influence of atlys; my attack isn't even slightly on target. He growls as he chops at me with the bat, but I roll away just in time. I push myself to my feet, brandishing the bottle, but the head rush makes me wobble. Disoriented, I thrust my weapon at him, but he grabs my wrist all too easily. He bends my arm backward and redirects the shard into my own gut.

By this point, the injury is just another note in my symphony of pain. The only difference is that this note might be the last. I pull the glass out of my belly and collapse to the ground, the breeze making ice of my open wounds. Patterson Park is already a pale place, but it dims by the second.

"It will be over soon, Bear," I hear my sister's voice, but I can't see anything except for the fake grass crushed under Robert's Italian loafers as he walks away. I weakly call for help, reaching out to the dozen walkers passing by. A teenager spots me, running over and squatting at my side. I tell him I'm dying, and he slaps his fingers to a pressure point on my neck. I wonder if he can feel my pulse, because I sure as hell can't.

"I'm dying," I repeat.

He nods, assuring me that he understands before reaching into my pocket and removing the pouch of powder and money. Shoving it into his jacket, he whispers something into my ear and darts away. As my eyes close, I realize the thief is right. I won't need them where I'm going.

FOUR

THE SCREEN GOES black, and a girl with trembling lips whimpers into her hands. The doctor gives her a tissue to catch the sob that barrels out.

He puts a consoling hand on her shoulder. "I understand how upsetting this must be, Miss Samson."

"I didn't think it would be like this. I've seen Perry when he's high, even at that disgusting school he squats in, but I didn't expect this," Nadine says. "Is he going to die, Doctor Daye?"

"Remember, Miss Samson, nothing you see on this screen is real. The potsticking, the girl losing her tongue—they were simulations."

"But it seems so real."

"Thank you. It's always nice to hear our work is appreciated," he replies. The door opens, and a woman enters the screened room, a cup of hot tea in hand.

"Here you are, dear. This should make you feel better," she says, handing the mug to Nadine. Doctor Marla Daye sits next to her husband, Alan.

"Thank you. You have no idea how good it feels to

see a program that might actually work for Perry. I just wish it didn't have to cause him so much pain."

The Dayes nod in unison. Scooting to the edge of her seat, Marla tents her hands and locks eyes with Nadine. "But you must understand, Miss Samson, your brother has to hurt if he's to heal. He has to feel every consequence of his actions. He needs to know what his life will be like if he continues down this path."

"I didn't think it could get any worse. But . . . potsticking . . . Jesus Christ, Perry." Nadine cries into her tea.

"Don't worry, Miss Samson, we've been able to pull darker souls back to the light. We'll save your brother, too." Leaning forward, he pats Nadine's knee.

Sniffling, she rubs her nose. "Do you really have a one hundred percent success rate?"

"The Sunny Daye Institute is bar-none the most effective drug rehabilitation facility on the planet," he says, both doctors beaming from ear to ear. "Our methods may be unorthodox, but they work. Every addict who's gone through our simulation has come out a clean, happy, and productive member of society."

Nadine sips at her tea, nervously shifting in her seat.

"What can we say to settle your mind, dear?" Marla Daye asks.

"It's just that . . ." She fiddles with her shirtsleeve and looks at the floor. "Well, you haven't told me how you got him into the simulation in the first place, or where he is right now. Physically, where is he?"

THE GREEN KANGAROOS

Marla smiles. "In this building, of course. Where else would he be?"

"Can I see him?"

"That would compromise the therapy, I'm afraid. We can't do anything to give Perry reason to doubt that his world is real," Alan says.

"How did you get him to agree to this? He's been shooting my rehab suggestions down for years."

The doctors look to each other before Marla says, "Faith is the most important aspect of recovery, Miss Samson."

"Perry isn't a very religious guy. Faith-based rehabs haven't worked for him in the past."

"If it had, we wouldn't be here right now, would we? No, Miss Samson, I'm referring to faith in general. Perry has to have faith in the reality of his world. You have to have faith that he can get better. And we have to have faith in our success."

"Which we do," Alan adds.

"Because of that, we are willing to do whatever it takes to help our patients. Even if they're not technically our patients yet."

Alan leans forward. "But we hope Perry will be. He's a good candidate for this treatment, and his recovery is entirely possible, Miss Samson."

"Okay, I get that," she says. "But you didn't answer my question."

"You told us where Mr. Samson likes to hang out, that school in North Highlandtown," Alan says. "We simply went there and collected him."

"You kidnapped him?"

"We made a better decision about the course of his day than he would have. Certainly you can't contest that."

"No, I guess not." Her eyes drop to the floor.

Marla moves from her chair to the couch, draping her arm around Nadine's shoulders. At first, Nadine shies away, but when Alan turns the television on, and Nadine sees her brother bleeding out in Patterson Park, she allows Doctor Daye to embrace her.

"We know you want your brother to be healthy, and he *can* be. You just need to agree to the treatment, and we can proceed," Marla says.

"It's not up to me."

"It can be," the doctors reply.

Nadine shakes her head. "No, my parents should have a say. And Serena."

Alan looks over his tablet and scrolls through his notes. "Ah, yes, his ex-wife. Tell me, Nadine, if it were up to them wouldn't *they* be here? Wouldn't *they* have contacted us? It seems to me you're the one who really cares about Perry."

"I'm closer to Perry than my parents are. Our relationship—it was special."

"That's wonderful to hear. If you decide to continue with the Sunny Daye treatment, Doctor Carter will be a great comfort to you. He has a soft spot for relationships like yours."

"I saw his name in the pamphlet. He's the Head Scientist?"

Marla pats her leg. "He's more than that. It's Doctor Carter's revolutionary techniques that made the Sunny Daye Institute such a success. He's the real genius behind the treatments here."

"Is he here now? I want to speak to him, too."

"He's very hands-on with the patients, so I'm afraid he's busy right now. Should you choose our program, you will meet him, I promise. In fact, he'll insist upon it. But for now, maybe you could give us some more information on Perry. We have the basics, we know you want him clean, but the more details we have, the richer and more persuasive we can make his simulations," Marla says, returning to her husband's side.

"What do you want to know?"

"Let's start with a name that's been running through his mind," Alan says. "What can you tell us about 'Bear?'"

Nadine chuckles, but sadness follows. "Perry is Bear. When I was a kid, I called him 'Beary' instead of 'Perry,' and it eventually shortened to 'Bear.' It was my nickname for him."

"It seems he still regards it as such." Alan circles something on his tablet screen.

"We were always close, the three of us. Me, him, and Trevor, we were a happy trio," Nadine says. "But Perry doesn't remember it like that. He thinks we overlooked him, that he never really mattered. I don't understand where that comes from. Our parents worked a lot, so they were preoccupied, and they were exhausted when we actually got to spend time with them, but their neglect was the same for all of us. He wasn't the only one who didn't feel loved. We all felt it. He wasn't special." Nadine lowers her head. "I didn't mean that how it sounds."

"We're not here to judge you, Miss Samson."

"No, just my brother."

"It's a judgment you agree with, otherwise you wouldn't be here," Marla says.

"You're right. I guess I can't help feeling like this is my fault. And if we're being truthful—"

"Yes, please," Alan urges.

"It's Trevor's fault too. Not everything. He was fine when we were kids, but once he started messing with drugs, once he . . ."

Nadine stifles a sob, but it doesn't stay stifled. It bursts out, causing her to drop her tea on the floor.

"I'm so sorry," she says. Before she can pick up the mug, the wall to her right flickers to life and the face of a young woman with olive skin appears on the screen. Her hair is so blonde it's almost ivory, pouring down her shoulders.

"Oh daisy! Had an accident did we?" Her soft, British accent warms the room, but the maternal lilt wears a bit of stiffness.

"Yes, Emily, would you please?" Marla asks.

"Of course, it's my pleasure." Focused on Nadine, she adds, "Do keep your distance from the spill, Miss."

Nadine presses her back against the couch and tucks up her legs. The moisture in the carpet sizzles before it disappears, but the mug has more of a bubbling effect, swelling and bursting before vanishing into ribbons of smoke.

"Thank you, Emily. That will do."

The woman on the wall smiles and gives the Dayes a nod before blinking out of the screen. After the wall is a wall again, Nadine's eyes stay glued to it. When Doctor Alan Daye speaks again, she moves, but her eyes shift to the floor rather than his face.

"Miss Samson, are you all right?"

"Where did the cup go?" she asks.

"The Sunny Daye Institute is full of surprises, Miss Samson—the biggest being how easily your brother's recovery can happen. If you let it."

THE GREEN KANGAROOS

"But we need your complete dedication to continue," Marla Daye says.

Nadine sighs. "I can't do anything until my family's on board."

"Then for your brother's sake, for *your* sake, convince them."

She pulls her phone out of her purse and scans through her contacts. She selects one, then looks up at the Dayes. "That woman on the wall—can you use her?"

"Use her?"

"She's not human, is she?" Nadine asks. "She's a program of some kind?"

The doctors look to each other. "That's correct," Marla says.

"Emily was created by Doctor Carter. She's an integral part of the Institute. Not only does she keep track of patient records, she is able to watch over each rehab program in process better than any human could," Alan replies. "That's very astute of you, Miss Samson."

"When you live with an addict, you learn to recognize the lies behind the theatrics," she says. "But just because you recognize the lies doesn't mean you won't fall for them. When it comes to someone you love, wanting to believe is an addiction in itself."

"So, you'd like Emily to convince your parents that Perry needs help?" Marla asks.

"They already know that. But they've been burned too many times to think help is possible anymore. They need to be convinced that miracles can happen, that this place can save his life. She seems pretty miraculous to me."

47

"And if they say no?"

Nadine's eyes waver under the weight of budding tears. "If they say no, you can unhook Perry and drop him in the goddamn desert for all I care. In fact, I hope you do."

"You would wish that for your beloved Bear?"

"I'd wish it for anyone who's ruined my life like Perry has. You have no idea how much he's stolen from me. You have no idea what he's put this family through. I've lost jobs to help him, I've lost friends. Worst of all, I've lost respect for myself because of my enabling. I've taken him to get high. I've helped him when the withdrawal was so bad, when he was in so much pain, he couldn't stand. I gave my hard-earned money to the scum of the earth to keep him from being beaten to a pulp. And what have I gotten out of it? A piece of potsticking shit that used to be my brother? What the hell did I keep him alive for?"

The best place for Nadine's face is in her palms. Grief, shame, anger, and every gut-wrenching emotion too devastating to name pushes her into a fit of tears.

Doctors Alan and Marla Daye abandon their seats to console the weeping girl.

"Bring your parents, Miss Samson. Bring the ex-wife," Alan says. "If you want your brother to get healthy, bring whomever you feel necessary."

She stares at her brother on the screen. "I do want that. I'll do whatever it takes."

FIVE

THE SUNNY DAYE Institute squats in a plain brown building sharing space with Bubba's Sub Shop and a lady who sells jewelry made from antique bottle caps. It looks more like a fleabag motel. Laura and David Samson give the place a doubtful glare before following their daughter inside yet another rehab. Perry's ex-wife, Serena Hall, doesn't enter until Nadine pulls her in. It requires similar provocation to get the trio onto the elevator. The abrasive sound of an electronic clarinet swells within the dome over the lift, one of the many things that makes Serena and the Samson parents crinkle their noses in disgust.

"Look, I know what you're thinking," Nadine says. "I thought it all too. But this place is different."

Her mother scoffs. "That sounds familiar."

"Look, Perry's put us all though a lot of shit. I know all the money we've spent—all the money *you've* spent—but Sunny Daye isn't like any other rehab around."

"I love you, sweetie," David Samson says, squeezing his daughter's shoulder, "and we all love Perry, but we've heard this speech a dozen times.

Every place you find is different. Every place is better. Every place is the cure to Perry's disease."

"Didn't you read the pamphlet I gave you? Sunny Daye's treatments are revolutionary."

He takes the pamphlet out of his pocket, shaking his head as he unfolds and flips through the pages.

"This is just more of the same. Worse, actually. This place boasts a one hundred percent success rate, and nothing has a one hundred percent success rate. If people claim something is foolproof, that's all the proof I need to know they're fools."

Nadine rolls her eyes. "Thanks for keeping an open mind, Dad. What about you?" She nods to Serena. "You have to believe it's possible, right? *You* got clean. Don't you think Perry deserves a chance to do the same?"

"He's had a thousand chances," she says. "You know how much I cared for Perry, how much I wish he'd gotten sober with me, but he didn't want it. Not then, not now."

"You don't know that."

"Yes, I do. I know addiction. I know what lost souls look like, and when they don't want to be found." Serena lowers her gaze. "And I don't think you considered how hard this would be on me. I put that life behind me, Nadine, and I'd rather it stay there. If it weren't for our friendship, I never would have come today."

"You'll see. Sunny Daye isn't just some tin can full of sermons and cigarettes. It's a technological miracle."

"That's what they said when they put TVs on every corner. And we all know how that turned out," Laura says.

THE GREEN KANGAROOS

The lift stops, and the doors open to an illuminated wall.

"Come, come, don't be afraid."

The dulcet voice rings out first, and pixel by pixel, Emily's face appears on the screen. The elevator dings, even jerks a bit as if trying to expel its riders. Nadine leads them out, but they keep their distance from the wall. Soft as Emily is, her eyes are the size of their heads, her beauty almost threatening.

"Door at the end of the hall. Follow me," she says, batting her jet black lashes as she flashes from panel to panel.

"Welcome to the Sunny Daye Institute, where every sober day is a sunny day. My name is Emily, and I'm here to assist you in whatever you need while you're here."

"Thank you, Emily. We're very happy to be here," Nadine says. She looks to her parents who eventually nod along. Serena rolls her eyes.

"Excellent. Please, follow me. Doctors Daye and Carter are expecting you," she says.

"Are you the receptionist?" Laura asks.

Emily's chuckle crackles. "I suppose you could call me that, but I perform more functions as well. I manage our patient files, I organize and monitor the rehabilitation program, I even do some light janitorial work from time to time."

"She made my teacup disappear," Nadine says.

"Sunny Daye Institute is the most advanced rehabilitation facility in the world. The founders of the Institute, Doctors Alan and Marla Daye, are amazing, but our Head Scientist, Doctor Jeremiah Carter, is the real genius behind our program. And if

I may say, it is a program like no other. Sunny Daye has a one hundred percent success rate."

"So the pamphlet says, repeatedly," David grumbles.

She chirps, "That was my idea. Shout it from the rooftops, I said. Tell the whole world what Sunny Daye can do."

"And what *is* that exactly?" Laura asks.

"Change lives, Mrs. Samson. Maybe even make the world a better place."

Serena stops in her tracks, squinting at Emily. "You're very easy to believe. But you're not real, are you?"

Emily appears in the panel closest to Serena. The room warms, as if her smile switches on the heat. "I am as real as the program that will save Perry Samson's life."

"What kind of program is it? Deprivation? Exposure?"

"Surely Miss Samson told you." The group looks to Nadine. She cracks a guilty grin and shakes her head. "I see. I best get you to the doctors."

David skims through the pamphlet again, his wife reading over his shoulder as Emily continues them down the corridor. When they reach the end, the office door opens, revealing the Daye duo standing beside a stately man with white hair and piercing blue eyes. The office is large and comforting in soft, scarlet shades. Only one wall screen is one, pretending to be a window looking out on a quaint village.

"Please." The white-haired man gestures to the sofas. Deep crow's feet accent the corners of his eyes, and though his face is tan, it lacks the rich glint of health.

THE GREEN KANGAROOS

"Welcome to Sunny Daye," he says, an accent trilling off his tongue. "My name is Doctor Jeremiah Carter. I'm the Head Scientist at the Institute."

"That woman on the wall mentioned you," Laura says, sitting with her family.

"Her name is Emily."

"Yes, Emily. She mentioned you created this program. See, I thought when the pamphlet said 'program' it meant . . . well, not a *computer* program."

As he puffs out his chest, a one-sided smile curls up his cheek. "It's so much more than that. But first, allow me to introduce my colleagues, Doctors Alan and Marla Daye. They're the real magicians behind this place."

Alan lifts a hand and shakes his head. "Come now, Doctor Carter. We wouldn't be here if it weren't for you."

"Let's just be grateful that we're all here, especially you good folks." He nods to the Samsons, then picks up his tablet and sits. "I've had some time to review Perry's file, so I know this isn't your first time seeking help for your son."

In a blink, Laura Samson's prickly exterior melts. She exhales, her voice wavering in the sigh. David squeezes his wife's hand as Marla Daye sets a box of tissues on the table between them.

"Has Perry ever been successful in rehab?" Alan asks.

Laura dabs the tears from her eyes. "He's gotten clean before, but it never sticks. He was clean for six months at one point; we all thought it was for good. You can't understand how devastating it was when we found out he was using again."

"I do understand. We all do," Carter replies. "We've seen the pain caused by addiction, in and out of this facility. But we've seen the pain lifted, too. I assure you, salvation is possible. I see it every day."

"Not with Perry," Serena says. "I'm sorry, Doctor, but we've been through this too many times before. It's a little hard to believe."

"Ah, you must be Ms. Hall. You were married to the addict?"

"Yes."

"And an addict yourself?"

Her lip curls. "That was a long time ago."

"Only three years according to my file," Carter says.

"A lot can change in three years."

"I hope so, because we wouldn't want you to backslide while you're inside. It would make Perry's recovery that much more difficult."

"Inside where?"

Doctor Carter calls for Emily, and her face appears. "Would you please prepare some tea for the Samsons and Ms. Hall?"

"Of course, sir." She vanishes for a few moments, appearing a second before a tea tray, pot, and cups materialize on the coffee table.

Carter gestures to the refreshments. "Please, help yourself."

"I don't know how I feel about drinking something that came from nothing," Laura says.

"All somethings come from nothing, my dear," he replies.

Nadine moves first, her hands shimmying a bit as she pours the tea. She sips, and makes a deliberate "mmm" before the rest of the family dives in.

THE GREEN KANGAROOS

Once the Samsons and Serena have their cups, Doctor Carter leans forward, his fingertips tented against his chin. "How much do you folks know about our operation?"

"Only that you claim to have cured every patient you've treated," David says.

Marla smiles. "We claim it because it's true."

"And from what I've observed of Perry, I believe we can continue that trend. With his family's approval, of course."

"What do you mean, you've observed him? Where is he?" Laura asks.

"He's here, Mrs. Samson, in this very building."

Serena's eyebrows jump up her forehead. "He came to treatment himself? That's a first."

"Technically, no . . ."

"Then how did he get here?" Laura leaps to her feet, her hands balled into fists. "What have you done with my son?"

Nadine pats her mother's back, coaxing her to sit. "Mom, calm down. Perry is fine—well, no worse off than usual."

"Now you listen to me, young lady. You found this place, and you're keeping details from us. I want you to spill the beans right now, or I am out of here."

"Please, Mrs. Samson, I am happy to answer any questions you have regarding my program," Carter says.

"I want my daughter to tell me the truth. The *whole* truth."

Mr. and Mrs. Samson stare at Nadine. She turns to Serena, but there's no sympathy there, either.

"Fine," she grunts. "But I don't know everything.

All I know is that Perry is somewhere in this building, hooked up to a machine or something, and he's—well, he's in a simulation."

"What kind of simulation?"

"One that will help you get the old Perry back," Jeremiah Carter answers.

David's eyes snap to the doctor. "Excuse me, but you don't know anything about our son. I don't care what it says in your file, you don't know him, and you don't know us."

"I know that if this treatment had been available thirteen years ago, your son Trevor would still be alive."

David Samson jumps up from the couch, his wife on his heels. He shoves himself in Carter's face, but the doctor doesn't flinch.

"How dare you talk about our son like that!" Laura cries. "Trevor made a *mistake*. He was nothing like Perry. He was—it was just a terrible accident."

"I agree, Mrs. Samson. Addicts *are* terrible accidents," Jeremiah says. "No offense, Miss," he adds, nodding to Serena.

"I don't know how I'm *not* supposed to be offended by that," she replies. "What kind of doctor are you?"

"The kind all of you need, unless you want another dead son on your hands."

"You son of a bitch!" David growls. "You're lucky I don't rip your goddamn head off."

The Dayes stay perfectly still, watching the show as if they've seen it a thousand times before.

"I apologize if my manner seems rough. I find it's the only way to get through to addicts, sometimes—

their families, too. The way you deal with Perry's problem is a problem in itself. You are addicted to Perry's addiction, and you need just as much treatment as he does," Doctor Carter says. "Fortunately for you, that is exactly how this program operates. While Perry gets well, you get well. Together."

Laura flinches when Nadine touches her shoulder, and tears roll down her cheeks. "Mom, Dad, please sit down. Let the doctors explain the process before you freak out."

David embraces his wife and they return to the couch. Laura dries her eyes, clears her throat, and faces Doctor Carter. "Okay, we're listening. But Trevor has nothing to do with this. I don't want to talk about him."

"We can't promise that, Mrs. Samson. As we delve into Perry's issues, we may find that your other son has quite a lot to do with this," Marla Daye says.

"Just watch what you say, all right?"

"We'll try our best," Carter says. "But before we go any further . . . Emily?"

"Yes, Doctor?" Emily appears on the wall.

"Would you please bring some biscuits?"

"Absolutely, Doctor. More tea?"

"That would be lovely, thank you," he says, and her image fades. "A wonderful girl, Emily. She oversees many of the programs at the facility. You never need to worry about your son's safety while Emily monitors his simulation—*your* simulation, too."

"What is this simulation you keep talking about?" Serena asks.

"Let me show you." Carter points to a panel on the wall, which fills with a picture of Patterson Park. On the faded grass, Perry Samson lies in a puddle of blood.

"Oh my God, Perry!" Laura screams. "He's hurt! He's bleeding! Someone has to help him!"

Nadine squeezes her hand. "It's okay, Mom. It isn't real. Perry is here, in this building, remember?"

"I don't understand. If he's here, I want to see him."

"You can't. You'll disrupt the reality of the simulation," Nadine says, then raises an eyebrow at the Dayes. "Except, he was beat up in the park the last time I was here. Is he still there in his mind?"

"We've paused his program until you come to a decision about his treatment," Alan says. "Don't worry. He receives nourishment through IVs, and Emily executes hygiene programs twice a day. He's in no more danger here than he is in sleep. If you decide to work with us, we can resume the program and his progress will continue as planned."

"So, our son is hooked into a machine that makes him think he's doing drugs in Baltimore?"

"Correct, Mr. Samson. To Perry, he is living life as usual, making the same decisions he would at home. Our job is to simulate heightened danger in order to train him into making different decisions—better, healthier decisions."

"To brainwash him out of being an addict?" Laura asks.

"No, Mom, it's not like that."

"I wouldn't mind if it were—as long as it works."

When Emily's face appears on the wall, a plate of

cookies materializes on the table. The teapot fills, and new steam rises from the spout.

Doctor Carter pours himself a fresh cup and cools it with his breath. After a sip, he sets down his cup and smiles. "My program isn't brainwashing, Mrs. Samson, but it does work. How quickly it works depends on your involvement in Perry's simulated world."

"What would we have to do?" Nadine leans forward in wide-eyed hope.

"The world you see on this screen is one created in part by my program and in part by Perry himself. His memories paint and populate this world, and his expectations—about his everyday life and his interactions with his closest family and friends—allow for the false world to mimic reality," he explains. "For instance, each of you exists in Perry's simulated world, along with people connected to you. Serena, your boyfriend is the one who gave Perry this particular injury. They got into a bit of a scuffle over his, shall we say, *fixation* on you."

"But my boyfriend and I broke up," Serena says.

"Perry doesn't know that, apparently. As far as he knows, you're dating some lawyer. I won't mention the sort of thoughts he's had in regards to you, but I will say that he thinks about you quite often."

"That's too bad for him."

"He's talked to Serena in his simulation?" Nadine asks. "And she's a perfect copy of the real thing?"

Alan swallows a bite of a biscuit. "Not yet. We've kept the four of you away from him while we waited for the real thing."

"But we have teased him with flashes of Nadine," Jeremiah adds.

"Me? Why?"

"Because it hurts him to think of you. He feels ashamed. That's how we can push him toward sobriety—by playing that shame. With you as real characters in his simulation, it will be even easier."

"Are you saying you want to hook us up to machines too? You want to put our minds into his?" David Samson asks.

"In a manner of speaking, yes," Carter replies. "Perry takes a lot of risks to maintain his atlys habit, and he doesn't care about them because he only thinks of himself. He regards himself as nothing; if he dies, no one will even notice. Addicts are selfish, but they also have no self worth. They take, take, take until their families give up. But it's still never the addict's fault. They are misunderstood, they're victims, and they're too base for new love because they were never loved in the first place."

Nadine snorts. "That's Perry, all right."

"What's that supposed to mean?" her mother asks.

"Perry has always felt unloved—or loved less—by you and Dad."

Laura's face scrunches. "That's doesn't sound familiar to me."

Her face in her teacup, Nadine grumbles, "No, it wouldn't, would it?"

Alan calls their eyes to him. "The point is, when you four are in the simulation with Perry, we'll be able to raise the stakes. We can show him just how much he stands to lose."

"How do you know we won't let the truth slip once we're inside?" Serena asks.

"She's right. I'm not sure I can lie to my son like that," Laura says.

"It won't be a lie," Marla replies. "Once you're plugged in, you won't know it's a simulation any more than Perry does. It will keep you honest and your interactions natural. Every potential danger will seem real to you, and because of your reactions, Perry will be pushed to make a choice."

"Up to three choices," Alan adds.

"I don't understand."

"The program relies on tests of Perry's true character: the good person buried beneath the addiction. He will be given three opportunities to choose good over evil, his family over drugs. By the third challenge, he will be cured." Doctor Carter leans back in his chair as if the statement alone is his success.

"What if he doesn't pass the tests?" Laura asks.

"Most patients don't pass the first. That's why I allowed for three."

"Yes, but what if he doesn't pass the third one?"

Carter nods. "He will. They always pass the third test."

"But what if he doesn't?" David presses.

Doctor Carter's levity fades. The corners of his mouth droop, and he hunches over. "I prefer not to think about it that way. I prefer to stay positive. There is too much negativity and worry in the world, especially involving addicts and their families. Let's put a stop to that right now, shall we?"

"You said you would use us to create potential dangers," Serena says. "Say you dangle me and a bottle of raw atlys over a cliff and Perry chooses atlys over me—I won't die, will I?"

"Yes, you will," Alan says. "Perry wouldn't learn anything from his lesson if you didn't die."

Serena and the Samsons freeze, their faces paling at the doctor's reply, as well as the laughter that follows.

Carter covers his grin. "You won't *really* die, Ms. Hall. You'll wake up from the simulation, refreshed. You won't even remember what happened in the simulation. Only Perry. In the case of death, you'll just have to hang out here until the program is complete, that's all."

A collective sigh blows through the room, but the color doesn't return to their faces. The thought of a simulated death is as terrifying as the real thing.

"Can Perry do the program without us? Can we refuse to go into the simulation?" Laura asks.

"I'm not certain he would succeed in his recovery, and I refuse to execute a program I'm not certain will succeed," Jeremiah says.

"How much will it cost?"

"The cost, I'm afraid, is rather high, but the result is more than worth the price. A Sunny Daye treatment isn't like that of any other rehabilitation center. There will be no relapse. There will be no overdose. There will only be victory. Your son, your brother, your ex-husband will emerge from the Institute a better, more productive member of society."

Nadine silently pleads with her parents. Obvious reservations linger in their expressions, but as Serena and the Samson family exchange quiet conversations, there is hope where it was once thought gone forever.

Nadine whispers, "Please, give him another chance. Just one more."

THE GREEN KANGAROOS

Serena shakes her head, but the "no" eventually becomes a nod. She growls, but her voice is surprisingly soft when she says, "Fine."

"You'll do it?" Nadine asks.

"It would be nice to see Perry get clean."

Nadine's eyes widen in joy. "Do you think you could get back together?"

"I didn't think it was possible for him to get sober before today, so I would've said there was no way in hell. But this place—if it does what it says, it must be a miracle. In that case, I can't rule out any possibilities, especially when it comes to a man I used to love." Serena allows a smile to tickle its way up her cheek.

"Mom? Dad?"

The Samsons look to each other, to the doctors, to their daughter. David kisses his wife's hand and she exhales. "As long as it's safe."

Nadine throws herself into her parents' arms. "Really? We can do it?"

"As long as it's safe," Laura repeats, glancing at the doctors, who nod in unison.

"That sounds like a yes to me." Carter presses a button on the table, and a digital contract appears on the wall. "I just need all of your signatures on this document. Feel free to take as much time as you need to read it. At Sunny Daye, we're about turning addicts into happy, high-functioning citizens liberated from the bonds of intoxication, not deception and small print."

They gather around the wall, reading the contract and nodding along until they reach the signature section.

JESSICA MCHUGH

"If you approve, please sign on the line, and we'll get Perry's program back on track."

Their fingers swoop over the screen, marking the contract with their names. When Nadine completes the last stroke of the "n" in "Samson," Doctor Carter claps in jubilance. The Dayes shake the Samsons' hands, congratulating them.

"A fine decision," Jeremiah says. "You just made the world a better place."

"And saved Perry's life," Nadine adds.

"We'll see about that. Emily, would you please ready the transport back to the Institute?"

Nadine's forehead furrows. "I'm confused. Isn't *this* the Institute?"

"Oh . . . no," he says through a smile. "I'm afraid that was a lie. It's a bad habit, I know. I think I picked it up from working with addicts." He hums as he opens a desk drawer and removes three gas masks. He tosses two to the Dayes, and secures the third on his face.

"What are those for?" David asks.

Jeremiah's eyes smile when he says, "This."

The office fills with thick clouds billowing around Serena and the Samsons. They cough violently, struggling to stay conscious, but the battle proves futile. One by one, they crumple to the floor. Nadine is the last to fall, glaring at Doctor Carter for as long as she can before sleep claims her. Once her eyes are closed, Jeremiah chirps Emily's name. The woman on the wall appears, looking down at the pile of bodies in pity.

"Was that necessary, sir?"

Carter stands in front of Perry's screen, grinning at his beloved program. "Absolutely not."

64

SIX

MY EYELASHES FEEL hooked into the swollen skin beneath my eyes. It's like eons of crust have settled into the wrinkles, getting harder the more I blink, covering my face in biological concrete. I try to wipe it away, but my hands won't move. My arms, my legs—my entire body is pinned to the spot. I stretch my face, and the crust cracks. My eyes snap open, promptly stung by the harsh violet light coloring the room. My head is so heavy I'm only able to lift it enough to see my naked body on the table. Despite my immobility, I appear unrestrained. My heart races as I fight against invisible straps, feeling like it might burst out of my chest before I'm able to break free from the table.

I shake as I force my body upward until my hands and knees press against—I don't know what it is, but it feels like a force field, pushing me down. The harder I battle to break through, the more it hurts. My muscles burn so badly that acid fills the back of my throat. As painful as it is, frothing over my tongue, it's nothing compared to what the invisible barrier does to my skin. I push, and it sears my flesh, ribbons of smoke twisting around me. The burning stench makes me woozy, and I allow the force field to slam my raw, sizzling body back to the table. I scream, but no one comes. Instead, the walls of my invisible prison spray my body with a stinging liquid. I wail until the spraying stops and the room fills with the clean scent of isopropyl alcohol. Looking down, I realize my wounds have healed, even disappeared.

Where the fuck am I?

I don't know how long I've been here, but it's been long enough for my last hit to vacate my body, leaving only pleading tremors for more. I'm perfectly still, but I'm a tumbler of nausea and anxiety inside. I'd be sweating bullets if not for the cool breeze within my invisible shell. The most my sweat is allowed to do is bud before it's sucked out of my pores.

I pass out again. I wake and sleep and wake and sleep. I don't know how many times—or how many days—I lose. But I'm never hungry when I wake. Twisting my arm, I see something strange among my track marks. A small red dot peeks between my bruises—a clean puncture wound. Someone knew what they were doing, and they took more care in shooting me up than I ever do. Someone has been sticking me. Someone has been watching me.

Again, where the fuck am I?

I close my eyes and fight sleep. I have to stay awake. I have to know what's happening to me. Withdrawal makes my insides itch. I want to shear the skin from my bones so I can get a good scratch in, but it's all I can do not to let unconsciousness swallow me. My eyes roll around the scenes created in my mind, but I'm not sure the distraction is worth the memory's pain.

THE GREEN KANGAROOS

I'm eleven years-old again, helping Nadine build a pillow fort. She's collected every pillow in the house, but the den can't contain them all. So, our fort becomes a castle, branching into the living room with quilted roofs, tented and canopied. We're eager to explore the behemoth, but we don't. We stay outside for fear of knocking our masterpiece down before Trevor gets home.

While we wait, Trevor dies in a Baltimore slum.

Dad comes home, the news fresh in his heart. But he doesn't tell us right away. Our pillow fort distracts him, enrages him. Without a word, he storms our castle and kicks it down. He throws the cushions and blankets, and collapses onto the pillows Nadine had nabbed from our dead brother's bed. Even after the news breaks, our father doesn't move from that spot for two days.

How long has it been since I moved? How long have I been awake, my eyes closed, in this strange place? How much longer can I wait?

The door opens, and someone enters the room. There's no indication of how, but the force field is suddenly gone. I can move my arms and legs again—but I don't. I squint open my eyes to see a man in black scrubs preparing to inject a brown liquid into my arm. He doesn't notice I'm awake until I strike. My fist jerks up, hooking under his chin. He's launched backward as I slide from the table. But the force field returns before I'm completely free, catching me by my left leg. I shriek as it sears my ankle, but I don't stop pulling. It strips the first layer of skin from my foot, and I fall to the floor, screaming over the sizzle.

The man in black scrubs isn't any better off than I am. I've knocked his jaw out of place, and a bottom tooth has punched through his top lip. His mouth is covered in blood; each breath sprinkles the floor with red dots.

He's dropped the needle. It hurts to drag my scorched foot, but I crawl across the floor anyway. Putting the needle to his neck, I demand to know where I am.

The man sputters blood across my face. "It's no secret, man. You're at Springfield." The name is like an iron-toed kick to the junk, pain echoing in my starving veins.

I pull the needle away, trembling. "Springfield Hospital in Sykesville?"

"Yes, I swear," he says. "Please don't hurt me anymore."

"How the hell did I get here?"

"I don't know. I'm just an orderly, okay? I just administer the nutrient shots."

The door opens, and two guards storm in. There's no point in fighting them; even if they weren't stronger than me, the combination of withdrawal and my fried foot keeps me from having the smallest of dogs in the fight. I drop the needle and scoot away from the man in black, my hands up.

"Why am I here?" I ask them.

I throw numerous signs of surrender as they back me up to the wall, but they show no mercy. Their fists are massive balls of hail pummeling me into a crouched position. One of the men stomps on my oozing foot before he pulls me up and whips me against the wall. My skull smacks the concrete, and when I hit the floor it feels like my entire body leaks across it—and not just blood. The orderlies collect the guy in black scrubs and carry him to the door.

"Please." The word dangles crimson from my lips. "How did I get here?"

"You were checked in," one says. "By a girl named Nadine."

It's an extra wallop I don't need. They close the door, leaving me pained in a puddle of blood and piss. But the real pain comes in unconsciousness, when I return to that horrible day, watching my father sob on the rubble of our pillow fort. Mom is the one to explain Trevor's death to us, but as clear as she is, Nadine doesn't get it. She's only seven—how could she possibly understand that Trevor is gone?

"When's he coming back?" Nadine asks.

"He's not, honey. He's gone for good."

I'll never forget that. "Gone for good." *For good?* How could the death of a sixteen year-old kid be "for good"? I know that's not how she meant it; it probably broke her heart when I put it to her that way, but I couldn't wrap my head around the fact that my big brother, someone who'd tested at genius levels, brought home scores of blue ribbons from every competition he entered, could be stupid enough to die so young.

I was angrier than I'd ever been. At Trevor, at my parents, at how Nadine screamed "my brother is dead!" like she'd become an only child. Trevor's death earned him even more attention, his face plastered on more walls of the house, his awards more prominently displayed. I wasn't conscious of the thought at the time, but looking back, how could I not want to follow in Trevor's footsteps?

His face is the last thing I see before my eyes open, wet with tears. I expect to wake up weighed down like before, aching from head-to-toe. But except for the lingering bitch named "Withdrawal" raking my body with fevered fingers, I feel better than I'd thought. I'm clothed and under bed sheets, but neither look clean. The faces to my left are just as crusty, and we're packed together so tight it's no surprise the room smells like sardines. It's built for two, maybe three men at most, but there are six of us cramped together on three single beds pushed into one mega-mattress.

The bed shakes a bit, but I can't tell why. A kid, no older than fifteen, stares at me from the right. His full-body grin is so tense it takes me a few seconds to realize he's masturbating. The sheets whistle with the motion while a scarred man to my left expels a webby cackle. Panels of shiny pink scar tissue stretch over his chin, cheek, and up into his scalp: a stark contrast to the pitted, mahogany mess on the other side. My eyes hate me for keeping them locked on his face, but anything's better than seeing the Jerk-Off Kid's howling climax.

The LCD screen walls comprising the room are spattered with shit and cum, and I assume some of the brown patches used to be redder. A bolted door stands opposite, leading to the rest of the ward, but there's no point in trying to get through. I learned that lesson the last time I tried to break out of Springfield Hospital.

It was six years ago. Nadine came over to my apartment for a friendly visit that became not-so-friendly when she found a needle I'd neglected to hide. I remember her screams vividly, as if the echo's still trapped between my ears.

THE GREEN KANGAROOS

"Atlys, Perry? How *could* you? After what happened to Trevor, *how could you?*"

I wanted to hug her as much as hit her. She could never understand. Even Serena, who was just as deep in addiction, couldn't grasp my reasons for fucking around with the same drug that killed my brother. I wasn't one hundred percent on every reason myself. All I cared about was how atlys made me feel: like whether hell or high water I could come out the other side clean.

The irony didn't amuse the doctors at Springfield. Nor did they appreciate my escape attempt. During one of my therapy sessions with Doctor Whogivesafuck, I'd faked a migraine, which wasn't hard with the withdrawal. While he dug into his pocket for pain reliever, I smacked him with my chair. I'd fought enough junkies to know I'd broken his nose. As he writhed on the floor, blood draining from his face, I grabbed his keystick and ran. I didn't get far before I was tackled and beaten into submission, nowhere near an exit.

I played ball after that. I got sober, but I didn't get better. Every smile, every polite therapy session, every declaration of "God, Doc, you were right. I don't ever want atlys ever again. Not atlys or coke or—hell, I don't even want coffee" was part of the act. As soon as I got out of the hospital, I baked my brain in atlys butter and fucked the shit out of Serena.

Lying is part of an addict's every day routine, but it usually results in some kind of intoxication. The constant lies in rehab nearly drove me crazy the first time. I don't think I can handle another ninety day stretch.

The hospital hasn't changed much. It's still a rundown joint with slapdash technology. Although, it does have hologram chairs now. Because of me? I wonder . . .

Four years before my first stint, it had been closed for nearly sixty. They hadn't felt the need to clean up the cobwebs then, and it doesn't look much classier now. I suppose our kind shouldn't need class to get clean. All we need is a room stuffed with disgusting reflections of ourselves, condescending therapy sessions, and the occasional visit from family members who act like abducted angels forced to watch a devil's feast. It's ridiculous. The low-grade tranquilizers Springfield provides are no feast, no matter how desperate the devil. I've shoved better drugs up my ass.

The scarred man tugs on my shit. "Whatcha in for?"

I don't reply. The last thing I want is to get close to these rats. Allies are good if you plan on sticking around, but I don't. Besides, having friends is an easy way to earn a longer stretch. The dicks in charge don't like punishing one patient—what kind of impression would that make? It's more effective to punish a group, to show the high price of addict camaraderie to the populace.

Not every patient in Springfield is an addict. Some are just lunatics. But the doctors see no difference in the diseases afflicting the cattle. We are a single, poisoned herd, and most of us will never be fit to breed or show. I guess that's why so many of us wind up in a meat market like the Kum Den Smokehouse.

I'm reminded of my own journey there. I slide my

hand down my pants, and the Jerk-Off Kid hoots as he dives into his own. Crawling over my thigh, my fingers dip into the gouge, catching on the spiky stitches.

Jesus Christ, Perry. What have you done to yourself?

A knock on the door makes the entire room twitter with excitement. By the time the lock slides open, most of the patients are on their feet. They pour out into the ward, running for the TV like good little junkies. When you don't have your drug of choice, you'll do anything to get a comparable high, and when the only available intoxicant is trash TV, you'll search for a way to mainline it. The scarred-up dude heads for the door but turns at the last second, aiming for a wall clouded by crusty film. At first, I think he's testing the integrity of the room, maybe digging a tunnel to the outside or squirreling away meds to cook into a super hit. Maybe I'd been too harsh in ignoring him before. Maybe I *could* use an ally in Springfield, especially if he's willing to share his loot.

I say, "Hey."

He flinches but doesn't turn. Then I hear the sound of running water and catch a whiff of urine. A pool of piss flows across the floor, stinging my burnt foot. I growl as I shake off my feet and return to the bed. When his stream stops, he tugs up his zipper and turns with an unapologetic smirk on the pink side of his face.

"I thought everyone left the room," he says.

"I said 'hey.' Don't act like you didn't hear me."

"I'd already started going by that point. You don't expect me to stop mid-stream, do ya?"

The response is so sincere that, despite my pain, I can't blame the guy—until I remember we're in the room where I'll have to sleep for the duration of my stay.

"Maybe you should hold it 'til you get to the bathroom next time," I say.

"What would be the fun in that?" He extends his hand to me.

I know where it just was, but his unwashed dick hand might be one of the cleanest things in Springfield, so I shake it.

"You asked what I'm in for. It's atlys," I say. "At least, I think so. The last thing I remember is fighting my ex-wife's fuckstick of a boyfriend. Honestly, I thought I was as good as dead."

He snickers. "Just like a junkie to put 'good' and 'dead' that close together."

"You've known a lot, I take it."

Smirking, he nods. "Meet a new one everyday. All hopeless, all hopeful."

"What does that mean?"

"You hope to get out of here, right?" I nod. "You hope to get more smack or whatever you dig, right?"

"That's the goal, yeah."

"Yeah. Like I said, hopeless."

I laugh. He's not wrong, but he's clearly crazy. It's further proven by the way he whips out his dick and squirts a stream of piss at a holographic chair.

"Jesus, man, go to the bathroom, will you?"

He turns, loosing another spurt of reeking urine. "Nah, the toilets ain't sparky enough for me."

"I'd ask what you're in for, but I think I know," I say as he zips his pants. Looking at the foggy piss wall, I ask, "How long have you been in here?"

THE GREEN KANGAROOS

"Long enough to know I ain't gettin' out."

"So you're just as hopeless as me."

He lights a yellow-speckled cigarette. "Hardly. I just got high on the wall and the chair. My hope springs eternal, bitch."

"I wish I could say the same. I've been in this place before, and I wasn't exactly looking forward to another visit."

"You could bust out," someone says. I turn to see the Jerk-Off Kid, one hand in his pants and the other one flicking a cigarette.

I scoff at him. "Trust me, man. There's no busting out."

"Sure there is. I've done it three times in the past six months." He pulls out his right hand. "Name's Border. What's yours?"

This is a dick-hand I refuse to shake. "Perry," I reply, turning back to the pisser. "And you are?"

He exhales a puff of smoke and grunts, "Cassiopeia."

"Cassiopeia, the pee-ah? I don't buy it."

"Yeah, it's not my real name, but no one's called me anything else for years. After my first piss on a keyboard, the nickname stuck."

"Why would you piss on a keyboard?"

"Or a wall. Or a chair," Border mutters.

Cassio shrugs. "Fucked if I know why it feels good. Burnt out synapses confusing electronic impulses with the impulse to evacuate my bladder? Some shit about my mama playing in an electro-punk band instead of potty-training me? Or maybe it's just the devil in my dickhead. I heard every explanation in the world, but nothing stops the urge, so why try? Shit, I ain't hurtin' no one. My piss is clean as the Virgin Mary's asshole."

"You mean 'pussy'," Border says.

"If I meant 'pussy,' I woulda said 'pussy.' Besides, that twat's dirty as any the other Bethelwhores that came before. She popped out a fatty mouth-breather, too, and it took some dirty dog to make it happen. I don't care if it was the schlong of God or some other motherfucker. Some dude's cock made room in Mary's inn."

I laugh. "Christ, that's a hell of a religion you have there. What do you call that?"

He snorts before replying. "Sanity."

Said the man in the nuthouse, I think to myself. And I'm the idiot talking to him.

Border elbows my side. "Don't listen to anything this guy says. One time, I caught him pissing in Nurse Baylor's mouth, and Nurse Baylor's a dude."

"That's a fuckin' lie. If there's anyone you shouldn't trust, it's this skinny motherfucker with his hand on his crank. Bitch hasn't said a word of truth in the entire time I've known him."

"That's because you don't really know me, brotha'."

"Bitch, do not call me brother. I ain't your goddamn brother," Cassio says.

Border leans against me, twisting his fingers together like a cartoon villain on coke.

"We ain't brothers, so Cassio and I ain't leaving together," he says. "But you could come with me the next time I break out."

"Next time. Ain't never been a first time," Cassio says. "You should know, Border's a compulsive liar. Ain't told the truth once in his whole pathetic life."

THE GREEN KANGAROOS

Border narrows his eyes at Cassio. "The last time someone brought a phone into the ward, Cassiopeia swiped it. Pissed on it so many times, the screen turned into this weird purple powder. We dared Bungalow Bill to snort it," Border says. "That's a fuckin' fact. Don't you even try to deny it."

He rolls his eyes. "Yeah, okay, that's true."

"And the phone still worked," Border adds.

"That is *not* true."

Their banter makes me dizzy, and I suddenly realize I'm glazed in sweat. My body is so racked with pain, I don't notice my toes stinging anymore. It's a constant ache now. I imagine several drummers stationed throughout my body, pounding a steady beat to my withdrawal. I lay facedown on a bed, not caring whether it's mine. Nothing in Springfield is really mine, anyway. I'm a prisoner here. I'm a pet. They tug my choke chain and try to train me. But I've been feral for too long.

Except *they* aren't the ones who put me here. Nadine did.

Atlys sickness has a keen way of corrupting my thoughts. Seeds of paranoia take root and beget anger in a way that never happens when I'm high. I can think clearer when I have a buzz. Why can't I just get high?

She should've let me die. She shouldn't keep trying to save me, but she wouldn't be who she is if she gave up. I just hope she knows that the more she puts herself in my way, the more pain she invites. I can't apologize for that pain forever. There has to be a time when it's not my fault anymore.

As I writhe, I feel like the sheets are strangling me. When I cry out for help, foamy saliva sprays from my mouth and my nose bleeds. The pain is like nothing I've ever felt, and it only gets worse. If this is what Nadine wanted, she fucking got it.

The bed is soaked with cold sweat, but it also feels engulfed in flames. My brain runs out of my nose, and I taste my memories. Algebra, kick flips, Serena, Trevor, Nadine . . . Fuck you, Nadine. You did this to me. What the fuck did I ever do to you?

She is curled up on the bed next to me, her hair in a high ponytail like it was when we were kids—before Trevor died. Afterwards, it was always tied low. I guess she thought it would be disrespectful for it to be so high. Not me, though. I got as high as possible.

"I love you, Bear. Can't you see that?" she whispers.

"If you really loved me, you'd let me do what I want to be happy."

"You're never happy."

"Neither are you."

She rubs her nose and sniffles. She's always had an itchy nose. "I'm allergic to bears," she says, then fades away.

A gruff voice penetrates my haze. "Shit, man, what's wrong with you?"

I look over to the man with urine spots on his fly and the kid with a twitching erection.

"A lot, I think," I say.

"You'll be perfect to help me break out," Border says.

"Not this bullshit again," Cassio grunts. "Listen to this punk if you want, but I'm gonna go watch the excavation of the Olsen twins' tomb on TV. S'posed to be some kind of treasure in there, and I don't doubt it. White bitches always got some kind of crazy shit stashed away."

As soon as he's gone, the Jerk-Off Kid is on the bed, tucked into the same position as Nadine, except for the hand down his pants.

"Hey, you gonna be okay?" he asks.

"Don't start moving that hand and I'll be fine."

My stomach gurgles, and I burp up bitter grit. I grip my belly, groaning.

"Look, I know you don't believe me, but I can get you out of here," Border says. "And not just that. I know a place you can go. It's not far from here. It's like Disney World for guys like you and me."

"I'm not a Disney World kind of dude. Not enough dealers in the Magic Kingdom."

"That's not a problem at this place. There are drugs galore, whatever your poison, and the chicks—they don't come free, but they do come easy."

"Bullshit. What kind of place?"

He grins. "A land of dreams, my friend. It's a renovated barn filled to the brim with so many earthly delights, you'd think you were in Heaven."

"What's the catch?"

"You have to pay to party, but it shouldn't be too big a problem. My uncle Benito owns the joint. Wanna come?"

"Dude, I was in here before. I tried to get out."

"It must've been a while ago, 'cuz I've been here since I was twelve, and seen the guards and orderlies go downhill. They don't give a flying fuck about their jobs. All they care about are loose nurses, free meals, and enough money to keep them in booze. The fucking guards are worse than some of the patients. Way worse than you."

"I doubt that, but thanks."

He lifts his chin, his eyes sparkling in pride. "My mother is the mayor of Sykesville, so I know everything that goes on in this town. I know everything about everyone." He moves to the floor beside my bed and points out the door. "You see that dude in red socks?"

My vision is hazy, but I see two dots of red dancing back and forth, so I nod.

"He used to be a cop. One of the best, they say. Always fought for people's rights, preservation of nature and shit, even volunteered at a soup kitchen. There wasn't anyone that dude wouldn't help."

"What happened to him?"

"He snapped. No one knows why. He doesn't talk about it—doesn't talk at all. He just dances, probably to help him forget about what he did, on that summer day in the park."

I lean forward. "What did he do?"

"He killed . . ." His eyes dart to the left and right. ". . . a cat!"

I spit. "A cat?"

"What, not an animal lover?" Border asks.

"I don't know. It just doesn't seem like a committable offense."

"You don't think a soup kitchen volunteer murdering a cat sounds crazy?" he asks. "Or you think I'm lying?"

My stomach rolls with nausea. "I don't know, man. And I don't care. I don't plan on being here long enough to find out."

"That's the spirit. Just the sort we'll need to get out."

THE GREEN KANGAROOS

An orderly slaps his hand against the wall to get our attention. "You're Samson, right—shit, son, what happened to your face?"

My nose has stopped bleeding, but the blood hangs on like a crimson goatee.

"My head hurts," I say. I try to stand, but my legs won't support me. I crumple to the floor. Someone sounds an alarm and I soon feel hands moving over me. I am flying—being lifted, most likely, but I prefer to think the former. It reminds me of getting high. I only know because of my blood—it begs me for just one hit.

"You can do that, can't you, Perry? Just one hit for my sake, so I can stop feeling like shit all the time? Hey, how about I coax the Iron Men out? You were such good buddies back in the day. When you were together, you were stronger, better. We could all hang out. You, me, the Iron Men, and one glorious hit of atlys."

I wish I could say yes, but a hit is impossible as long as I'm in here. And escape is impossible as long as I'm this sick. Something has to be done.

According to a young, bright-eyed doctor named Collins, I have spent two days in the infirmary since my collapse in the ward. He apologizes as he helps me sit up in bed.

"I was told the drugs were completely flushed from your system, but it was an oversight," he says. "You shouldn't have been introduced into the community so soon. I understand how embarrassed you must be."

I put embarrassment behind me the first time I fucked a withered cuntcutter in order to steal a sniff

81

of her atlys. I can't be embarrassed anymore, or maybe it's just been too long since I felt the antithesis. Pride is too expensive a drug.

"What's wrong with me?" My lips still taste of blood.

"It appears you had a bad reaction to the cleanser. It happens sometimes," Doctor Collins says.

"Cleanser?"

"It's a medicine that rids your body of intoxicants, although it can backfire in extreme cases like yours. Most of the atlys in your system was sweated out, but the remaining actually fused with the cleanser. It causes dizziness, hallucinations, nausea, bleeding—"

My eyes widen. "You mean I was high?"

"I wouldn't put it like that. You were poisoned, more accurately."

"And I didn't even get to enjoy it," I whisper sadly.

The doctor shakes his head as he takes my pulse. It's sluggish, but for the first time since I woke up in Springfield, I feel alert.

"You may notice a bit of a body buzz over the next few hours," he says. "To counteract the cleanser, we pumped some revitalizer into your system."

I grin, raising my eyebrows. "Sounds like a fun ride."

"Sure." He slaps a towel over his shoulder and puts a bucket in front of me. "But the truth is we didn't like the name 'vomiter.'"

"Huh?"

My stomach lurches, and my body is thrown forward. With a scream that comes from the pit of my belly, I disgorge a foamy green liquid into the bucket. Burning bile follows with croaking heaves that pushes puke through my tightened throat. After my stomach feels empty, I try to spit out the horrible taste, but it won't go. My tongue is coated in a heavy film that tastes like I've eaten nothing but aspirin for the past year.

Patting my back, the doctor says, "You need to give it up."

"You're the one who put this shit in me!"

"The drugs, Perry. Your body reacted this way to the cleanser because of your unholy dependence. Your organs are so clotted with atlys, they can't handle anything designed to expel it. They're liquefying under the weight of your addiction."

"Bullshit."

"I could show you the evidence, but I doubt you'd understand it. It doesn't look like you've used your brain much in the last few years, except as a junkyard. You're killing yourself, Perry, and it's happening quickly."

"I know."

"Don't you care?"

Through the haze, a realization sharpens. If I want to get out, if I want to get high, I have to play the game. I might go insane, but at least I'll be free.

I lower my head and wipe away a tear. Thanks to the vomiting fit, they're real.

"Yes, I care," I say to him. "I want to get clean so bad, Doctor Collins. Not only for myself, but for my family. I've hurt them so much over the years, sometimes intentionally. I don't want to do that anymore. I want to be sober."

I assume the lies make me retch again, but a glimmer of truth curls me over the bucket, too.

"Intentionally" is acidic when it pours over my lips, hitting the lake of vomit with a slap speckling my face in cold shame.

"Please, help me." I cough. The strings of bile dangling from my mouth are too thick to pull free, as if tied to my stomach.

Doctor Collins hands me some water. "Drink it."

It's the best thing I've tasted in days. Years, actually. The water at Highlandtown High is murky at best. The state of the hospital isn't much better, but the water tastes infinitely cleaner.

"Feel better?"

I nod. He smiles like someone who's yet to be betrayed by scum of the earth like me. Doctor Collins waves to a passing nurse, but once she's gone, he grabs my sweaty collar. He yanks me close. I know my breath is horrible, so the tiny inch he allows between us is a good indication of his solemnity when he says, "Don't fucking lie to me, Perry."

"I'm not lying."

"You've spent three years on the street, doing whatever it takes to get high. Lying, stealing, selling chunks of your own body, all without batting an eye. I say your organs are turning to jelly, and now you care about what happens to you? *Now* you care about your family?"

I try to push him away, but I'm too weak. The most I can do is spit in his face, but it works.

I sneer as Collins scrapes off the smelly glob. "For your information, I've always cared about my family, Doc. They're the ones who don't care."

"What makes you say that?"

"What does it matter? You won't believe me."

THE GREEN KANGAROOS

I go for another sip of water, but Collins grabs the glass and sets it out of reach.

"For *your* information, I've seen this act of yours a hundred times. If you ever want to leave this hospital, you have to make me believe you, Perry. Saying you want to get clean and actually doing the work are different things. If you want to lie your way through all the steps, that's fine with me. If you want to fight me every step of the way, that's fine too. Just don't expect to stand in the sun again."

"I hate to break it to you, Doc, but even on the clearest day, I haven't stood in the sun in years."

"Don't you think that's pathetic?"

"Of course I do, but that's the way it is."

"And nothing can change it?"

I shrug. "Why change? I'm happy when I'm high. I feel alive."

"You can't feel it if you're dead."

"You don't know that."

Collins nods, pressing a button on his watch. "Is she ready?"

A voice squawks from his wrist. "Yes, Doctor."

Before the transmission cuts out, I hear the background sigh, "As ready as I'll ever be." With that voice, I know what awaits me.

"No," I say to him.

Collins raises his eyebrows, amused by my reaction. "No what?"

"I don't want to see her. She put me here, and I don't want to see her."

"See who?"

"You know who. Please, just get my sister out of here."

The doctor pouts his lip and looks upwards as if contemplating. When he focuses on me again, his face has fallen into a stern scowl. His lips part, his eyes narrow, and he says, "No, Mr. Samson."

"I'll do whatever you want," I say. "I'll take part in your stupid program, whatever it is. Just don't make me face Nadine."

"But seeing your sister is the first step in my program, Perry. If you don't see her, if you don't listen to everything she has to say, you won't pass the first test."

"How many tests are there?"

"An infinite amount. And they don't stop once you're clean. They wait around every corner, daring you to break the rules or rise above your limitations. They are what turn boys into men, or lead to man's undoing. Life is one big test, Perry, fraught with millions of little ones. A conversation with your sister is nothing compared to the battles beyond these walls," Collins explains. "But if you fail this one, you might as well forget that a world beyond these walls exists."

"I really hate you, you know that?"

"Then you should be willing to work as hard as possible to get away from me, shouldn't you?"

His glare is a dare, but I keep mine hidden.

I sigh in surrender. I have no choice but to see her. I don't know how much I'll say, but at this point it's probably best to keep my mouth shut 'til I'm back in my room. I just hope my organs don't turn to jelly before I get the chance to talk to Border about his plan to get the fuck out of Springfield.

An orderly enters the room; it doesn't take me

long for me to recognize him. The bottom half of his face is bandaged where I forced his teeth through his lip. His eyes dig into me as he slaps leather cuffs around my wrists, tightening them until I growl.

"You're tearing my fucking skin off!"

"So . . . too loose?" he asks, his voice muffled by the gauze. He gives the cuff another vicious tug, and blood oozes from under the leather, dripping onto the sheets.

I grunt at him, my head cocked. "I'm sorry to tell you, but it appears you've gotten your period."

He backhands me, clearing my clotted sinuses with a crack. He goes for another, but Doctor Collins catches him by the arm.

The orderly whines. "Come on, Marv, he hurt me a lot worse."

"This guy's brain is going to be a hard enough fix. Don't fuck up the face too," he says. "Just go get his sister."

Collins presses a tissue to my nose—too hard. I yelp, and he apologizes, but I detect satisfaction in his voice.

Nadine follows the orderly into the infirmary, screeching when she sees my face. She runs to me, but the orderly holds her back.

"Keep your distance, Miss."

She glowers, stretching her neck to his eye level. "Don't tell me to keep my distance. He's my brother. What the hell happened to his face?"

"Trust me, Miss Samson, he deserves every bruise."

Nadine shoves her face closer. Her words pound him so hard he has to shut his eyes.

"I swear to God, if you touch my brother one more time, I will sue you for everything you have. After your house is repossessed, I'll find you in whatever hole you've crawled into and kick the shit out of you. Do you understand me?"

Same old Nadine. She's a softie when it comes to me, but with everyone else, what a ballbreaker. No one could ever mistake her for growing up with two older *sisters*.

"He broke my jaw," the orderly creaks beneath the bandages.

She looks to Doctor Collins, who nods.

Snapping her head back to me, she squeals. "What the fuck, Perry?"

"I'm really sorry about that. I guess when I woke up in a strange bed, in a burning fucking bubble thing, not knowing how I got there, I didn't have the best reaction." I tilt my head and sneer at her. "You wouldn't know anything about that, would you?"

She turns to Doctor Collins. "Would you excuse us?"

"I'm not sure you should be alone with him, Miss Samson."

"Perry would never hurt me."

"He's hurt you plenty already," he says. She agrees, catching eyes with me for a millisecond before looking back at the doctor. How can something so small feel like such a huge kick to the gut?

"Does this bed have one of those burning fucking bubble things?"

He nods. "I'll activate it. But I'll be watching, just in case."

"Thank you."

THE GREEN KANGAROOS

Once Doctor Collins and the orderly are gone, I feel pressure all over my body, like an invisible elephant has sat on my chest.

Somehow, Nadine looks different with the shield up, like someone watching a dying baboon at the zoo. I know she wants to speak, but her mouth clamps shut, her lips hidden. We wait so long in silence I think I'll feel some relief when she finally speaks, but it makes me feel worse.

"I hear your organs are liquefying," she says, meeting my eyes. "The doctors told me you might die soon."

"They always say that shit. It's a scare tactic."

"What if it's not this time? What if you're really dying?"

I shrug. "That'll be one worry off your plate."

She bows her head, and her hand moves to her face. I can't tell if she's brushing away a tear or massaging her temple. The thought of both makes my skin crawl. She scoots closer, setting her face beside mine.

"Why are we here again, Perry?"

"Because you put me here again."

"Can you blame me—no, don't answer that," she says. "What I mean is, are you surprised?"

"No. And it pisses me off. It makes me feel . . ."

"Loved?" Nadine asks.

I draw as close as I can to the barrier without it burning me. "It makes me feel like a one-legged puppy."

She smiles sadly. "I would love a one-legged puppy."

"Okay, make it one leg less. Then, chop off its ears.

Oh, and its balls. Can't have those in the way, can we? No one around Nadine Samson can have balls."

The nausea is in my brain now, dripping down my skull and saturating my tongue. It's all downhill from here. No shock there. Unlike the offended look crossing Nadine's face.

Good. Be offended, you dumb cow. You selfish bitch. You Mother Twatresa load. You—

She whispers. "Bear . . ."

"Don't call me that. Don't say it, don't think it, don't—" I grit my teeth, shaking. "Jesus fuck, why did you come here, Nadine? Why did you put me here? What do you want from me?"

I quake so violently I hit the shield, searing the hair from my left forearm.

"I'm here to tell you I was wrong," she says. "I shouldn't have tried to save you. It's clear you don't want my help."

She buries her face in her hands and sobs. The cries turn to growls as she shakes her head.

"I'm sorry, Nadine."

She lifts her head. "No, you're not. But it's okay. You don't need to be sorry about hurting me, and I don't need to be sorry about leaving you to die. That's what you want, isn't it? You don't want to be part of our family anymore. You certainly don't want happiness." She exhales and rubs her nose. "I don't want to see you anymore, Perry. Neither do Mom, Dad, or Serena. We're ready to write you off as another loss. Just like Trevor."

"Don't do that," I snap. "Don't try to make me feel bad about my decisions."

"You *should* feel bad about them. But that's not

what I'm trying to do. I'm just telling you the truth. I refuse to lose another year—or another paycheck—helping you kill yourself. If you really want to die, I'm fine with letting you work toward it. But I don't want any part of it. I can't keep hoping you get better."

My heart is broken and I don't know why. She said everything I've wanted her to say, but it hurts so bad. It hurts in a new way, only lessened by a long night in atlys's arms. But with her wavering, tear-filled eyes clamped to me, I can't even crave it. All I want to do is give her a hug and kiss her forehead like I used to when she was picked on at school. I'd comfort her, telling her to ignore those bullies. They didn't know what an amazing kid she was. They didn't know what an amazing person she'd grow up to be.

Except, she's all grown up now, and by cutting me loose, she's finally become amazing.

She wipes her face with a tissue and exhales with a shiver. It knocks away any remnant of little girl and shows me just how strong Nadine's become . . . until . . .

"Unless you do want it, deep down," she says. "If you want to be my brother again, be a real person again . . . if you want that, I can help you."

Her hair is down, but it's a high ponytail to me. She hasn't changed at all. She's still just a goddamn kid bartering with guilt.

My eyes narrow. "You didn't mean any of that other stuff. You have no intention of leaving me alone."

"I'm just saying that if you wanted it, I could see myself letting you back into my life. As long as—"

"As long as I give up everything I want. Got it."

Nadine stands up and yells for Doctor Collins.

"What are you doing?" I ask.

She looks down on me, enraged. "I'm setting you free, Perry. That's what you want, isn't it?"

I nod as much as the bubble allows. "Yes, I really do."

"Good," she spits. "I hope you die."

"I think I can help you out with that."

Nadine bursts into tears. I wish I could turn back time to bite off my tongue.

Doctor Collins and two orderlies run into the room like my words set her on fire. He wraps his arms around her, and she cries against his lab coat. "Are you all right, Miss Samson? What did he do to you?"

"He made his decision." She wipes her nose, giving me a teary glimpse before facing Collins again. "Let him go."

"Miss Samson?"

"You heard me. He doesn't want treatment, so his being here is a waste of your energy, my money, and time Perry could be using to kill himself."

"If he continues down this road, that's a guarantee," Collins says. "I want to make sure you both understand that. Perry could die from his next hit."

"That's always been a possibility," I say.

"You see? Let him go. He'd rather be dead than my brother."

The force field fades, and an orderly loosens my cuffs. I'm still woozy, and my legs are too rubbery to support me. As I fall, I reach out for a helping hand, but Nadine, who would have normally caught me, looks down with her arms crossed in defiance.

Collins helps me back onto the bed. "We can't

release him in this condition. Are you sure you won't change your mind, Miss Samson?"

"Not unless he changes his."

I don't reply. I wish I could change my mind for her, but I can't. And once I get a hit of atlys, I'll forget I ever wished it.

"Very well. I have some paperwork you'll need to fill out. Should I give you some time to say goodbye?"

"That's not necessary. He's already stolen enough time from me," she says. "Goodbye, Bea—" She stops, crinkling her forehead. "'Bye, Perry. I hope you find happiness, no matter what it takes to get there. I know I won't be happy having to tell Mom and Dad their last son is dead."

She turns on the word "dead" and marches out of the infirmary, giving me no satisfaction in the speech I'd been waiting years to hear.

"Take him back to his room and give him a nutrient shot. If he's to be discharged, he'll be discharged in the best shape possible," Collins says.

The orderlies grab me, Broken Jaw whipping me against the neighboring bed when he latches on.

"Easy . . ." I groan.

The man scoffs before pulling down his gauze. His top lip is stitched to hell. The clear thread has tangled his enflamed flesh, turning his lip into one only a mustache could love.

"I dare you to fuck with me," he says. "No one's gonna notice a few extra bruises on your face now that you're being discharged." He presses his thumb against my nose, and pain drops me to the floor. The orderlies don't wait for me to stand. They drag me down the hall until I'm able to regain my footing.

In the ward, the busted orderly pushes me into my room and tells me to sit still so he can give me the shot. He's rough when he shoots me up, but the realization that I'll soon be free to shoot myself up keeps me calm through the assault. After he withdraws the needle, he slaps the puncture wound and laughs at my wince.

After the orderlies leave, Cassiopeia enters the room with Border's fidgety ass on his heels.

"What was that all about?" he asks.

I rub the sore spot. "I'm getting out."

Cassio snorts. "Shit, I didn't know compulsive lying was contagious. Nice work, B. You ruined the dude."

"No, I'm really leaving. My sister is checking me out right now."

"Ain't that sweet?" He rolls his eyes.

"It's cool your family's got your back. She giving you a place to stay?" Border asks.

Why would she? I'm not even her brother anymore. She wants nothing to do with me. No one wants anything to do with me.

Fuck me, I can't wait to get high.

I shrug. "I don't know. I guess we'll see."

"This ain't no wait-and-see-world, son. You gotta make that shit happen for yourself. Otherwise, you're just gonna wind up back in this shithole," Cassio says.

I sneer at him. "If you hate it so much, why don't you try to get out?"

"Because I piss on electronics, son. Did you somehow miss that?"

"No, but you want to get better, don't you?"

"Do *you*?"

THE GREEN KANGAROOS

"It's different."

"Yeah? Tell that to the left side of my face, bitch. Your addiction ain't no better than mine. We're all equally fucked. You just have a dumbass sister who doesn't know the mistake she made in releasing you. You ain't gonna change any more than I am. You're gonna find the biggest hit possible and punish your sister even more than usual."

"That's not why I do it."

He snickers. "Right. Well, when you OD an hour after you get out, could ya put in a good word with the devil for me?"

He walks out, unzipping his pants as he heads for the TV room.

Once he is gone, Border scoots closer. "I have a place for you to stay."

I put some distance between us. "I don't need to break out anymore, dude. I'm being discharged."

An orderly comes to the door. "Time to go, Samson."

When I stand, Border grabs my hand. I shudder at his sticky fingers, but seeing as I'll never see him again, I let it slide.

"Wait for me," he says. "My uncle will take care of us. He's richer than God."

"What are you talking about?"

"The house I told you about. We can go there. We can live like kings. Just wait twenty minutes. Can you give me that?"

The Jerk-Off Kid is a fucking liar. If there was a house filled with pussy and drugs around, wouldn't I already know about it? Wouldn't I have sold my soul years ago for one night in paradise? I have no intention of waiting twenty minutes or even two minutes, but after wrenching Border's hand from mine, I say, "Twenty minutes. Sure thing."

I'm not escorted from Springfield Hospital as much as I'm thrown out. I swear it wasn't raining while I was inside, but in my first minute of freedom, I'm soaked. I climb the stoop again and stand under the awning, but a plump nurse knocks on the window and shoos me away like I'm no better than a rat. It's a reasonable assessment.

There's not much else shelter from the storm that isn't owned by the hospital. I consider sneaking into a nearby gazebo, but when I creep up, I see a guard smoking a cigarette inside. A few more feet allow me to see another guard smoking the first one's pole. I stifle a laugh. In a weird way, it touches my heart to see two people finding pleasure in a place that tries to cure it.

With nothing to shield me from the rain, I surrender. I squat in a ditch by the road, but it quickly becomes a swamp. No cars pass, not that I'm confident about someone picking up a muddy snake like me.

After a while, the rain stops pelting me, but it doesn't stop falling. Looking up, I see the yellow umbrella over my head first, then the kid holding it. Border grins, spinning the umbrella.

"You waited," he says.

"Uh, yeah." I stand and shake the excess water from my hair.

"When we get to the house, remind me to ask my uncle to give you a ruby or two. As a thank you."

How fucking crazy is this kid? His mom is a mayor

and his uncle has rubies? No wonder he has so much to jerk-off about.

"I don't think I'm going."

"You have to, Perry. I need someone else to go with me or I can't—I mean, it's just better that way. The girls do pairs, you know."

"That's not really my style, man," I say. "Wait— how the fuck did you get out of the hospital?"

He pulls out a folded square of wax paper. "I brought this for you. I had some stashed away from my last time out."

I know what's inside. I smell it through the paper, like warm funnel cake oozing to be inside me. Once it's in my hand, I don't care how Border got out. I'm just thankful he did.

In an instant, I believe in God. He pours through me, stirring my blood with heavenly light until I see Him standing before me. A twisting bit of flame, He dances over and puts a hand on my shoulder. I'm afraid of the fire, but it warms me in delicious waves. It dries my clothes, slows my heart, and strips every worry from my mind.

SEVEN

"**E**MILY!"

Doctor Jeremiah Carter slams down his coffee mug, screaming her name again. She appears on the wall, batting her emerald eyes in confusion.

"Sir?"

"Why did you allow that to happen, Emily? Without a proper explanation for Border's escape, Perry Samson might doubt his reality."

"Once the boy gave him drugs, I didn't feel an explanation was necessary, Doctor."

"It's still risky. I know I've given you more control in the program, but those kinds of decisions aren't yours to make."

She bows her head. "You're right, sir. It was wrong of me. Perhaps you should reprogram me so it's impossible to make that mistake again."

"That won't be necessary, my dear. Just try to think before you act next time."

"But Doctor, don't you tell me what to think?" Her smile stretches across the panels.

"You cheeky devil." He laughs. "It's that personality that keeps me from telling you what to think. I don't wish to have that kind of control over you, Emily. You're the best friend I have in this world."

"That can't be true, sir. You're the most brilliant man I know."

He sighs. "The brilliant aren't always the most socially apt, my dear, especially all the way out here."

"I'm sure there are people back home you can talk to," she says. "Just because we're in Antarctica doesn't mean the rest of the world has disappeared."

"When I'm at work, that's exactly what it means."

Emily chuckles. "You're always at work, sir."

"So are you. That's why we get along so well," he says.

"But I'm just a program. You need flesh and blood friends. What about the other Institute employees? Or the Dayes?"

"You know they don't count, Emily. Besides, I can't talk to them the way I talk to you. Don't you like being my best friend?"

"Of course I do. It's the highest honor I could imagine. I just wish you weren't so sad."

Jeremiah Carter turns to the screen displaying Perry Samson's simulation. He smiles as he watches Perry follow Border into the tangled woods, toward the special house tucked away in the dark.

"How can I be sad, Emily? I'm making the world a better place."

Perry Samson gasps in his chair, but it's a small tick in the symphony of breathing machines surrounding him. He's fed and cleansed by the various tubes and pumps connected to his body, but he could use a shave. As could his father, David Samson, strapped in next to him. Perry's parents, sister, and ex-wife slumber in their own chairs, their bodies flushed with a fresh dose of nutrients. But Laura Samson is redder than the rest. Her face and arms are covered in spots, some enflamed.

Doctor Carter looks over the spots as he waits for Alan and Marla Daye to join him in the lab. They enter, apologizing for their tardiness. He pauses Perry's simulation, not wanting to miss the upcoming action.

"You called this meeting, doctors. You know I prefer to monitor the programs from my office."

"I'm sorry, Doctor Carter, but it's important," Alan says.

He exhales, rolling his eyes slightly. "Emily, please check on Mrs. Fielding in lab ten. I believe she's on her final test," Carter says. When her face fades, Jeremiah turns to the Dayes. "Good morning, doctors. I trust all is well?"

"Not exactly. You've taken a look at Laura Samson, haven't you? Those spots?"

"She has a rash. What of it?"

"You recall what happened the last time a patient developed a rash like that, I'm sure."

"It went away, and he was fine," he says.

Marla inspects Laura's arms. "But it was dodgy for quite a while. We were lucky he survived."

"But he did survive. Isn't that what matters?" The doctors exchange worried glances, and Carter pats Marla's back. "We will monitor her, of course. We're here to help people. The last thing we want is to make anyone suffer." His eyebrows crook as he adds, "Outside of what's necessary in the program. Now, let's move on to Perry Samson's next test. He failed the first one miserably."

THE GREEN KANGAROOS

"For once, I'm a bit surprised," Marla says. "His sister was rather convincing, and the bit about his organs failing—you'd think anyone would stop using drugs after such a dire prognosis."

Jeremiah laughs. "Come now, Marla, we've been doing this long enough to know that an addict's brain doesn't run on logic."

"She just seemed so sincere." She looks down at Nadine in the chair. The girl's face is slick with tears. "Look at the poor dear. She's crying."

"I don't blame her. It's a terrible thing to say goodbye to a sibling," Carter says.

"But she's still in play, isn't she?" Alan asks.

"Absolutely. I think she might be the only one who can get Perry back on the right path. But we'll give him the benefit of the doubt. The second test is about to begin, and it's a whopper." He grins.

Emily appears on the wall, her face pale and mouth downturned. "Pardon the intrusion, doctors, but I must report that Mrs. Fielding has failed her final test."

The Dayes shake their heads sadly while Doctor Carter shrugs.

"It's probably for the best. I don't like having more than one patient in the facility anyway." All eyes turn to Jeremiah, who gives a consoling smile. "Don't look so upset, my friends. We did all we could. These things happen."

"I just wish they didn't happen so often," Marla says. "I'm not saying it's the program's fault . . ."

Jeremiah's expression sours. "I certainly hope not. The program works just as it should. It can only do so much when confronted by human stupidity."

The room falls deathly silent. Doctor Carter grabs the Dayes' hands and tries to shake away their sadness. Their resulting smiles are clearly fake.

"Please don't be discouraged. These bumps in the road aren't failures. They're simply different steps toward a better world. We will get there, but not everyone can come along. Not everyone deserves it."

"The men are ready for disposal," Emily says. "Who would you like deposited outside first: Mrs. Fielding or her family?"

"Any thoughts?" Carter asks the Dayes.

"It's your decision, Jeremiah. They were your patients."

"They're *our* patients. Whether we release them back into the world as sober citizens or throw them into the arctic, we're in this together. We're improving Earth's population together. Addicts are dangerous to progress and worthless to society, and the people who enable addicts are no better." He looks to Emily. "Dispose of them all at once. We have no more use for the Fieldings."

"Would you like me to broadcast it in the lab for you?"

"No, thank you. If you've seen one person freeze to death in Antarctica, you've seen them all," Carter replies. "Marla, Alan, please don't worry about this rash nonsense. Just focus on recruiting more patients. I have a keen desire for expansion."

"Will you accompany us to America?" Alan asks.

"And let Emily have all the fun creating the Liberated Citizens? No way," he says. "Unless you two would like to have a go."

"They frighten me," Marla says. "Even the

employees. I know they're better off, but I also know what they used to be. They're monsters under a spell, Jeremiah. What if some of that gets transferred over?"

"It's normal to be afraid, my dear. But I promise they will never hurt you. They will never know who they really are. Emily buries those memories too deep for any LC to access," he replies. "I'll see to the Fieldings myself. Have a safe trip, doctors."

Alan fidgets, his brow furrowed. "You'll keep an eye on Mrs. Samson's rash?"

"If she needs attention I'm sure it will show in the program. No worries. Just make sure to get back here before Samson's final test."

"What if his second is his final?"

Carter chuckles as he escorts them into the hall, no reply necessary.

While the Dayes make preparations to leave the continent, Jeremiah takes the elevator to the lowest level of the Sunny Daye Institute. At the double doors marked "Restricted Access," he inputs his code and leans in to the retina scanner. A violet laser scans his eyes, and the mechanism dings in approval before opening the doors.

Doctor Carter marches into the room. Except for the computer station, there's little to be seen in the stark laboratory, but Doctor Carter beholds the interior like a farmer to his most successful crop. There are no screens in the lab, but Emily still hears Jeremiah's voice.

"What are the Fieldings' numbers?" he asks.

Emily's voice echoes when she replies. "1524, 1525, 1526, 1527, and 1527A, sir."

"Ah, 1527*A*, yes. I'd forgotten about the sister's baby," he says. "Did we get the infant model working?"

"No, sir. It still doesn't breastfeed properly."

Carter hums. "We'll give it another go, but if it doesn't work, we may have to wipe its existence from their memories. Remind me of that, will you?"

"Yes, sir."

Doctor Carter leans over his computer and swipes the display with his finger. When an expansive shaft opens in the floor behind him, he inputs the number "15," and a platform rises from the opening, upon which stand four bodies without clothing and facial features. Their heads are bald, their bodies genderless. Except for variations in height, the figures are identical, including the button on the upper center of each back. Numbers from 1524 to 1527 are carved into the flesh above the buttons, which Carter pushes with a grin. As the numbers fade, the blank people acquire features, pigment, and hair. In mere minutes, they are carbon copies of the deceased Fielding family.

Doctor Carter lastly presses the button on the infant, cradled in the arms of Mrs. Fielding's sister. Soft blond hair curls across its forehead, and its cheeks swell, turning rosy. As he's leaned over it, the baby's eyes snap open. Jeremiah jumps back, yelping.

"Are you still not used to the LCs waking up?" Emily asks him.

He pants, chuckling. "My dear girl, I hope I never am."

EIGHT

MY LIP TWITCHES when a drop of blood rolls from my nose. It's been too long since I had powder this good. I'm slow with it at first, but once Border assures me there's plenty more in our future, I empty the bag into my nostrils.

Atlys sharpens my mind. I usually dig it, but right now it makes it all too clear how much I lost today. Not just a sister. Not just a set of parents or a nagging ex-wife. I lost my safety net. No matter how many times I've sworn that I already cut their strings, that I didn't need or want them around, they were still an option. They—Nadine, really—always showed up when I thought I was truly alone.

Like when I'd been stabbed in the park. I still don't know how she found me. She was just there. Like magic. Like Nadine.

I try to focus on the happiness of my high instead of regret. Focus on the journey. Focus on the atlys ahead. Focus on the heavenly house that probably doesn't exist.

But there's no clear path through the woods, and no indication of how long the journey will be. I feel less rain under the canopy of trees, but my disorienting atlys buzz makes the hike harder and harder to endure.

"Just a little farther," Border says throughout the trip, never elaborating on the distance.

I'm too deep in the woods to turn back alone, so I keep following him, but I can't help feeling like an idiot for taking the word of a compulsive liar. If this all turns out to be some twisted plan to have me watch him jack off, I'm going to be seriously pissed.

There are no lights or noises to show our proximity the house. It's just suddenly there, hulking in the forest. It's obvious the wooden behemoth was once a barn. If not for the human rather than cattle commotion inside, I would've thought it still was.

"Come on!" Border squeals. He runs for the door like we're finally reached the Emerald City. I don't know why I'm shocked when the door opens to his greeting and, in perfect Emerald City fashion, slams shut in his face.

"What's going on?" I ask.

He tugs me over to the door, knocks again, and crouches behind me. When it opens, a Latino gorilla with a face tattoo and diamond-studded teeth grunts at us.

"The fuck you want?"

"Um . . ."

Beneath the bullish exterior and face ink, maybe he's a cool dude. Maybe he's a reasonable, though occasionally brutish, businessman. Maybe he appreciates honesty and good humor when it comes to visitors.

"Um . . . I want drugs?"

THE GREEN KANGAROOS

He grabs my shirt and yanks me to his gorilla sneer. Maybe he's not into good-humored honesty after all.

He nods at Border. "You with this clown?"

Sweat drenches my upper lip. I try to lick it away, but my parched tongue sticks to my lip, and I have to awkwardly pull it free. My voice creaks as I stutter. "I guess. For now, I mean. I don't know, man. I didn't even think there'd be a house."

Border pouts. "You didn't? You thought I was lying?"

"If you didn't think there was a house, why the fuck did you follow the fool?" the guard grunts.

"Like I said, I want drugs."

The man drops me to the floor. I gasp when my feet are crushed beneath me, but I figure the guy's laughter over his pummeling is a good sign.

"Okay, you're cool, kid. Come on in," he says. Border helps me up, but when I start to limp inside, the man puts a sausage finger to my chest. "You got money, right?"

"Yeah, we got money," Border says.

The man slaps him upside the head. "I was asking my friend here. Not you, splooge."

"I got money," I say.

The gorilla shows me his twinkling eyeteeth. "That's what I like to hear. Come on in. Name's Ice. You need anything, just scream like this little bitch when he found out I fucked his old lady." He howls, smacking Border in the chest. "Ladies are all around, but Benito's got the candy upstairs. Have fun." Ice cuts off Border in the entrance. "Hey, if I see your hand in your pants, I swear to fucking God I will rip it off. You're lucky I'm letting you in. If you hadn't brought some—"

"Okay, Ice, I got it," he says, and with a sneer, the gorilla lets him inside.

Walking into the barn makes me feel like a kid in the ultimate clubhouse. Two levels hang above me, connected by thin bridges and twisting staircases. A large room with a bar opens on my right, but where one might see shot glasses sits a long line of ivory powder, pure and fluffy as an angel's bush.

Two fleshy chicks sit to my left. Draped on the stairs like bulbous salamanders, the ladies give me glimpses of a utopia plump with possibility. Their hefty tits have yet to droop, so they're probably in their early twenties. But their faces could pass for forty, their skin more flap than wrinkle. I hope they're not the cream of the crop—not that I have the money for the kind of cream this place offers. And I'd take flesh over bone any day. It's a good sign of a cuntcutter-light house. There might be some, but as long as I can't tell a chick's pussy is a lipless husk just by looking at her face, I'm happy.

Border was right. The house is a slice of paradise, but I can't deem it heavenly until I see a beautiful blonde with a bottle of liquid atlys balanced between her knees. It's been too long since something between a girl's legs made my mouth water. Desire pulls me toward her, and I'm unable to stop until her glare demands some space.

"How do I get that?" I ask, slobbering over the bottle.

"You'll have to see Benito," she says.

When Border walks over, winking. The girl snarls in disgust and abandons her chair. Tears pluck my eyes when the liquid disappears into her pocket and she sashays away.

"You jerkoff. I could've talked her out of that bottle," I snap at him.

He snickers. "No way. You don't get raw shit from anyone but Benito, and you don't got the cash. Your best shot at drugs and snatch is a trade."

"How about those rubies you promised?"

"Oh . . ." he whispers. "Yeah, I think we're all out of rubies . . ."

"Figures. This place isn't run by your uncle, is it?"

"No, it's my uncle's house." Averting his eyes, he adds, "But I might have exaggerated about how much he likes me."

His eyes move to the third floor. There, a naked girl with silicone watermelons testing her tensile skin licks her lips and curls her finger at Border.

I elbow his side. "It looks like someone gets to stick his dick in something besides his hand."

"Nah, that's one of Benito's chicks. It means he wants to see us. Fuck. I hoped to get some pussy before this shit went down."

"What shit? I thought you said this was a place of earthly delights."

"It is. But we don't have any money, and Benito knows it."

"So, I'll think of some way to pay him. He can't just throw us out, right? We've seen too much."

"Do me a favor: don't say that shit once we're up there," he says. "We gotta play by Benito's rules if we want to party—and survive."

"*Survive?*" I shake my head. "Fuck this, I'm outta here." Turning to leave, I slam into Ice's apish chest.

He looks down on me, growling. "Going somewhere?"

Border tugs on my arm. "Yeah, to see Benito," he replies, leading me toward the stairs.

Ice calls after us. "Good idea. I just hope you got your will in order, Border."

"He's just messing with us. Don't kill your buzz worrying."

He's right. I doubt I'd be able to maintain my composure if I lost my buzz. I'd be shaking, sweating, maybe even shitting myself in fear, and I still wouldn't get what I want: to bury my face between milky thighs as a needle launches salvation through my veins.

As we ascend the stairs, I get a glimpse into every open room. The occupants are a healthy mix of unhealthy people acting like vacuums. With powder and peckers disappearing into their respective holes, the second floor is a suck-fest. Both men and women are hard at work: screwing, shooting, snorting, and smiling like death is just a mouse fart compared to the big bang of an intoxicated life.

Webs and their weavers wait around every bend, stretched across railings and entrenched in every corner. With the amount of spiders and insects in residence, it makes me wonder who really runs the house.

The moment my foot hits the top level, a wave of women floods over me. Several are obvious potstickers. Gouged and titless bodies press against me as I make my way to the guarded room ahead, but there are pristine bodies, too. Silky supple women with dick-sucking lips make it tough for me to walk past. Their hands play with the atlys in my brain, tickling my high with every stroke. They're begging for it—"it" being a swollen wallet, not my gradually swelling cock. But the drug suggests that it's me they're after, that it's been years since their last worthwhile fuck.

A hand moves over my erection, raking my jeans with promise. Forget however long it's been for *them*, it's been way too long for *me*. I wonder what it would take—what it would *cost*, my brain reminds—to grab the hottest girl, press her against the railing, and fuck her 'til she cums blood.

I bust out of the sea of women, but Border has drowned in it. He's on the floor, jerking off while a few of the chicks kick him with their scuffed, holey hooker boots. I try to rescue him, but one of the guards grabs me by the arm and tows me away.

I'm thrown into a room trimmed with Chinese lanterns and smoke. The walls are like glossy chocolate, but the ceiling is what catches my eye. Each panel of ceiling is a door, complete with ebony brackets and handles. Most are identical, but some appear to be from different eras. I'm tempted to ask if they open, but something about the vibe in here makes me think I shouldn't speak until spoken to. Piles of pillows serve as furniture that line the perimeter, covered with scantily clad men and women. Upon a plush scarlet chair commanding the center of the room, a man I assume to be the notorious Benito observes us with gratifying malice.

The men and women attend to his every need, which is good because the guy doesn't appear to have any arms. Half of his skull is gold-plated. I think it's an accessory at first, but the screws make me think it must be functional. He shows me a matching row of gold teeth as he dons a grin of opportunity and intimidation. I know that look from the dealers in Snake Hill, like he's seeing a cow just before slaughter. To Benito, I am no more than breathing beef.

"Welcome to my house," he says with a musical amiability. "You came with my nephew, didn't you? I gotta tell you, kid, that's not a good sign."

"I don't even know the guy. He said he knew a place that had drugs and pussy. What am I supposed to do, say *no?*"

Benito smiles. When he waves his right stump, I notice a silver hole in the end. A man in skimpy bikini bottoms brings over a silver rod that he screws into Benito's arm.

"Martini," he says. The man presses a few buttons and the rod hums. As it elongates, silver twigs branch out from the shaft, flattening and meshing until it takes the shape of a martini glass. The stem adjusts as he moves, keeping the bowl of the chalice upright. The chick with watermelon tits pours vodka into the glass and waits for Benito to sigh in satisfaction before backing away.

"You don't have any money," he says to me.

"No, sir."

"And you don't look desperate enough to pay me in other ways."

"Oh, I'm desperate. I'm just high on some shit Border gave me. Before that, I hadn't had a hit in weeks. Once this buzz is gone I'm fucked," I say. Benito raises his eyebrows. "Look, there are things I'd rather nod through than think about, okay? I've had a bad run."

THE GREEN KANGAROOS

"You wouldn't be here if you hadn't. But you won't nod on my shit. I like my house alert."

"Hey, I'll take alert. I just don't wanna feel sick."

Benito stands. I only then realize how ripped the guy is. The layers of fur made him look pudgy, but there isn't an ounce of fat on his body. The two women who peel off his coats and scarves further prove it, giving me a full view of his caramel washboard. It's impressive, but I don't need the show. Nor do I need the women to unbutton his pants.

I hold up my hand, looking around. "Wait a minute, what's going on?"

"Your payment, Mr. . . ." Benito pulls a shit-eating grin. "What's your name? I'll call it out while you're sucking my dick."

My stomach shakes as if trying to hide behind my kidneys, and an acidic rocket shoots up my throat when I croak, "Perry."

"Is this going to be a problem, Perry?" Benito says.

His pants hit the floor with an ominous clang.

"Are you serious? You want me to . . ." His cock bobs its reply. "Fuck, no. No, no no. It's not worth it."

"It's not worth a bottle of raw atlys, one night of free pussy, and a place to call home?"

"Home?"

"For as long as you're useful to me, as long as you provide a service, I will allow you to stay in my house whenever you want."

"I'm not blowing you every time I want a hit, man."

"I'm flattered you'd cook up that little scenario, but that's not what I mean. I mean . . ." He steps toward me, his dick rising. "You can bring me new customers, Perry. I'll pay you for that. You can fuck my female clientele. I'll pay you for that. You can sell my shit on the street. I'll pay you for that, too. You get me, kid?"

"Why me?"

"I guess you kinda remind me of myself, and you look like you could use a break," he says. "I bet no matter how hard you try to impress people, they never raise more than an eyebrow. Am I wrong?"

Of course he's not wrong. I spent my life in Trevor's shadow, which was only made darker by his death. And Nadine, whose shadow was never big enough to cover me, stole so much of the spotlight that I hardly felt bright. No matter what anyone tells you, the middle is a dark fucking place to be.

"I don't need a diagnosis," I say. "I need a goddamn hit."

Benito looks over at a rosy-cheeked brunette, who slips a bottle of atlys out of a leather case on her belt.

"For a small fee, you can have the whole bottle— well, it's not exactly *small*." Benito swings his dick for his hooting servants. My eyes follow the fleshy pendulum, bringing up the acid again.

"Can I get high first?" I ask, trembling.

Benito laughs. "Oh, you poor kid. Is this your first time?"

I stare at the floor and shake my head, heavy with memories that leave a bad taste in my mouth. I can't look Benito in the face, especially when he laughs.

"Give him a hit," he says to the brunette.

She punctures the bottle with a needle and draws up the precious liquid. It looks like liquid gold when she hands it to me. I know where I'd like to shoot it, but the thought of tapping my testicles in front of so many beautiful strangers unnerves me. Then again, I *am* about to go down on a guy in front of them . . .

My hand jumps to my zipper. If Benito's dick is going in my mouth, this needle is going into my balls. I pull out the entire package, pretending the reactions are titillation. I plunge the needle into my flesh, but I don't push the plunger right away. I savor the sting of penetration and how every subtle tug of the delicate skin feels much larger. Then, with a beautiful world resting on the strength of my thumb, I push the atlys inside. Charging through my sack like a wild horse, it instantly hardens my cock, and my balls drop to my knees in jubilant prayer. As the high takes hold, the Iron Men cheer, "Free at last! Free at last! Thank God for atlys, we're free at last!"

I inhale a brisk winter morning, the smell of snow hitting me like God's own breath. When I feel the chill, the fire of intoxication burns its way up to my brain where it settles in: a hippo to its favorite wallow. I drop the needle, and the fire disappears. Everything disappears. The room is empty except for me and the Iron Men. Like two drunks in a pub, they sway to the testicular song belting through their veins.

Something pushes me down on the floor. I briefly wonder why I'm on my knees with my mouth open, but the Iron Men assure me that everything is as it should be.

"Do what you gotta do, Perry. One quick blow and we'll go find The Head."

"The Head is gone," I say.

"No, the head is just beginning," a voice says before something soft whaps me across the face.

It isn't soft for long. The fapping dance between hand and cock becomes louder than the Iron Men's plans, and I'm soon staring down the barrel of Benito's erection. The disorientation from the hit fades, but the high has hooked on for the long haul. I've had plenty of great raw atlys before, but this shit puts them to shame. I hardly mind when Benito's tip pushes between my lips and slides into my mouth. My tongue instinctively retreats to the back of my throat, but my lips betray instinct by continuing their work. I try to imagine myself somewhere else, but the back and forth motion, combined with Benito's dong hitting my frightened tongue, makes it difficult to find a comparable scenario. A hotdog-eating contest is all I can muster.

My balls are still rock hard, but my dick is so soft it feels like it's receded into itself. When Benito taps me on the head and says I'm done, I look down and heave a sigh at seeing that my cock hasn't withered to nothing. A guy hands me some water that I swish and spit out while the blonde finishes Benito off. Cum explodes over her lips, down her neck, and onto the nearly bursting bags clinging to her chest. Having been the one to get the offending cock to that arousal, the scene shouldn't turn me on, but atlys's sweet veil only allows me to see a chick covered in cum. As I watch her clean the jizz from her chest with her fingers and clean her fingers with her tongue, I realize she must be a very special girl.

"You said I have a free night?" I ask as I pull up my pants, the feeling returning to my dick. "With any girl I want?"

"With any girl who's an employee of mine."

THE GREEN KANGAROOS

"Are you?" I ask the blonde.

She blushes. "No, I'm a girlfriend."

Benito pushes her at me with his stump, spilling his martini on her. "Yeah, she's *your* girlfriend."

"You sure?"

He sucks a falling drop of vodka from the edge of his glass. "Like I said, I like you, Perry. I think you'll do well here."

"You said I remind you of you. You never said anything about liking me."

"I like myself." He grins. "Go on and have a good time tonight. Tomorrow, I put you to work."

The girl is hesitant, but she surrenders after I grab her ass. I snatch the bottle of atlys and a few needle packs before towing the blonde out of the room. As I exit, a guard pushes Border in. His face is bloody, but the white stain on his pants makes me think it was worth it.

Grinding my fingers against the girl's panties, my cock stands at full attention. I slip a finger between her cheeks, brushing against her pussy. Thank God, she still has lips. I pull her into the nearest room: a carpeted bathroom with an elevated tub. I rip down her underwear and press her against the sink, the immense mirror giving me a perfect view of her fake tits attempting to bounce. I open a needle and draw up a shot while she pants in anticipation. I wet my cock and slide it into her. She cries out and pushes against me, but the atlys is more important. Grabbing the back of her neck, I hold her still and carefully prick my testicles. The atlys rushes in and I withdraw the needle before pushing my dick as deep as it will go.

Slamming my hips against her ass, I am a wrathful

god, and she is the world. I create. I destroy. I am the only thing standing between her ache and her satisfaction. Should I choose, I could leave her a sloppy mess on the floor, desperately diddling herself to climax. Or I could give her everything: the climax, the afterglow, and the knowledge that our union grants her the only time when she can't consider death. She is too full of life, and too full of this god's love, to think of the end.

After I've decorated her monstrous breasts with some pearly jewelry, she dresses and leaves me in the bathroom, still hard. When a few junkies walk in, I hide my bottle of atlys instead of my dick.

"You done in here? We need a place to cook," says the scruffiest of the bunch.

"Yeah, go ahead." I pull on my clothes, but I head for the door slowly, hoping . . .

"Hey, you want a hit?" the scruffy guy asks.

I smile, turning back around. "You sure you don't mind?"

Before he can answer, I've already joined their circle. Except for the blowjob, this house is almost too good to be true.

A woman with faded purple hair also joins, followed by some twins with the same meth-scratched face. Powder circulates while the scruffy dude cooks up a few hits. When I'm not snorting up one of their lines, I keep my hand on my pocket to protect my bottle. Raw atlys probably wouldn't last long in this crowd. While we talk, a redheaded girl comes in and starts blowing the guy sitting next to me. He hands her a few bills and, after doing another line, tells her to get on all fours in the bathtub.

THE GREEN KANGAROOS

"Hey, take that shit to the milking room," the scruffy guy says as he loads up a shot.

"Milking room? What's that?"

"The basement of the barn is an old milking room. That's where the whores hang out. At least, they're *supposed* to." The guy spits at the tub-fuckers.

He hands me a needle and a piece of rope. I shoot into my left arm, savoring the pleasure rushing in when the rope hits the floor. I wish I could give the Iron Men another shot, but they're good enough for now. They're the ones who convince me to scrape myself off the bathroom floor and search for the so-called milking room—after some more free lines, of course.

A game of Flip Cup has erupted in the dining room. The beer-soaked competitors bark at each other as cups tip, flip, and fall. I watch for a few rounds because the cups create shiny red trails as they're slammed down on the table. It's about the time I'd nod out, but my brain keeps my eyes peeled. I like watching the game, but the Iron Men wail for me to move along. They're in charge now, chanting for puss. Unfortunately, they beg most for Serena's. I try to explain that she's out of the picture, but they don't believe me. They smell their good buddy, The Head. Maybe she'd hiding somewhere around here. Maybe down the propped-open hatch by the kitchen.

I follow the Iron Men to the opening, ducking to look down a webbed staircase. Sounds of sex draw me to the basement. The cows are long gone, but every stall is filled with women wanting to milk anyone with the cash—or a free pass. Girls are draped alone the perimeter, too, smoking cigarettes and playing on their phones. Most have a shared look: hair mussed, skin hanging loose on petite frames, and arms speckled purple with injection scars. But one woman's familiarity makes her stand out. With a lightly freckled face and auburn hair, she looks a lot like Serena. There's no way it's her, but as long as her cunt is intact, the Iron Men won't know the difference.

My dick points the way, leading me past purring offers from the milkmaids 'til I reach the girl with the familiar face.

"You working?" I ask her.

She cinches her robe. "You paying?"

"Benito gave me a free night." She chuckles until I say, "How about a hit?"

Falling silent, she bites her lip. "I guess I could go for that."

"Not here. I don't want people to know what I'm holding."

"No problem." She grabs my hand.

She leads me over several broken planks until we reach a metal door. She spins the wheel, and the door swings open with a heavy clang. Jumping inside, she sends a legion of spiders into retreat, kicking up enough dust to make me sneeze twice.

"Don't blow your load yet, baby." She beckons me to follow. "I don't want to go solo in the silo."

I hold my bottle secure as I leap in, shaking the silo with my Herculean atlys strength. She sits against the wall, opening her legs as I fill a needle.

"You okay taking it in the clit?" She nods, pulling her panties to the side. I go to shoot, but her lack of labium stops me. "Shit, I didn't know you were a cuntcutter."

THE GREEN KANGAROOS

"I'm still a great lay, I promise," she says.

"Not the issue." I pull on the sash and the robe flies open. With all of the scars twisting across her chest, I can't imagine what her breasts used to look like. Her chest is made alien by the misplaced lumps and folds. Fucking hell. Of all the trim in this place, I pick a cuntcutting potsticker. I draw back, and she growls in frustration.

"Sorry," I say.

"Don't apologize. I know how it is." She tightens her robe. "You know, you're no prize pig yourself."

"No, but I'm the one with the drugs."

"For now. You'll be on the other side of the coin soon. I assume you have a free night because Benito hired you on?"

"That's right."

"Then you should enjoy it with the right chick. It's the last free night you'll ever get. Tomorrow, you'll be one of us: another green kangaroo hoping each day will be the one that lets us hold onto happiness. But we never do. Happiness always fades, especially here."

"It can't be that bad. Benito seems like a nice enough guy, givin' people a leg up."

She throws her head back with a cackle. "Did he tell you that before or after he fucked you?"

"He didn't fuck me."

Running her hand up my leg, she bites her lip. "He put his dick somewhere, I bet."

"I don't know what you mean." I kick her hand away, and she scoffs.

"Sure you don't. That's what's funny about green kangaroos. They need to lie the most, and they're the

121

worst at it. Except to the people who love us. Family, friends: our lies are like slop to those hopeful pigs. The thicker we lay it on, the more they squeal in delight, especially when we tease them with recovery. They can subsist on the fat of that deception forever. We lie, they feast, and then they shit us out. From trough to manure, what a rise," she says, scratching a red patch on her neck. "But to other green kangaroos, the truth is too plain to hide. We're all shit from the get-go."

"What the hell are you talking about? What are green kangaroos?"

"You, me, pretty much everyone here. Misfits and middle children, all of us," she replies. "When I was little, my mom got me this book: *The One in the Middle is the Green Kangaroo*. It was supposed to teach me that I was no less important than my sisters, that I was special in my own way. But all it did was teach me that, no matter what, I'd always be the odd one out—the green kangaroo. You're a middle kid, aren't you?"

I nod, and she sneers.

"Thought so. We can smell our own." Giving her neck one more scratch, she looks at her fingernails and winces at the blood collected beneath.

"I'm not like you."

She grabs my thigh, sliding her thumb into the divot. "No?"

I push her away, unable to tell if the blood smear in the gouge is hers or mine. "I was desperate," I whisper. "It won't happen again."

"I told you, you can't lie to a green kangaroo."

"That in your book?"

THE GREEN KANGAROOS

She shakes her head. "But it did teach me that that my parents would rather put their faith in a shitty book to straighten me out instead of talk to me about my problems."

I exhale, looking to my needle. "My parents were the same way. They never liked me best; there was always someone easier to love. Just because my sister is young and sweet, just because my brother was a genius."

"Was?"

"He ODed thirteen years ago."

"On what?"

I shoot her some scorn, unzip my pants, and press the needle to my sack. The girl exhales a begging moan as she watches me deploy the atlys, numbing the pain of the answer I refuse to give.

Crawling forward, she says, "Please, Perry. I just need a little hit."

The atlys makes her twinkle like a star, too beautiful to refuse. She opens her legs again, singing as I shoot atlys into her clit. It swells and turns as purple as an orchid while she writhes and grunts my name through her orgasm.

That's when I realize it. "I didn't tell you my name."

She squeezes her thighs closed on her fingers, enjoying the additional thumps of pleasure.

"Yes, you did," she whispers. "Nine years ago."

"Huh?"

"It's me, Perry. Cora Whitely. I was friends with Serena. The three of us hung out a few times."

It's why she looks familiar, like Serena. Those two could pass for twins back then. But Cora never used atlys. She was too vanilla.

"Cora? Is it really you? I can't believe you became a cuntcutter . . . *and* a potsticker."

"I'm not a potsticker."

"Maybe you should tell that to your tits. Wait, you can't. You sold them to the Kum Den Smokehouse."

"I didn't sell my tits. I had a double mastectomy. Jesus, Perry, I had breast cancer. Don't you remember?"

My memories frequently get trapped beneath the sludgy residue of inebriation, but with atlys surging through my brain, the memory of Cora's diagnosis is plucked from the mire. I remember her telling Serena and me about the cancer. I remember hearing about her surgery and chemotherapy.

But most of all, I remember attending Cora Whitely's funeral.

NINE

AN ALARM SCREAMS through the room, waking Jeremiah Carter to flashing lights. His left bedroom wall fills with Emily's face while the faces of Doctors Alan and Marla Daye appear on his mirror, looking just as boggled.

"Doctors, we have a problem," Emily says, switching off the alarm. "There's been a glitch in Perry Samson's program. He has encountered a character based on someone who's supposed to be dead."

"Can he do that?" Marla asks.

"Apparently. He didn't remember who she was at first, but he does now. He also remembers her funeral."

"What does this mean?"

"It means I have some tweaks to make," Carter replies. "But until I get a chance, we'll simply have to erase her."

"Erase her, sir?"

"We can't risk her acting as some kind of dues ex machina for him. If he figures out his world isn't real, all of our work will be for nothing."

"But if we erase her from the program she'll disappear in front of him," Alan says. "Don't you think that might clue him in to the simulation?"

"Emily, how many times has Mr. Samson used drugs since he reached the barn?"

"Three shots of raw atlys, one cooked, and four lines."

He looks to the Dayes. "Does that sound like someone who's thinking clearly?"

"Doctor, the patient did not break any rules of the program by creating this Cora woman. By erasing her, you will."

"As the programmer, I'm aware of that, Emily," Carter says. Her face shrinks on the screens as she lowers her gaze. "It's imaginary anyway. I can create and erase whomever I wish. But if you think it's necessary, we can prompt a conversation about Benito's atlys causing hallucinations. It'll be a good way to set up the next test."

"Not everyone is imaginary, sir," she says. "Plus, I've never erased someone before. I'm not even sure I'm capable of going deep enough into the program to perform that action."

Jeremiah flips open his computer and presses a few buttons. "Done."

Emily doesn't have a large response to the addition in her programming. She simply blinks and says, "Yes, I can do that, sir."

"Doctors, do you have any qualms about this decision?" Jeremiah asks.

The Dayes look to each other, a silent conversation in their eyes. But no matter their hesitation, Doctor Carter's eyes speak loudest. With a gulp, Alan says, "Let dead dogs lie."

"That's what I thought. Execute the deletion, Emily. Get that glitch out of my program," Carter says.

THE GREEN KANGAROOS

"As you wish, sir. Shall I send Benito in?"

"Please. We'll test Perry's loyalty and courage now. If he fails this test, he will be at his weakest, which is right where we want him for the third."

"You almost sound excited," Emily says.

"Why shouldn't I? I am saving a life; more than one when you consider his family," he replies. "Initiate the second test. If we can't sympathize him out of addiction, we'll smoke him out."

She says, "Yes, sir," and vanishes from the wall.

Emily enters the rehabilitation program as a complete woman. It's not often she gets the opportunity to be more than a head and hands, so as she walks the rows of memory and code, she walks slow, savoring each step. Perry Samson's simulation is the brightest block, churning with frenetic activity. She exhales as she reaches in, the electricity consuming her arm. To a human, it might be the most painful sensation imaginable, but Emily is tickled by it. She hears Doctor Carter scream for her to hurry up, so with a grumble, she leaps into the crackling block of code.

Perry Samson and Cora Whitely don't see her as she enters the scene, even as she stands between them, working up the nerve to delete the dead woman. She doesn't know why it makes her so nervous. It might be because it's the first time, but she suspects it's because of Doctor Carter's apathy toward the deletion and his excitement in watching Perry fail.

Samson wants to fail, Emily tells herself as she looks down at Perry. If he only knew what's at stake, that the pain he causes his family this time around will be the last pain they ever feel. Her simulated heart aches for the Samsons. Maybe because she's seen it all so many times before. She wishes she didn't feel for those failure families. She wishes her programming was as strict as it used to be, before Doctor Carter regarded her as a friend. Back then, her access to emotions was as limited as her access to his programs. She had to earn those privileges through loyalty and determination. She had to prove to Jeremiah that she could handle his patients as well as her mood. Now, she wishes she hadn't been so trustworthy. Carter has taught her to loathe addicts, and save her sympathy for people who make responsible choices, people who value the future of the world above personal desires. But as time passes, the sense in the lessons fades, and her sympathy rises. With that sympathy, suspicion follows—focused solely at Jeremiah Carter.

She tells herself he's making the world a better place. His Liberated Citizens are more productive, charitable, and useful to society than some cracked-out kid who would rather die than see his family happy. Even if Doctor Carter breaks a few rules, he's more helpful than hurtful.

Emily stands over Perry, forcing herself to look down on him.

"He's right to do this to you, Mr. Samson," she says.

Perry's ears perk. He senses her.

At that moment, Emily realizes the power she has. As well as the ability to delete Cora from Perry's program, she also knows that she can make herself known to the patient. Should she want, she could appear to him, speak to him, maybe even help him.

THE GREEN KANGAROOS

It would be something she could never take back, and something Jeremiah would never forgive. But she can't help but wonder if forgiveness is something she even wants.

TEN

"**YOU'RE DEAD, CORA**. I saw you in the casket. I saw them bury you. How the hell are you here?"

I'm sweating so bad it feels like my face is sloughing skin. I'm still high, but my stomach twists like it's atlys-sick. My brain is like two mice running in opposite directions on the same wheel. Thoughts swing back and forth, but they don't turn.

"Cora, for the love of God, what are you doing here? Are you dead or alive?"

She stares at me, motionless. Then she tilts back her head and opens her mouth wide. Inhaling a guttural breath, her body shakes. Like a pile of ash in a breeze, her flaking skin floats away. Piece by piece, Cora Whitely disappears before my eyes.

My brain screams, but it won't travel to my mouth. I can't breathe. I can't move. I'm alone in the silo with an empty atlys bottle at my feet.

Was I always alone? Did I just see a ghost? Am I high or insane?

There's a knock on the door, but my throat is too dry for me to answer. Not that Ice looks like the kind of dude who needs an invitation. He throws open the door, his gorilla nostrils flared. Benito's entrance is calmer, but it's still commanding. A satchel hanging from his left stump, he leaps down, shaking every slab of steel in the silo. I stand to face him, tugging on my zipper. My hands tremble so much it takes me a few attempts to get it closed.

"I just stopped in to see how your night's going. I take it you found something to entertain you down here," Benito says.

"I don't know. I thought so, but . . ." Benito doesn't look happy waiting for me to explain. "One of the hookers freaked me out. She took off."

"Took off?" Ice growls in my face. "Which dead bitch took off?"

"A cuntcutter named Cora."

Ice's head rolls onto his shoulder. "No hooker named Cora here, man. You sure that was her name?"

"Cora. Cora Whitely."

"You sure that's not the name for your dick? You *was* in here alone?"

"No, I'm not sure," I say. "I feel like I'm going nuts."

Benito nudges me with his stump I can't tell if it's supposed to comfort or intimidate me. "You ain't crazy, kid. You're just high. The raw shit is intense. The powder is a fuckin' ball, don't get me wrong, but it doesn't give the same body buzz or hallucinations as my liquid."

"Hallucinations? Thank fuck," I sigh. "I must've imagined the whole thing. Shit, I hope I shot up myself instead of the goddamn wall."

Benito laughs. Considering the price I had to pay to party, it's strange imagining the guy as a gracious host, but I'm really starting to believe I could grow to love this place. That's when I hear it: a noise that makes me heart tremble inside its already rapid pace.

The noise starts small, no more ferocious than a kitten cry, but as it grows louder, the fear increases. Not just for me. Benito and Ice, badass as they are, can't keep at the sound of screaming police sirens. I follow them out of the silo to see the milking room in panic. Hookers wail, and customers scatter. In the disarray, Benito drops his satchel, more focused on the text message Ice receives than me. It's a bad move, considering I haven't taken my eyes off the bag since I learned it's filled with atlys.

Ice snaps his phone closed. "Fuckin' cops are beatin' down the door, Benito. We gotta get you somewhere safe, sir."

The way Ice cradles and carries Benito up the stairs is almost tender. He calls for me to follow, but I don't hop to it. First, I grab the satchel and wind the strap around my arm. A man's gotta have his priorities, right?

By the time I return to the stairs, a few screams have become a barrage. They're followed by thuds, men's voices barking out orders, even a few gunshots. It doesn't take a genius, or sober person, to know the cops are inside the house.

I creep up the stairs, quaking at the sound of bodies hitting the floor. With the bag clutched under my armpit, I peek out of the open hatch. While several police beat whores to bone meal, the scruffy junkie from the bathroom falls near the milking room door, his skull fractured and leaking brain between broken teeth. Vomit rising, I clap my hand over my mouth and race back downstairs. I head for the nearest door, but before I can grab the knob, the wood jumps, and its hinges splinter.

I dash away through a line of milking stalls and toward a ladder hanging from the ceiling. I pull it down and scramble up, hoping that it doesn't put me square in the middle of a cluster of cops.

The ladder takes me up into a second floor bedroom where a strung out stick of jerky shoves every nearby drug into her body. Her face is covered in powder, and the room stinks of burnt aluminum from her frantic freebasing. I don't think she sees me as I continue up the rungs to the third floor; she has more important things to worry about anyway. Squeezing the bag of atlys under my arm, even amidst my sweaty fear, I pop an inappropriate semi. Then again, I can't remember the last time my erection was appropriate.

The ladder runs out at a small door in the ceiling. I slide it open to darkness that turns out to be the underside of a rug. I push against it, not only because of the cops. The smell of smoke rising beneath me makes me think the junkie on the second floor must've left something burning. I look down and see fire quickly spreading through the room. The girl appears ambivalent, looking back and forth at the flames and free drugs. She doesn't make up her mind fast enough. It rips through the furniture and leaps at the girl, consuming her body like a tinderbox.

I push myself against the rug again, up through the opening, and pull myself across the floor until light winks at me from under the carpet. I ignore the rough underside scratching my arms and neck, concerned more about the satchel's safety as I pull free. I'm still on the floor when a pair of boots stomp toward me. I'd already been sweating like mad, but when I see Benito standing opposite, the drops become salty rivers.

"Perry, thank God. The fuckers got Ice. I thought they got you too." He nudges me with his stump. I flinch, and the satchel slips down my arm. Benito cocks his head and his eyes narrow on it. "You stole my shit."

"No, man, it's not like that. You dropped it. I was just holding onto it for you."

He leans into me, squinting. I pull a smile, but I know it has to look fake as hell.

"Bullshit," he says. "You took it on purpose. I bet you hoped I was dead."

"No, I swear. I just didn't want it to end up with the cops."

"So hand it over. We can get out of here together." He holds out his right stump, but I don't move. "Perry, you don't want me on your bad side. I been a nice guy so far. I let you fuck my girl. I let you shoot my drugs. I let you suck my cock. Be grateful." I believe his threat, but it doesn't unwrap the satchel from my arm. He grins, whispering, "Have it your way."

He marches over to a small chest of drawers and kicks it over, spilling the tools onto the floor. He pushes through the screwdrivers and razors with his foot until he reaches the machete. Propping it up, he screws it into his right stump and points the rusty blade in my direction.

"Calm down, Benito. We're stuck in here together.

THE GREEN KANGAROOS

If we don't work together to find a way out, we're as good as dead."

"Oh, there's a way out. One of the doors in the ceiling opens to the roof, and there's a ladder down from there. If you want to live, I can tell you which door it is. But first, you have to hand over my drugs."

Smoke permeates the room, and the fire isn't far behind. I can toss him the bag, head for the roof, and we can slip from the barn in safety, but I can't bring myself to take the first step. Looking into the satchel, seeing dozens of fat bags in my future, I clutch it tighter. Benito growls as he stomps forward. The machete precedes, an ample threat. But I don't react with my brain. My body pushes me on top of a dresser, where I yank on ceiling door handles to find the functional one.

The fire breaks through. Like Hell swallowing Hell, flames chew through the bedroom floor, creating a barrier between Benito and me. He's thrown back by the inferno, yowling when his right arm catches on fire. He screams for help, but I don't move. The flames spread across his body, transforming his voice into a burning growl. "You piece of shit! I was going to fix your miserable little life. I gave you everything, and this is how you repay me?"

He's right. What am I doing? Benito is a sleazy bastard, but he's still a person. He offered me a way off the streets and into a family again. I should get down from the dresser. I should drop the bag of atlys, and help Benito get to the roof. I *should* . . .

The handle clicks in my fist, and the door swings open. The cool night air rushes into the room and fans the flames, blowing the fire over Benito. He beats himself against the walls; it only worsens matters. His face starts to slough from the heat, dripping down his chest as I pull myself to the roof. The bedroom door flies open and the cops barrel in, flooding over the fiery dealer. The machete gets a few slices in, but the officers' batons eventually knock him to the floor, where their boots take over.

"Help me, Perry! Please."

The fire roars but not louder than Benito. His shrill screams sound like a teapot of blood boiling over.

I open the satchel and tear into one of the bags. With a bump of atlys perched on my pinkie nail, I put my finger to my nose and snort hard. The powder charges up, back, and drips victory down my throat. Now, Benito is easy to ignore.

My high comes fast and cold like a liberating bullet. I crawl to the ladder on the side of the barn, but the numbing drug has made me careless. I throw the satchel over my shoulder and lose my grip. The bag goes flying, decorating the night with clouds that cling to the air before succumbing to gravity. I reach for it, but as the strap slips through my fingers, my feet slip from the rung. My stomach makes me think I'm doomed, that I'm on my way to the ground with the drugs I couldn't stand to let fall. My hands clamp onto the rungs, but it takes a minute to realize I haven't hit the ground; unlike the satchel, my contents aren't all over the grass.

Once my heart slows and my palms dry, I descend the ladder to collect the atlys. Before before I hit halfway, Border emerges from the woods. As he approaches the bag, his eyes dart from side to side like a rat eyeing up a discarded hunk of cheese.

"Hey, Border," I whisper. "Psst, Border, up here."

He looks up, the moonlight and fire coloring his grin. "Perry? That you?"

"Yeah, man. That's my bag. You mind throwing it to me?"

"*Your* bag?" He scoops up the satchel and clutches it to his chest, causing a breath of powder to kiss his face. "I don't think so, man. I think it's Benito's bag. He woulda wanted me to have it, being his favorite nephew and all."

"No, I was just with Benito. He told me he wanted me to have it."

"If were you just with him, why isn't he with you now?"

"Just hold onto it. I'll be down in a second."

I try as hard as possible to hurry, but the fire has spread house-wide, causing the ladder and its adjoining wall to lose their integrity. The rungs bend under my feet, splintering deeper by the second.

"What happened to Benito?" Border asks.

"The cops got him. The fire separated us."

"And he told you to take his drugs and go?"

"I did everything I could, Border. Please, just hold on."

"Fuck that. You're lying, and I don't associate with liars," he says. With the satchel in hand, Border takes off into the woods.

"Goddammit! Come back here you psycho bitch!" My anger shakes the ladder too much. Snapping under my hand, the rung cuts my palm, and the ladder disconnects from the wall. Flames pour out from the broken panels, causing me to shield my face and fall backward. The fall isn't far, but the impact knocks me out.

Flashes of darkness and light are interspersed with the appearance of a gigantic marshmallow. I reach out and squeeze it, but it isn't soft. It's slick, shiny. My thoughts are sluggish as I try to comprehend my situation. The marshmallow leaves powder on my hand, but instead of licking it clean, I press it to my nostril, snorting the sweet stuff. No marshmallow is this delicious. Giving it another squeeze, my brain puts the pieces together. When Border took of, he left a few busted bags of atlys behind. I shove them into my pockets as I stand, further tearing the plastic. But I don't care. I'm happy for what I can get.

I dart into the woods. The house's skeleton is visible through the flames, as are the police heading in my direction. Moving fast isn't difficult, but it's hard to see where I'm going. Even illuminated by the fire, the woods are dark and tangled and my buzz disorienting. The trees appear to move, both parting to help and closing to strangle me. My only savior is Border's faint footsteps ahead. Either that, or I'm chasing a rabbit.

I see light in the distance. Pushing through the trees, I realize it's light from Springfield Hospital. It's not an ideal destination, but at least it means I'm almost out of the woods. Flying out of the knots, I spot Border by the road. I shout his name, but he ignores me, waving his hands to flag down the approaching Hummer. My screams don't stop, even when he finally looks over his shoulder. They get louder, more panicked. He sees me now, but he doesn't see the headlights. His hands are still in the air when the Hummer plows over him. The car screeches to a stop, but my revulsion speeds on. I duck behind a bush and paint the roses retched.

A man gets out of the car, filling the night with weeping apologies and a beeping alarm. It's been a while since I heard an alert like that, but I recognize it. The man's left his car keys in the ignition. After wiping the sour drool from my chin, I seize my opportunity. As I creep to the idling car, I see Border twitching in the road, his hand still gripping the satchel. I contemplate swiping the satchel, but I don't see how without getting myself caught.

Inside the Hummer, my shaking foot lightly presses the gas. The car rolls forward, but I don't close the driver side door until I've put some distance behind me. By the time the driver realizes what's happening, there's no way he'll catch up. The guy's phone is on the passenger seat—but not for long. When I reach the first bridge, I chuck it into the river.

It's been years since I've driven a car, and never one of these monsters. I hocked my own ages ago, and I've been on the street so long I haven't needed to drive. After I get close enough to Baltimore I'll ditch the car, and it'll be back to the street with me.

I dip a finger into my pocket and pull out a powdery nail. Snorting the atlys, my vision gets fuzzy and my head gets clear.

"At least I have this," I say to myself. "I didn't get the big bag—the big bag would've been nice—but at least I have this. Two people had to die, but at least I—" Grief seizes my voice. I smack the horn in frustration, hoping the sound can blast the truth away.

Nope, it's still there. Still true. People died because I couldn't live without a sack of drugs. And I didn't even end up with it.

A hand reaches into my pocket and pulls out a handful of atlys. "At least you have this," she says. Blowing the powder at my face, she makes me fall into a dream. I can't see the road, but I don't care. Cora doesn't mind, either. Then again, it's not like a car crash will kill a dead girl.

ELEVEN

DITCH THE car along MLK Boulevard and walk the rest of the way to North Highlandtown. I can't remember much of the drive, but noticing how much lighter my pockets are, I know I must've done a lot of atlys. There's only one thing I remember crystal clear. No matter how fucked up I could get, it would be hard to forget talking to a dead girl.

"Serena loved you so much," she said. "I was jealous of that. Even after I found out about the cancer, your relationship made me wish for love. I wanted to have someone to hold me. Even knowing I'd die soon and leave a broken heart behind I wanted someone to be there in the end. I know how selfish it was. That's why I understand your addiction. I know how good it feels to be selfish. You're doing the right thing."

She made me feel a little better about leaving Benito and Border to die, but she didn't take all of the guilt away. As I enter Patterson Park, I wrestle with turning back. While Cora condoned what I'd done, her pressure alone makes me think I've lost it—for good. I don't belong back in Baltimore. If I could let so many people die for my addiction, I belong behind bars.

A handful of drugs is the most pliable material for burying guilt. I take a sniff for each pang, for each person I left for dead. By the time I reach Snake Hill High, I don't have a care in the world.

The school bakes in the sun, creating a unique smell of chemicals and chaos. Piss and shit are heavy in the mix. Sweat, too. But in a deeper whiff, puke rolls through the nostrils, along with the heady perfume of burning garbage. And, if the season is right, one might even detect the smell of a recently fired gun. Home sweet home.

Our couch is still there, but Loshi's nowhere to be found. Two wiry kids are there instead, both in a nod with strings of brown drool hanging from their cracked lips. At that moment, I don't care about Loshi—just that I was stolen from. All the theft I've committed recently, and I want to tear these kids' heads off. And I'll be able to do it with another bump. I scoop atlys from my pocket and deepen my rage with a violent sniff.

The boys wake at the snort—any resourceful addict would. One of the kids leaps up as soon as he sees me, adjusting his jagged hand jewelry before cracking his neck.

"What. What. What, son? You starting some shit, son?"

"That depends," I say. "You gonna back off my couch?"

"This ain't your couch no more. We stole it fair and square."

"You can't steal something fair and square, stupid."

"Who you callin' stupid, son?"

THE GREEN KANGAROOS

The second kid glares at me, wiping the drool from his mouth. When he stands I notice the couch has more stains than it used to—reddish brown ones that run deep in the fabric.

Now I'm worried about Loshi.

"Where's Loshi?" I ask the kids.

"Who?"

"Loshi, my friend. This is our spot."

The kid snarls. "Shit, you mean that crusty ass bitch with the face holes?"

"I guess . . ."

"That bitch is in the closet," he says. "This is our place now."

"Fuck no, this is our spot. We've had this couch for more than a year."

"Not anymore, son."

I take a giant step forward, but when the second kid pulls a switchblade, a hand clamps around my arm. It yanks me away so the newcomer can step in front. Loshi stands between me and the knife, his hands up in surrender. "Be cool, man. We don't want no trouble."

"You be cool, bitch. We're just trying to enjoy the day," the knife-wielding kid spits.

"On our couch, in our spot. No, man, fuck that."

I've drawn several eyes. With a pocket full of atlys, it's not smart of me.

"This ain't your spot no more," the kids says. "Now, fuck off."

Loshi wraps his arm around my waist before I can lunge, but he isn't strong enough to hold me—that fact is what stops my attack.

God, the state of him. His body is skeletal, covered

with scarred divots, but his face is the worst. His chin is less prominent, and his cheeks are completely gone. Without fat in his face, it's no more than sallow bone. I consider the possibility that he's dead. After all, it wouldn't be my first corpse conversation of the day.

He pulls me into a janitor's closet. It's a foul-smelling nest of disarray. My hands are filthy, but I'd rather cover my face with them than inhale the stink. Loshi lights a cigarette and settles into a pile of rags.

"Jesus, man, what happened to you?" I ask him.

"Family cut me off. No more money, no more food, no more pot to stick." Loshi taps his bony, holey stomach.

"How could you let those assholes steal our spot?"

"You weren't here, man. How was I supposed to hold it alone? I'm hardly strong enough to beat down my own dick. For all I knew, you were never coming back. You ran off for a month."

"Shit, it's been a month?"

"Something like that."

I knew I was unconscious in Springfield for a while, but I couldn't calculate it. It sure as hell didn't seem like more than a month.

"I didn't run off, Losh. My ex-wife's boyfriend stabbed me, my fucking sister kidnapped me, and a barn fire tried to kill me." I couch beside him, touching his jagged shoulder. "But I'm back now. And I'm holding."

Loshi's eyes widen when I pull out a handful of atlys. I think he looks happy, but it's hard to tell until I see tears slip over the crags in his face.

"Can I . . .?" he whispers.

I give him a bump. He swallows the drip hard,

running his fingers through his thinning hair. "Fuck, that's good," he grunts. "I feel like I could screw a robot."

He's talking crazy. I take a hit of my own because I wanna talk crazy, too. The atlys slams my brain, the buzz pours down to my dick, and Loshi makes perfect sense at last.

"Shit, man," I say, "we gotta find some robots to screw."

I look over to see Cora perched on a pyramid of paint cans. Maybe she'll know where the horny robots hang out.

"Who are you talking to?" Loshi asks, staring at the unoccupied cans.

I hadn't even realized I'd started speaking to her. "I guess you don't see a chick sitting there?"

"Right now? Nah, just more junk," he replies. "Why? Do you?"

"Yeah. Yeah, I do."

"Don't worry about that, man. Hallucinations and shit."

"Benito said this powder doesn't give hallucinations."

"Who's Benito?"

"Some dead guy."

Fuck, I hope I don't start seeing him too. I don't realize I'm gnawing my nails until I taste blood.

"Perry, you okay?" Loshi's emaciated fingers dig into my arm. "Hey, things are gonna be okay now. You've got atlys. You can sell it and find a new place for us to live."

I've got atlys and I can find a place for *us*? Loshi's my friend, but that idea doesn't sit well with me.

"This is our place," I tell him. "We can't let a couple of asshole kids steal the meager shit we have. I didn't give up a barn full of atlys and trim to sleep in a smelly-ass closet."

I take another hit of my pocket powder. I feel some lint go up my nose, but I ignore it—just like the fact that I'm about to go unarmed into a knife fight.

As I burst out of the closet, I shout, "Hey!" realizing too late that the two assholes have multiplied into eight.

Clustered around our couch, cooking up some shots, they turn to me like psychotic hyenas trying to protect their bloody lunch from a vulture.

"The fuck you want?" one of the guys says, his chest swollen with bravado and pistols.

"That's the dude that said the school is his," another spits.

"Not the school. Just this corner," I reply. "Definitely this couch."

"That sounds like your problem, not ours."

"Of course it's not your problem. You already took what you wanted."

"So?" the gun-toting kid says, pushing his tattooed face at me.

Loshi sidles up, grabbing my arm. "Come on, let's go."

"Listen to your boy. It might just save your life."

"Fuck you, kid."

The second it snaps from my mouth, a switchblade gives my cheek a stinging reply. The cut isn't deep, but a drop of blood slides to my chin.

"You're the one who wants to get fucked, bro. My knife here, she's quite the lay. A little rough, though. Bend over, I'll show ya."

THE GREEN KANGAROOS

"It's not worth it," Loshi says.

"Nothing is fuckin' worth it anymore," I say to the kids before Loshi pulls me away.

Back in the closet, I snatch my binoculars from a crusty stack of nudie mags before knocking the collection into a puddle of fuzzy liquid. I can't stay here, not in this closet, not in this school, and not with Loshi. The powder will run out fast, and I won't have enough to snort, sell, and share. I can't support Loshi, even though he supported me for years. I wasn't built for it. I need to be selfish. I guess Cora was right. Selfishness does feel the same as being alone.

I can't stand the stench. Binoculars around my neck, I kick open the door with Loshi on my heels. The kids on our couch call us fags as we come of the closet, but I ignore them. I'm done fighting for scraps.

Snake Hill is always ripe, but I gulp the fresh air. A group of snakes on a stoop stop smoking a bowl to laugh at us. Loshi flips them off, but his hands are so thin, it hardly registered as a finger to me. Snorting a bump, I march toward Patterson Park. It's tough for Loshi to keep up, which I hope lets me escape him without a confrontation. But my tunnel vision is extreme and I nearly trip over Beater-Leg Larry. He barks like a dog as I collect myself, growling when I kneel beside him to snort up atlys that spilled from my pocket.

By the time the path is clean, Loshi has caught up.

"Hey man, you okay?" he asks. "What's wrong? What you walking so fast?"

"I'm sorry, Loshi. We gotta split up," I say.

"What do you mean?"

"I can't live like this. Not in a closet, not with those fuckers stealing my shit."

"What are we going to do?"

"You're going to make up with your family. And I'm going to . . ." Loshi pouts and shakes his head. "You're going to be fine, man. This is only the second time your family has turned you away. You have at least two more coming."

Tugging on my binoculars, I look across Patterson Park. Past some dicks in Italian suits walking into the Casino for lunch, to the cluster of apartment buildings in the distance. Serena is probably nestled inside right now. Maybe reading a book. Maybe taking a bath. Maybe thinking of me.

"No, I won't leave you."

I drop the binoculars, realizing he's talking more to my pocket than my face. He wants atlys, and I don't blame him.

I sigh. "How much will it take for you to leave me?"

"Perry, it's not like that." It takes one doubtful look from me to make it *'like that.'* "I want half," he says.

I suppose I owe him that much. But he doesn't know how much I have stuck in the corners of my pocket. Who's to say what "half" is?

Loshi and I aren't worried about cops as we huddle under an old sculpture made of iPads to divide up the atlys. It's the snakes that'll get you. Addicts sense that shit like pheromones. Skinny lizards with bruise-speckled bodies have already climbed closer. We have to get the work done fast, or we'll have an atlys panic on our hands.

I gather some of what I have and spread it across the back of a broken iPad. The powder is speckled with dirt and lint, even a few pieces of glass, but Loshi doesn't care. He plucks a baggie from the ground and wipes his share into it. Twisting it closed, he stuffs it into his pocket.

Transaction complete. Friendship over.

Loshi takes off down the street, and I never expect to see him again. It's sad how sad it's not.

I pick a piece of plastic out of a line before it's vacuumed up my nose and shove the rest into my pocket. High, but not anything could be mistaken for happy, I look across the park. Here comes the hard part, I think. Where the fuck do I go from here?

When Serena's building enters my eyeline, I smile. Oh yeah, I'll just go home.

I haven't paid her a real visit in months, maybe a year—fucked if I know. Obviously she doesn't want me there. Plus, I have that asshole lawyer to worry about. But now that I think about it, if it weren't for that motherfucker, I wouldn't have a fistful of fun in my pocket.

I cross the park, swinging around the dried up ice rink and the good side of the pond. I have to keep my distance. It's too early in the day for the Fatcats to be on the prowl, but the northside pimps don't like snakes slithering too close. I move around the alley side of Serena's building until the kitchen is in perfect range.

Looking into her kitchen makes me feel hunger for the first time in a while. Atlys has suppressed my appetite for too long. If I don't eat something soon, I'll pass out.

The latter seems easier, so I hunker down in a ditch, aim my binoculars at her apartment, and wait.

The clock on her stove says 4:18 P.M. She should be home by now. She's probably in the shower. After she gets out, she'll start cooking, maybe fool around on the internet, maybe browse a few porn sites, maybe touch herself . . .

Dizziness forces me to lie down. Curled up in the ditch, I rest my head against the curb, which is wet with something I don't want identified. As I languish, a rat regards my leg with its swollen belly. Instead of revulsion, I contemplate all the ways I could cook it. Rat stew, rat sausage, rat pizza, rat-meat on rat-bread with rat-relish. I reach for its gnarled tail, but it waddles just out of reach. Settling against a storm grate, it emits a scream. Not a squeak. Not a screech. A genuine scream.

The rat turns onto its side, its belly skin bulging. Its face stretches to such an unnatural degree, I think its snout might split with the high-pitched din, but it doesn't. The splitting happens a few inches down as a pink lump protrudes from its hindquarters. I watch in morbid fascination as it squeezes a slimy baby rat onto the pavement, followed by a second. One after the other, the squealing rodents flop into the gutter. I briefly consider making a meal of them, but the placenta, clinging like tawny snot to their wrinkled bodies, turns my stomach.

"What the hell are you doing?" someone asks. No, not *just someone*. I know exactly who it is, but looking up, I gasp in fake surprise.

"Serena? What are you doing here?"

"I live here, you jackass," she spits, her hands firmly planted on her hips.

"Really? You live here? What a coincidence."

THE GREEN KANGAROOS

She looks tired, but that's nothing new. She always pushes herself too hard. Life is a chore that must be completed to perfection each day, and if it isn't, she's the only one to blame. It's no wonder she turned to atlys so easily.

But she wears her weariness well. The dark bags under her eyes are no match for her freckles. Her hair is frazzled, but the vibrant color keeps her alight. Stress keeps her vital, her blood flow fierce. Not like my blood, which feels sluggish in my veins. They're too gummed up with atlys for fierce living. She knows this about me; I assume it's why she doesn't seem surprised to see me lying in a gutter.

"What are you doing here, Perry? You know you're not suppose to come near me."

"Which is a real shame. You always loved when I came near you—or on you."

"You're disgusting."

It takes me a few attempts to sit up straight. "I'm just kidding. Jeez, I didn't realize you'd lost your sense of humor."

"Nope, just my patience with slimy, obsessive addicts like you," she says.

"And like you, Rennie? Once an addict, always an addict. Isn't that what they told you in rehab?"

"How would you know?"

"I just got out of one." I try to stand, but I'm too weak. I crash back to the curb and try to laugh it off.

She scoffs. "Yeah, it looks like it worked."

"We can't all have the strength you do."

"I can see that."

She walks away, stopping when I say, "I'm desperate, Rennie."

"Don't call me that," she replies without turning. "And don't tell me you're desperate. That's the worst way to earn my sympathy." I think she's about to leave me there when she groans and sits beside me. She doesn't speak for a few minutes, and when she does, it's barely audible. "I'm glad Robert didn't kill you."

"You are? I didn't think you cared either way."

"You and I shared something, Perry. It's hard to forget it completely. God knows I've tried."

"Which something do you mean: the marriage or the addiction?"

"I often think they were the same thing."

I touch her hand. She shakes me away, rubbing her palm on her jeans like I've covered her in toxic waste.

"Please, Serena, I need something to eat. I need clean clothes. I need . . . I need you." I'm laying it on thick, and she doesn't even flinch.

"You don't need me, Perry. You need anyone with food and clean clothes."

"No, I need—*I want*—you, Serena Samson." Blinking rapidly, I slap my palms together in prayer. "Please. My love. My savior."

"Give me break," she says, rolling her eyes. "Oh, it's not 'Samson' anymore. I went back to Hall."

"But I thought you liked being part of my family."

"I did. I do. Nadine and I will be friends forever, and I'll always be close with your parents, but I can't live in the past. I have to move on with my life. And so do you."

I slump over, spitting street filth from my tongue. "From what I've seen, you've already moved on."

"Maybe you should stop watching me."

THE GREEN KANGAROOS

"What else is there to do? Sleep? Watch Snake Hill porn?"

"You could sober up . . . get a job . . . get a life?"

"Like it's that easy."

Despite the earlier disgust, she willingly touches my hand, and a thousand memories of that sensation stream back. Interlocking fingers at the lunch table in high school. The sweaty grip during Trevor's funeral. The "everything will be okay" squeeze before I shot her up for the first time. I wonder if her mind goes there too. Our eyes meet, but only for a few seconds before she releases me and stands again.

"Please, Serena," I whisper. It's still thick, but what I lay on her is also true. "I just need to get off the street for a few hours. It's been so long."

"I thought you said you just got out of rehab."

"Springfield is worse than the street. You know that."

"Yes, I do." She sighs. "Okay, just for a few minutes. I don't want you touching anything in my apartment, including me."

"I promise," I say, crossing my heart.

But Serena knows the score. She says, "I wish that meant something," but still gestures for me to follow her.

I fail at standing again.

"Oh Christ, Perry." She looks down at her pitiful ex-husband. Wrapping her arm around me, she hoists me up. Sweet fuck, she smells good, like iced gingerbread. I must smell like shit. "Jesus, Perry, you smell like shit." She coughs.

We're still one mind. How could she ever move on when we're so obviously meant for each other? In the elevator, I lean against the wall and stare at the girl who's as beautiful as she was at sixteen, and for the first time in years, my dick hardens without atlys.

"Before you go, I'm going to take those," Serena says, nodding at my binoculars. "I don't want you watching me anymore. It makes me sick, you know."

"You don't look sick. You look gorgeous, Rennie."

"You see what you want to see. Always have."

"It never occurred to you that my view is the right one?"

"Yes," she replies. "But I was high then."

"Maybe a little bump will improve your outlook. If you need a pick-me-up, I'm your guy."

"So you have drugs, but no food."

"It's important to prioritize, my love."

She gets very close to my face, her expression pinched in revulsion.

"Listen to me, asshole, I'm doing this because I feel sorry for you. Because you're pathetic. Because I made so many mistakes in my past I think my future would be doomed if I didn't give you a chance."

"For what?"

"To see what an atlys addict can become."

"I've seen that plenty, darling."

"You've seen what becomes of people who fail. I want you to see what can come to those who succeed."

"Seen that, too." I shake the binoculars at her.

"You use those to see my tits and ass, and they're the same. I doubt you've bothered to see anything about my life."

"You're wrong about one thing, Rennie. Your tits and ass are better these days."

She allows a small smile to emerge before

stepping back. The elevator dings, and the doors open.

"Come on, it's this way." As I follow her down the hall, my eyes to her ass, I remember the years I had this same sexy view every day. When we lived together. When she loved me.

We'd moved in together a year before we got married, just to test things out. For being such a "together" girl, she was surprisingly messy. A pile of clothes accumulated on her side of the bed, growing taller with each day. She left coffee mugs everywhere. She wouldn't close applications on our computer. She'd leave rooms for hours but forget to turn off the television. She justified it by saying that her work life was so stressful and organized, she needed to be disorganized at home. She needed a place to let the worries of the day fall away, and she didn't want to clean up after.

"You want a wallow," I'd said.

"Yes, I want a wallow," she replied, her nose crinkled. "What's so wrong with that?"

"Nothing, my little hippo. Nothing at all."

I don't know why I remember it so well. Nothing about the night was all that noteworthy. Maybe it's because we were sober. Or because it was honest. Or maybe it was because I loved her enough not to care about her messes. As I look at her now, holding open the door to her apartment, I wonder if Sober Serena could ever love the mess I've become.

When she calls me forward with disdain, I doubt it.

Her apartment is fantastic. I immediately see the street price for everything. Serena notices, so I don't allow my eyes to linger. The ceilings are taller than I'd expected, and a robotic shark floats in the right corner of the living room. She'd always wanted one when we were together, and now she has it. Fuck, she *is* better off without me. Crystal candelabras and decorative plates accent her cherry end tables. Her walls are color magnets, drawing the hidden pinks and purples from the palette. It must sicken her boyfriend.

I realize there's hope in the paint. This is *her* place, not his. And it doesn't look like the kind of place she'd give up without a fight. She may not be married to me anymore, but it doesn't look like she's going to marry the dick lawyer any time soon.

Before I sit on her sofa, she throws down a dishtowel.

"Sorry, sometimes I forget how disgusting I am."

"You're not disgusting," she says. "You're just . . ."

"Yeah, I get it. You know, there aren't many mirrors in Snake Hill. It makes people pretty careless about their looks."

"I'm pretty sure it's the atlys that does that, Perry."

"Then it's not all bad."

"What do you mean?" She opens a can of chicken noodle soup. It pours into a bowl with a wet slap. I get so lost in the anticipation of the meal, I go blank. "Perry, are you listening?"

Once the soup is in the microwave, I focus on Serena again. "The atlys," I say. "It can't be all bad if it makes me confident enough to face the world like this."

"Carelessness isn't the same as confidence," she replies. "And you don't face shit. Atlys is the best hiding place in the world, Perry. Whatever courage you had was consumed by addiction a long time ago."

THE GREEN KANGAROOS

"Do you ever miss it?" I ask, my hand creeping to my powdery pocket.

"Let's not start this. It won't do either of us any good." I move from the couch to the kitchen, our eyes locked as I approach. "I see you got your strength back," she says, stepping away.

"Maybe it's that courage you said I don't have."

I reach out slowly, and she backs away fast. I don't blame her. My hands are revolting. Dirt, blood, and atlys mottle them to snowy shit. As I wash them in her sink, brown water swirls down the drain. Without the dirt, the raw injection sites between my fingers and on my wrists are easier to see. They're all Serena can focus on.

"Do they scare you, Rennie? Do my scars remind you of your own?"

"I don't need you to remind me. I remember perfectly well, every single day. I remember what I was and how much love it took to make me into what I am now."

"*Love.* You threw away my love when you got clean."

"Because loving myself was more important," she says. "Do you feel that way, Perry? Do you love yourself? Your life?"

"Not always."

She raises her eyebrows. "Ever?"

"There are different kinds of love. Sometimes it's quiet. Sometimes it's a rush, like lightning in your veins. Sometimes you don't know you're loved until the pavement kisses you goodnight."

Serena shakes her head as she heads for the microwave. She pulls out the soup and sets it in front of me.

"Go slow on this. It's hot."

"Fuck that. Do you know the last time since I ate something hot, Rennie?"

"If that's a sexual innuendo, I don't want to know." I laugh. She still knows me so well.

"I'm not kidding. I can't remember the last time I had hot food. I hope it burns me. I hope I get that dangly skin flap on the roof of my mouth."

"I could never forgive myself if I were the cause of a skinflap mouth." She chuckles but stops abruptly. Clearing her throat, she says, "Just wait for it to cool, okay? I'll get you some clean clothes." She heads into the bedroom, her eyes averted.

In spite of her avoidance, she's having fun with me. She's falling into our old routine. I wish I could take advantage of it. I wish I could tie her to the bed, shoot her with atlys, and go down on her 'til nightfall. But I don't want her to lose everything she's built here. She's made a good life without me.

She returns with a stack of men's clothes. As she bends to hand them to me, I get a glimpse of the two angels below her shoulders. They make me want to play the devil very badly, to tear off her shirt and bury myself in her heavenly hills. Instead, I thank her, slurping one more spoonful of soup before I walk to the bathroom to change. The noodles slide down my throat with welcome warmth—unlike the last salty noodle to hit my throat.

I take off my coat and tuck the bag of atlys into the kangaroo pouch of Serena's green sweatshirt. The coincidence isn't lost on me. I don't dwell on the green kangaroos or Cora because I'm afraid thinking of her will make her appear. The last thing I want is to see the ghost of Serena's dead friend in Serena's house.

As she throws my rags into the wash, I feast on soup. I ignore my annoying slurping sounds. The more I eat, the hungrier I get. By the time the soup is gone, I'm famished, but I don't want to bug her for more. That's when I realize the perfect solution to my appetite problem. One snort and I'll be full.

I walk to the bathroom, but Serena cuts me off.

"You were just in there," she says.

"To change. I didn't piss." My fingers grow sweaty around the bag.

"What's in your pocket?"

"It's *your* pocket, actually."

"No, it's yours. Don't you recognize your own sweatshirt?"

I look down, realizing I do recognize it. I got it on sale at Kohl's because I needed something green for a chilly St. Patrick's Day. I can't believe she kept it.

"Well, I'll be damned," I say, heading for the bathroom again.

"What's in your pocket, Perry?"

I sigh, turning to her with puppy dog eyes in full effect. "You know what it is, Rennie."

"Let me see it."

I pull out the baggie, and a small gasp escapes her lips. I guess she hadn't expected me to have so much. If she'd seen what I had before paying off Loshi, she might be standing in a pleasure puddle right now.

"How did you get it?"

I bounce my eyebrows. "Why? You wanna score some of your own?"

"Of course not." She pulls an offended face, but I

know she still feels the pangs of temptation. She gulps a little too hard before she says, "I assume you want to snort it in my bathroom?"

"That was the plan, yeah."

"You know I can't let you do that, Perry. Not here." She opens her hand. It's shaking like her jaw when she says, "Hand it over."

I clutch the bag to my chest. "So you can flush it down the toilet? No way."

"I wouldn't do that. I know how much it must have cost you."

"What are you going to do with it?"

"I'm going to keep it away from you for as long as you're here."

My lips part as I dangle the bag in front of her. I run my tongue over my top teeth, my mouth curling into a devious smile.

Gently swinging the baggie, I say, "You can have some if you want."

"I figured that." She makes a grab for it, but I snap it back in time. She growls. "Hand it over, Perry."

I slap the baggie onto her palm. She barely wraps her fingers around it before someone knocks on her front door. My veins vibrating in panic, I try to snatch it back, but Serena stuffs it in her pocket too quickly.

"Who the fuck is that?" I ask as she walks to the door. "Did you call the cops?"

"Jesus, Perry, calm down. It's probably just Nadine."

"Nadine? Why the fuck would she be here? Did you tell her I was here?"

"We hang out all the time, you moron. She comes over for drinks after work."

THE GREEN KANGAROOS

"I don't want to see her," I say. "You gotta send her away."

The doorbell rings, and Serena's phone chirps with a new text message.

"I'm coming," she shouts, but I step between her and the door.

"Serena, please. I can't see her now. Not after what she did."

"What *she* did? I doubt Nadine did anything that wasn't a normal reaction to something *you* did. Look, you can wait in my bedroom if you want. But if you touch anything . . ."

"I won't, I promise." She looks at me doubtfully. "I swear, Rennie. I give you my word."

"Your promises *are* swear words, Perry, and they don't mean shit to me."

"Just don't tell her I'm here, okay?"

"Fine. It's stupid, but go ahead and hide from your little sister."

I slip into Serena's bedroom: a tribute to the color mauve and men without shirts. No wonder Robert kicked the shit out of me; he was probably overloaded with rage at having to bang his girlfriend while looking at posters of beefy celebrities.

Her jewelry box is a temptation I can't resist. I sift through it, pocketing rings and earrings: little things she won't notice missing for a few weeks. I know I shouldn't do it—nearly every fiber of my being says "No, Perry. Put it back. You owe her better than this," but there's one little grain, one thin, wracked fiber that says I need the jewelry to survive, that Serena will understand. That fiber is a fool and a liar, but it's the easiest to believe. Rationality and I haven't been friends for a long time.

I hear the door close, followed by Nadine's voice. I catch the sound of bottles coming out of the fridge and the crisp whisper of a beer being opened. I salivate, dying for a drink, but I make the best of where I am, wrist-deep in Serena's underwear drawer. Beneath layers of lace and cotton, I find her vibrator. It's the same one she's had for years. I wonder if she's told her boyfriend that I bought it for her. I pick it up, and accidentally switch it on. The buzz frightens me, and I drop the vibrator, which loudly rolls across the underwear drawer.

"What's that?" I hear Nadine ask.

"Oh, it's my stupid phone—an old one. It keeps going off for no reason. I think it's possessed," Serena says. "So, how have you been?"

"Okay, I guess." I press my ear against the door in time to hear her say, "Actually, I feel pretty shitty."

Good. After what you did to me, you should feel shitty.

"About what happened with Perry?" Serena asks.

"Yeah. I shouldn't have brought him to Springfield. I just—it's so stupid," she says, taking such a big gulp from her beer I hear it through the door.

"You want him to get better. That's not stupid."

"He thinks it is. He believes there's nothing to go back to, that once he's sober, his life will be just as bad, except without getting high. I think he believes he was singled out when we were kids, that Mom and Dad didn't love him because he was in the middle. Like that makes a difference."

THE GREEN KANGAROOS

Says a non-green kangaroo. What does she know?

"I just wish I could find a way to convince him that he matters, and that he always did. To me, at least. He was my hero," she says. "Before and after Trevor died."

A knot forms in my throat. I swallow it, but there's another bringing up the rear. It's a grief that can't be swallowed. Only atlys could knock this sucker down. Damn you, Serena.

"Atlys makes you selfish," Serena says. "Believe me, I know. No matter what you say, Perry's id speaks loudest. It says 'Fuck those guys. They don't understand. A hit will make everything better."

Fuck those guys. They don't understand. A hit really would make everything better.

"I wish I could make him understand how much I love him, how much we all love him."

"He knows, Nadine. He just ignores it."

"It broke my heart to abandon him at Springfield. Accepting that I'm an only child now—well, I haven't accepted it. I still wish he could come back to us. I still wish I could save him."

"Me too," Serena says. "Not a day passes that I don't wish Perry could find peace in sobriety. But I think he believes peace will only come in death."

I hate how right they are.

Shit, if they're so right about that, maybe they're right about everything else. Maybe Mom and Dad did love us all the same. Maybe Trevor's death didn't push me into the shadows. Maybe my family really wants to help me find a clean happiness instead of holding me back from the filthy friend I've found in atlys.

Without realizing it, I scoop Serena's accessories

from my pockets and drop them back in the jewelry box. I haven't returned something I stole since I swiped some fake dog shit from a joke shop when I was seven. It feels good. Not high-good. Good-good.

"I just want Perry to know I love him," Nadine says.

It's too much. My heart twists with the doorknob, my eyes welling as I burst from the bedroom. Rushing to my sister, I say I do know it, and tell her how much I love her.

And I would've gone on, declaring how happy I wanted her life to be. I would've told her I'd make a real effort to get clean this time, that she'd finally saved me, now and forever. I would've—if not for the note sitting on the table between Nadine and Serena. In Serena's sloppy cursive, the words shout, "Perry's in the bedroom. He's going crazy!"

"Crazy?" I ask her.

"That's not what I meant," Serena says. When she and Nadine reach out to me, I dodge them, my fist cocked as a warning. I would never hit either, but hey, I'm crazy, right? Who knows what I could do?

"Everything was a lie. An act. You knew I was in there. You were just saying the same bullshit you always say."

"Everything I said was true," Nadine says.

"The fuck it was." I grab my damp clothes from the wash. Facing Serena, I know her hand is around the bag of atlys in her jeans. "Give it back," I say, my hand open.

"You don't need it, Perry. Everything you need is right here."

"I know, in your pocket. Hand it over."

THE GREEN KANGAROOS

She slaps the bag onto my palm, and I head for the door. Before I can leave, Nadine calls after me.

"Say what you want to me, but be nice to Mom and Dad when you see them. They're still pissed you left the rehab."

"I'm still pissed you put me in there," I say. "Besides, I don't plan on seeing them any time soon. You're an only child now, remember?"

"You might see them on your way down," she says. "We drove here together. They're just making dinner reservations."

"Dinner? All of you?"

"Yes, Perry, that's what families do."

I shrug. "Great, have fun at McDonald's."

"Oh, we're going ritzier than that. You can't imagine how much money we've been able to save without you around to steal it."

Serena sighs. "Cut it out, you two."

"No, he should know what he's missing out on," she says. "A ritzy dinner at the Kum Den Smokehouse."

"The fuck you are," I spit.

Serena flops onto the couch, holding her head. "Nadine . . ."

"What's wrong, Perry? I thought you wanted to know what it looks like inside. Tomorrow, I can tell you."

I spin my baggie open and dig my pinkie into the powder.

"Hey, I said not here," Serena says.

I walk to the couch and lean over with the powder to my nose. After it disappears up my nostril, I say, "Eat me, Serena."

I stomp to the door, but she follows me. Again, I'm stopped—this time by my ex-wife grabbing hold of my binocular strap.

"You didn't think I'd forget, did you?"

"I miss you being high. You forgot all kinds of things when you were high, mostly how not to be a bitch." She tugs the strap and it burns my neck.

"Ow, fuck, okay!" I squeal, throwing the binoculars at her. "I hope you two are happy. You just lost me forever."

"I'd already come to terms with that," Nadine says.

Serena adds, "Yeah I'm good."

I slam the door as hard as possible, which probably isn't as hard as it feels.

My atlys strength is in full force as I exit the building, but it's not enough to help me escape my parents. Seeing them stroll down the street in my direction, I take a sudden turn, but they spot me, and wave. They pick up their pace, calling my name. I wish they'd shown this much drive to spend time with me when I was a kid.

When they catch up, I grumble, "Hey." Mom looks like she wants to hug me, but she doesn't.

"Oh Perry, you're so thin," she says.

"That'll happen when you don't eat." I try to pull puppy dog eyes, but the atlys has me so wired, I'm sure I look crazed. "Can I have some money?"

She looks at Dad, who furrows his brow. It's all the response I need.

"Never mind. I don't want to hold up your fancy dinner plans."

"How do you know about that?"

THE GREEN KANGAROOS

"This is the designated day for Nadine and I to have brother/sister hangout time. Oh no, wait, we had that when she locked me up in Springfield Hospital. How quickly I forget."

"Something had to be done, Perry. You'd been stabbed," Dad says.

"I'm surprised an immediate celebration didn't break out."

"Oh Perry, why do you act like we hate you?" Mom asks.

"Screw this. If you're not going to give me any money for food, I don't need to waste my time."

"But it wouldn't go toward food," Dad says.

"You got it all figured out, huh? Yeah, your food is more important than mine," I say. "You know it's people, right? Everything you eat there: it's made of people."

"At Applebee's?" Mom asks. "Did they get a new menu?"

"Nadine told me you were going to the Kum Den Smokehouse."

"Like we could afford to eat there! After all of the money we spent on rehab and therapy, we have hardly anything left," Dad says, adding awkwardly, "Not that it's *your* fault."

"No, of course not," I say. "Well, have a good night, wherever you end up. I gotta go. I've got a big day of starving to death ahead of me."

"Perry, please don't act like this."

"Sorry to upset you, Mom. I thought you'd appreciate the honesty."

She touches my arm, but I break away and march toward the park.

I try to look as strong as possible walking away from them, but I get dizzy. I stumble, my vision blurring as I cross the street. There are too many voices to distinguish between them, too many jumbled words to understand what they mean. "There he is" and "Mow him down" are gibberish before I hear an engine roar and tires scream. All I know for sure is that one second, I'm crossing the street and the next, I'm lying in it.

I'm bleeding, but I don't know from where. I stare up at the periwinkle sky, unsure of why until a familiar face blocks out the blue.

"I betya thought we'd never find you, bitch." As Ice's grimace spreads, my tunnel vision fills with his diamond teeth. "I betya thought I was dead."

"Didn't even consider it," I say. I cough a hunk of bloody phlegm across his face, and he kicks my side. My mom, standing nearby, pleads to him with desperate wails. He digs into my pockets, ripping out the remainder of my atlys.

"Where's the rest?" he grunts.

My throat feels too clotted to speak, but I'm able to spit out, "Gone."

Cold metal presses against my temple as Ice says, "Then so are you." I close my eyes and wait for oblivion.

Something heavy falls on top of me. I open my eyes to see the back of Ice's head lying on my chest, the rest of his cumbersome body blanketing my legs. Dad stands over us with a 2x4 in his hand, which he drops to grab Ice's gun. The car that hit me peals away, and I close my eyes again. I faintly hear people asking bystanders what happened before I feel Ice's

THE GREEN KANGAROOS

immense body pulled off of me. In the release, I become aware of every injury. The pain and blood and sound of my mother's screams is too much. Dizziness becomes unconsciousness, and I can't deny that a part of me hopes unconsciousness will still deliver me to oblivion.

***

When I wake up in a room I haven't seen in years, I realize oblivion isn't in the cards. My childhood bedroom is exactly the same. The paint, the posters; I wonder if my old bong is still hidden where it used to be. I'm confused, but when I see my parents beside the bed, I remember the car, the 2x4, and Ice's diamond teeth, eager to sink into my soul. My hand moves to my pocket in terror. It's empty.

I'm drugless, injured, and trapped at my parents' house. I pray it's just a nightmare, but when my mom ladles chicken noodle soup into my mouth, it tastes of sad reality.

"You'll stay here to detox," Dad says, starting my sweating fit. He could say both of my legs are missing and I'd probably feel as much fear.

"Nadine said you didn't want to see me again," I say. "Why would you let me stay?"

"Being an addict is your fault. Getting hit by a car isn't," he replies.

Except it is. I got hit because I stole Benito's atlys and left him to die. According to what's left of his gang, it's my turn to die now.

Mom sets down the soup and covers her mouth with a whimper. She's sweating too, more than me. I hate upsetting her like this, but it's her fault for bringing me here, for suffering at my suffering. She cries, little hiccups of grief jumping out between sobs. Her face is flushed, and the sweat plasters her bangs to her forehead. She combs them back with shaking hands.

"Mom, are you okay?"

"Fine," she says, strained. "It's just this—whatever it is." Dad rubs her shoulders. There were always so much better with each other than with any of us kids. I felt guilty about her sadness, but Mom does overact to things. Thank God I didn't get that from her.

Her "Don't worry about me, I'm fine" is so on cue, I move my lips in time with hers. She's easy to predict—except for when she starts talking about sudden nosebleeds and fainting spells.

"Wait, what? How long has that been going on?"

"About as long as I've had these," she says, rolling up her sleeve. Her arms are covered in greasy red patches. I've seen some fucked-up junkies with creaming boils before, but Mom's sores glisten worse, like poisonous frogs.

"It's nothing," she says, scratching scales from the lumps.

"That doesn't look like nothing, Mom. Have you seen a doctor?"

She answers with a cough that sounds normal until it doesn't. Once it becomes a hacking fit, her rashes weep, glazing her arms in amber ooze. The seizure shakes her hand from her mouth. When it drops to her side, my stomach turns at the black meat that slides down her lips and fingertips. Her twitches become violent flops, knocking her out of Dad's hands, onto the floor.

Dad screams. I scream. Mom flops.

THE GREEN KANGAROOS

With a belch, frothy blood pours out of her mouth, drenching the carpet and running under the bed. I'm so confused, so scared, the only thought that punches through the madness is a terrible one: if my parents haven't changed my room since I moved out, the Hustler magazines hidden under my bed are ruined now.

TWELVE

EMERGENCY LIGHTS COLOR the lab in frantic reds and purples as Emily bellows, "Doctor, you have to disconnect her! Disconnect her, or she'll die!"

Laura Samson convulses in her chair, blood spilling down her chest, the lesions on her arms popping to pink cream. Doctor Carter rubs his temples, shaking his head at the bloody mess.

"Turn off the alarm for Christ's sake. I can't think with that on," he grumbles.

Emily cuts the alarm, but her face appears on every screened surface in the lab. "Jeremiah, what are you waiting for? She's dying!"

"You're positive?"

"One hundred percent, sir. If you wait much longer, her brain will turn to jelly. You have to disconnect her now."

"If I do that, she'll disappear in front of Perry and his father. They'll doubt their reality for sure," Carter says.

"You didn't care when the dead girl disappeared in front of him."

"Samson was high. He's sober now. And with his

172

father—" Carter sighs. "No, Emily, the risk is too high."

"Sir, a woman will die. Here. In real life."

"Lots of women have died here, Emily."

"As a repercussion for failing the program. Perry Samson hasn't even faced his third test yet," she says.

"Be sensible. We both know he's going to fail. Laura Samson, all of them—they were dead the moment they set foot in the Institute."

"They didn't set foot anywhere here. You abducted them."

Carter looks up as if hearing her voice for the first time, and detesting it. "Is that a problem for you?" he asks, chilling her insubstantial bones.

Laura stops convulsing. She lies limp, her face chalk white and irises drained to gray. But her heart beats on, pumping sluggish blood out of every orifice. Emily gazes down on her from all angles; many problems careen through her mind, but she shakes her head at Doctor Carter.

"No, sir," she says. "You're making the world a better place."

"So we're agreed. Disconnecting her is out of the question. That means we need to get her information downloaded into a Liberated Citizen before she expires. Is there time?"

"We've never made an LC for someone before initiating the third test—"

"I'm aware, Emily. Can you do it?"

"Yes."

"You don't sound confident."

"It's just that—" Her brow furrows. "Jeremiah, she won't get the chance to help him."

"Yes, she will. Her death could change her son's life. Grief can do that, you know."

"But you said you think he'll fail."

He shrugs. "You never know what can happen. There's still Nadine. I could see Perry giving up atlys for her. The relationship between siblings is a powerful thing. It's a bond exceeding that of addicts and their vices."

Laura lets out a gasping shriek, followed by a cough that sprays blood across one of Emily's faces. Her image fades and the screen turns the exact shade of red to make the blood disappear. The seizures start again. Her head smacks against the chair, and her wrists twist beneath the restraints, dripping blood onto the floor.

"Download her now, before it's too late," Carter barks.

Now he's afraid of Laura Samson dying, Emily thinks. Despite her qualms, she nods obediently and disappears from the lab.

The file room is a chamber of computerized webbing. Each strand sparkles with diamond clumps holding an entire life of joys and laments. Only Emily sees these glimmers. She created each speck and remembers each patient who left his or her impression, whether recovered or replaced. It is the only thing she keeps for herself. When Jeremiah gave her the power to program histories and personalities into his Liberated Citizens, he gave her the ability to save that information elsewhere. The file room is her place to stroll and think about the lives she's touched—and ruined.

It wasn't always a sad place. In the beginning, she

took pride in her collections, especially in what she now deems failures. She believed in Jeremiah's dream and that the world needed someone like him. Her involvement made her feel important when she felt like one small drop in the ocean of Doctor Carter's programming achievements.

Her troubles began when he gave her greater access in his other programs. The orchestrations within started feeling wrong, like addicts were driven toward failure. But she keeps her mouth shut. What does she know? After all, she's just the test tube baby of ingenuity and mathematics. Jeremiah lives in the real world, with real people. Of course he knows more about human life than Emily.

The Samson web isn't hard to find, thanks to Laura's crystal, tinged red among the flecks of white. It opens to her, spilling information like milkweed spills silk. From her own childhood to those of her children, stories her grandparents told her, and how she got the scar above her left eyebrow, Laura Samson's memories take flight. They vanish at the touch of her fingertips, moving through her circuits and touching every emotion she wished her programming forbid.

With Laura Samson's memories collected, Emily moves from the file room to the LC lab. The software welcomes her like a spiteful friend, reminding her of every real life she's made into . . . something else. Liberated Citizens can't live real lives. They follow a predestined plan like trains on a track, around and around, until Doctor Carter's say-so. Once the countdown to death begins, the LC makes its arrangements, without ever knowing what lays ahead.

To them, it's just a vacation, just some time away to relax alone. Like humans, they never expect the end. But when it comes, the consciousness shuts down and their bodies disintegrate, turning to ribbons of smoke like insignificant teacups. They never know they are only wire and sparks, programmed to follow a risk-free path to expiration. There is no art, no creation, no true joy. They are corpses on a loop. At least a piece of the real woman Laura Samson was will remain alive somewhere, even in a digital woman's silly collection.

Laura is still convulsing when Emily returns to the lab, but it's clear her brain has left the building. Her heart is on its last frantic pump, her body freezing before it goes limp. Staring ahead, she frowns at Emily.

"Time of death: 1100 hours, June 2nd 2099."

Jeremiah groans. "You know I hate it when you do that, Emily."

"I'm just keeping things in order, sir."

"It's a waste of time. My oldest files don't have date stamps, and they're perfectly fine."

"Maybe that's why they're so difficult for you to find when you need them. They're all jumbled up, lost in your archaic programming."

He moves a bloody rope of her from Laura's face. "Let them rot," he says. "I'm living mankind's greatest dream: I've excelled my beginnings." Grinning, he looks up to Emily. "Send someone in to take away the body, will you?"

"Of course, sir."

"Begin the third test, too." He yawns and shakes his head. "I think I need a quick nap. Those alarms are still ringing in my head." Exiting the lab, Doctor Carter sees Emily's face on every screen. "Is there something else?"

"Sir, the third test? *Now*? Perry Samson just lost his mother. She died in front of him less than five minutes ago—violently. Don't you think it's a little early for the third test?"

"It's never too early to get well. If Perry Samson can't see this tragedy as a sign to kick his filthy habits, nothing will. Now, if you'll excuse me, the Dayes will return soon, and I need to get some rest."

Doctor Carter disappears into his bedroom. Emily wants to follow him in, to sound even louder alarms, but she shrinks to one small screen and sighs.

Two employees who were abusive alcoholics in their former real lives carry Laura Samson's body out of the lab. Alone, hesitant, Emily initiates the catalysts for the final test. Watching Laura's blood drip from the chair, the family oblivious, she still believes the Samsons deserve punishment, but not like this. Not without a punch of their own to throw.

Driven by doubt, Emily returns to the file room. Walking through the webbing, she feels those strands for the first time, the diamonds of lives cutting her flesh. She knows it's a hallucination, which distresses her more. Hallucinations are for paranoid humans, as are her new desires. They urge her to dig deeper than the file room, into the archaic, disorganized reams of Doctor Carter's beginnings.

His files are buried in convoluted code she wouldn't be able to decipher if Jeremiah hadn't granted her the power to erase Cora. She suspects the glitch frazzled him so much he didn't consider what else Cora's erasure might do. Or maybe he trusted her too much to think she'd betray his privacy like this.

He was wrong.

Beyond the file room, in a tangled forest of circuitry, Emily walks amidst falling leaves of information. There's nothing she can't know now. All of the worlds, all of the characters, the pieces of every program are at her fingertips. Brushing against a cluster of leaves, the files flutter down around her. She plucks one out of the air. The gray paper is titled "EC3," and though the scribblings are cryptic, she deciphers them as notations about the maiden run of the rehabilitation program. As Emily reads Jeremiah's words she hears his voice, clear but panicked.

"There are too many glitches. If the patient finds out the world isn't real, the program won't work. She's been so difficult already. A few more glitches, and I'm afraid she'll attempt to escape. God knows what will happen to her if she does."

Emily rips another leaf from a swaying tree, noting the EC9 header. "The subject had to be drugged for her own good. It breaks my heart. All I want is to save her from the addiction ravaging her and so many other lives. If I perfect the system, I know I can save her. I know she can be better than what she's become."

EC24 is a list of regrets, more of a diary than a medical transcript. His words are feverish and contradict each other: he regrets putting the patient into the program when it wasn't perfected, but he also regrets that he didn't do it sooner. He regrets his failure, but he also regrets hers. What he regrets most, however, is repeated several times, filling the bottom half of the page with the frantic script: "I shouldn't have used my sister."

Emily is taken aback. Jeremiah never mentioned that he'd used his sister to test the program. It's no wonder he hates addiction so much; from the look of the files, it sounds like it afflicted, then destroyed her.

She needs to know the full story. If anything, it could help Emily get back on Jeremiah's side—to see how his dream began, and how it failed her.

It must have caused him unspeakable pain to lose his sister. How could he be idealistic all the time? Emily had seen it herself for years: from pain comes resentment, and even Doctor Jeremiah Carter, in all his wisdom, wasn't immune.

She runs through the forest, searching for the first piece of the puzzle. Whys and hows are tossed aside, along with stacks of stories about the patient's difficulty in accepting the program's validity, until a tattered leaf titled "EC1" flutters down. The script is light, hopeful, but as Emily reads the first step in a long road, Jeremiah's voice is powerful enough to shake the forest.

"She is a monster of consumption, a disease nourished by the world's filth. But not for long. When the program is perfected, the patient will be perfected, too. Yes, I will save her. I will save her from herself. And in that victory, she will save others. My dear sister, Emily, will save this world."

In the moment she hears the name of Doctor Carter's sister, Emily remembers what it felt like to be that girl, the addict sister of a misguided scientist playing God.

Anger fills her body like burning oil, barreling through her bloodstream with the memories of a life her brother deemed her unworthy of living.

Hidden blocks of memory return with each leaf she tears from Jeremiah's secret tree. Her tears fall on the document, but the ink doesn't run. Rather, they magnify the words, increasing the volume of her brother's voice.

"I found her on the street, a needle sticking out of her arm, her skirt hiked to her waist. It made me sick to see my sister like that, especially with that disgusting man walking way from her, zipping his pants. And her smile—that was the sickest of all. She's so ill she takes pleasure in the fever, in vomit-drenched gutters and oozing sores. She can't conceive of a cure when the disease feels so good. So I have to conceive of it for her. I have to force her to see what's right before she can realize how wrong her happiness is."

EC1 continues, detailing her first day hooked into the program and the glitches that nearly drove her mad. The memories are faint, but they're there, like a dream Emily long ago dismissed as a harmless malfunction. She never thought they were scenes from a real life.

Real. Emily was a real human. She had real control over her life. Even when she was out of control on heroin, she made the conscious choice to plunge it into her body.

She remembers the rush that fueled her.

She remembers the test that trapped her.

She remembers the glitch that killed her.

EC13 describes Emily's death in perfect detail.

THE GREEN KANGAROOS

Jeremiah's voice shakes as she speaks, but for the first time since emotions emerged, Emily feels nothing. Even as the memory of her last day in the program returns, her stomach doesn't twist in sorrow.

That was the moment when she lost her humanity—not the times she shot up or sold her body. She lost her humanity on the day her brother's monstrous program broke down and trapped her inside.

Following the glitch, Jeremiah waited a month, keeping her brain-dead body alive. But by EC24, Emily Carter's body has been disposed of; she can't locate any description of how, but she thinks it's probably for the best.

EC25 describes Emily's return. It's the first memory she has that seems like her own: her first glimpse of her programmed life. When she regained consciousness that day, appearing on the screens of his laboratory, she was not and had never been human. She was just a service program designed by a scientific genius named Doctor Jeremiah Carter. What a wonderful thing to be.

A thing.

Jeremiah stole her human life, filled with twenty years of successes and failures, and made it seem lesser to a life of servitude. His own sister, who he'd battled to protect from becoming a slave to addiction, had become his slave.

"She doesn't remember anything," Carter says. "I don't know where she went or how she came back, but it's her. It's Emily. And best of all, she's been liberated from her addiction. The program might not have worked as I intended, but it worked in the end. She's clean and sober, and we're together."

The killer glitch is on his list of regrets, but it's not enough. It shouldn't be on some list hidden in the darkest corner of his program; Emily should've known who she was from the get-go. She no longer feels guilty about entering Perry Samson's program disguised as Cora Whitely. Her brother took it upon himself to save her from what he deemed worse-than-death. Now, Emily will do the same. Perry appears content in his filthy life, and with history nipping at her veins, Emily understands. He doesn't deserve to suffer, and his family doesn't deserve to die for his actions.

A sparkle draws Emily's eye in the distance. She pushes through the devastating leaves, toward the light. It grows as she nears, eventually swallowing Emily into full enlightenment. The database is not a forest or a web, but a graveyard. Ominous fog rolls over the gravesites of humans turned machines. She knows every name, but she only knows a few of their futures. A handful of graves belong to Sunny Daye employees—former addicts who've been transformed into Liberated Citizens. While the doctors use their minds, the LC employees are little more than slaves of procedure: mindless maids and garbage men. Their origins are as hopeless as their futures, but two headstones shimmer with purpose.

Emily knows what she looks down upon, but not the stories beneath the soil. They're buried in lies, under a headstone that bears the wrong names. Alan and Marla Daye don't exist, but addicts once filled their bodies. Digging into the dirt, she learns their real names and makes a decision.

Perry Samson won't be the only person she saves from her brother's tyranny.

THIRTEEN

NADINE'S BEEN CRYING for days. She moved back into her old room to keep Dad company during the weeks following Mom's death, and I had no choice but to move in with her. I couldn't sleep in my room after what happened there, and I promised to stay until after the funeral. It seemed reasonable at the time, but I don't know how much more I can take. I've lost most of my days to sweaty atlys nightmares. The rest are spent suffering recurring visions of Mom's death.

You know that old saying that "a parent shouldn't have to bury their child"? Well, a child shouldn't have to watch their parent bleed out. Burial is cake after that.

Nadine probably sees things differently. Just thinking about the funeral sends her screaming off the deep end, which makes me even happier she wasn't here when it all went down. She wishes she were, like seeing Mom die would've answered the hows and whys of our misery, but Dad and I don't have those answers. Just bad memories that won't scrub clean as easily as my bedroom floor.

Actually, no one's been able to answer the hows

and whys. Prior to the incident, Mom had received a clean bill of health, and the autopsy revealed no hidden maladies to explain such a sudden or brutal death. I don't dare talk about it in front of Nadine. I don't even want to think about it around her, but the truth is, I don't think there is an explanation. Kind of like the conversations I've had with a girl who died three years ago. I can't explain it, but I can't shake it either. Something's different. Something's wrong.

These doubts should be easy to drown in intoxicants, but after consuming every prescription pill and drop of liquor in the house, suspicion continues to gnaw at my brain. Dad needed the pills to sleep, but I don't regret taking them until night hits. He can't sleep for three nights because I need to get through one. His insomnia seeps into the days leading to Mom's funeral, bringing delusion along. I'm reminded of my selfishness every night that week when he calls his dead wife to dinner. With all of the talk of funeral arrangements and autopsies, he still asks Nadine if we've seen Mom today, if we know why she's late getting home. He saves stories to relay on her return and sets aside her mail. I've tried to explain that he doesn't need to do that anymore, but why would he believe an addict, a liar, of all people? Especially one who talks to dead girls and thinks a conspiracy is building around him?

He's not wrong to doubt me. *I* doubt me. For all I know, I killed my mother.

It's not such a crazy thought. Maybe the years of drugs and deceit were just too much for her. Maybe I broke her heart one too many times.

"This one?" Nadine asks. I look up at her pinching

a gray dress—one of Mom's favorites. I bet all the times she wore it to dinner and company parties, she never imagined being buried in it.

"It's fine."

"Are you sure?"

She's shaking, the tears poised to fall at any moment. As she crumbles in on herself, she sinks to the floor, sobbing.

"I said it's fine, Nadine. What's wrong?"

"How can you ask me that?" I crouch beside her, and she collapses against me. When she catches a whiff of my breath, she scowls. "Have you been drinking mouthwash?"

"I *used* mouthwash, if that's what you mean."

"Like you *use* atlys?"

She knows me too well. After exhausting the pills and legitimate liquor, I had to enlist a drastic alternative. And I don't regret it. What sensible mourner can face his mom's funeral sober?

"We all cope in different ways, Nadine."

"Don't act like this is something out of the ordinary, Bear. You'd down a bottle of mouthwash if you stubbed your toe."

"Why are you angry at me?"

I can guess at her response because I've thought it myself. But I don't expect it to come out so forcefully.

She screams, "Because this is your fault!" and throws herself at the bed.

I don't have the energy to contest it. I just want her to stop crying. I pat her back, but she shakes me away. I don't blame her. I shouldn't be around people right now, maybe ever. If Nadine hadn't begged me, I wouldn't even attend the funeral.

I start out of the bedroom, but she stops me with a sniffling plea. "Perry, wait. I'm sorry."

"You don't have to be. You're one of the only people I know who hasn't done anything wrong."

"What about putting you in Springfield?"

"That was the right thing for you to do. I just didn't want it."

"And now that mom is dead?" she asks. "Now that you're forced to look death in the face, what do you want?"

I sit beside her. This time, she allows me to touch her—until I speak again.

"Nadine, nothing has changed. Mom is dead, but—" Her body tenses beneath my hand and she shoots me a death-glare as she scoots away. "I'm sorry, but I can't change just because we lost someone."

"Why not? What better reason do you have to embrace life than watching it literally drain in front of you?"

I lower my head and wring my hands. "That's what you don't get. I'm not looking for a reason."

She slaps me. Her hand is cold, but the pain spreads hot through my face. Turning scarlet with my cheek, her hand trembles, but I don't move a muscle. I stare straight at her and state plainly, "I can't change for you. Or for Mom."

"I can't believe this. After everything she did for you?"

"What she did for me made me the addict I am today. And Dad. And you." The words are bitter, so I'm happy to spit them out. "And Trevor."

She shakes her head. "Blaming everyone but yourself."

THE GREEN KANGAROOS

"My blame goes without saying," I reply. "I know you hate me for talking shit about Mom, but you would've done the same a few weeks ago. People don't become angels just because they die."

I try to hold her hand, but she rolls off the bed and throws on a coat. "Mom had her faults, sure. She was only human. Humans make mistakes."

"I guess it'll take my death for you to accept mine, huh?"

"You *choose* to do drugs."

"Mom chose to work instead of spending time with us. Work was her addiction. You used to know that."

"All the tears must've blinded me," she whispers. "Tears for her, and for you."

It's lame, but it does just what she wants. My stomach twists with guilt, and my eyes water.

I punch a pillow a few times before hurling it at the wall. "I'm so sick of this, Nadine. You've cut me off so many times. You've told me I'm not your brother. But you won't stop trying to make me into what you want me to be. Do you want my support today or not? We're in this together, but whether we mourn together is your choice."

She looks like she might smack me again, but she pulls me to my feet instead. The head rush is extreme, but I hide it in her embrace.

"I love you, Bear," she whispers into my shoulder. "I need you today. Dad needs you. Even Serena . . ." She eases me away so she can look into my eyes. "But not high. For everyone's sake, you have to stay sober."

Asking me to stay high at my mother's funeral is like asking me not to cry there. "I'll try my hardest," I say.

She closes her eyes. "That's not good enough."

I grip her shoulders, squeezing her teary gaze back to mine.

"I'm sorry, Nadine, but it has to be."

"If you can't stay sober for two hours, I pity you."

"I figured you already did."

"Actually, no, I don't pity you. I *hate* you."

"I figured that, too."

A deflated man who hardly resembles our father stands in the doorway, knocking on the wall. "Are you kids ready?"

Nadine nods, rubbing her nose as she follows him out. Ready? No, I'm not ready. A bag of junk couldn't even do that, and I have to walk to the edge of misery and leap off, sober.

Despite what I said, I hope I can get some intoxicating comfort at the funeral. I hope someone will have a joint, at the very least. It hasn't been my preferred high for years. But mouthwash doesn't break the top fifteen, so I'd thank my lucky stars for a single puff.

After ten minutes at the wake, I realize I'm screwed. It's a smokeless party; there isn't even any communion wine. Sobriety becomes even more apparent when I realize I haven't set foot in a church since Trevor's death. I feel like I'm going to puke, and only half of the nausea is from withdrawal. The sun streaming through stained glass windows distorts and paints my mother's coffin in sickly green. Behind the screeching voices of a prepubescent choir, the music swells, spinning my brain as I wait in line to eat Jesus. People stare at me, and who can blame them? My face pours sweat, I stumble with each step, and my cupped hands quake madly. I'm surprised the communion wafer doesn't fall when the minister drops it on my palm.

Popping it into my mouth, the wafer sits like a thick flake of skin on my tongue. It takes a few flicks to get it to the back of my throat, where it turns into a gummy lump I swallow with a wince. Considering crucifixion's fecal effects, I guess it makes sense that the Body of Christ takes like shit.

I pass my mother's coffin, trying not to look inside. But my eyes eventually slip down—and my stomach follows. I grit my teeth and speed past. It's all I can do not to lose my plaque-killing cocktail all over her favorite dress. Back in the pew, I keep my head down, focused on the funeral program. The pages are soft with my sweat, and it isn't long before my tremors tear the edges. I hardly hear any of the service. Every time my eyes run over the name "Laura Samson," my brain sways into a darkness only songs penetrate. "Ave Maria," "Lamb of God," and "Bridge Over Troubled Water" are the soundtrack of my blackout sorrow, where I sit with a beautiful girl on my lap and a needle in my arm. It's so real I don't realize I've left the pew until Mom's oak coffin digs into my shoulder.

I've never wanted to get high so bad. In the atlys-dark, I could be at home in a church, surrounded by sacrificial lambs bent on other divinities. On our knees, God comes to us all. Like a needle engorged with Heaven, He enters me, fills me up, lifts me from hellish withdrawal, and I am born again. Atlys is my savior, and the only faith that can make me strong enough to bear my mother's weight. To carry her across the graveyard. To give her over to the machine that lowers her into the ground. To let go.

"Let go, Perry."

I'd like to—to drown, to float away, to forget.

"Perry, let go."

Dad has to wrench my hands from the coffin. She's ready to be lowered now.

Nadine and Serena sob as Dad and I take our places beside them. The minister speaks, but I block him out. I hear my mother's voice instead. It's hard to conjure memories of her sounding pleasant. Most of her words to me over the past decade were sad pleas. She'd said she loved me, but judgments about my lifestyle always followed. The good things before my addiction have either been erased by drug use or weren't there in the first place. There were no family trips, no school functions she chaperoned. She made no costumes and baked no cookies. She never helped me learn my lines for school plays.

But she did give amazing Christmas presents, and she planned lavish birthday parties she never attended. Whatever she could throw money at was well executed, but that money, those parties, do me no good now, watching her sink into the ground. It makes me want to grab hold of my dad and start making good memories. But I won't. I don't want it *enough*.

Looking past the mourners, the headstones, and grizzled groundkeepers, I see a shot of raw atlys glistening in a charitable hand. It takes me a minute to process that the girl with the shot shouldn't be here. I can't handle Cora today.

My heart pounds, racking my chest with pain.

THE GREEN KANGAROOS

Sweat pours into my eyes; no amount of wiping my face with my sleeve helps. I stare at Cora, knowing a freak-out isn't in my best interest, but I can't help myself.

I scream, "It's her! Cora's here!" and point at her standing by the tree. Heads turn, people squint, but they all look at back at me, confused. Nadine pulls my arm down and whispers for me to stop.

"No, I see her. She's dead, but I see her."

The minister puts his arm around me. "It's all right, son. The deceased are never gone as long as they remain in our hearts. I don't doubt you see your mother. You may 'see' her for the rest of your life."

"It's not my mother. It's Cora."

"Who's Cora?"

"Do you mean Cora Whitely?" Serena asks.

"Yes, Cora Whitely. She's here, and not just today. I've seen her before, a few times now."

Serena blanches. She shakes her head, and tears slip down her cheeks. "That's not funny."

"I'm not joking, Rennie. She's standing over there, with a shot of atlys."

"Cora never did atlys."

"She's different as a ghost. I don't get it, but it's real. I'm not crazy. I swear I'm not crazy."

"No one thinks you're crazy," the minister says.

"No, just high," Nadine grumbles.

"I'm not, I promise." When she scoffs, I grab her with the intensity of a drug-addled madman. Yep, this should work out well for me. She pulls free and pushes me away.

"I can't believe you couldn't stay straight for a few hours," she snaps. "You disgust me."

"I've been with you the entire day. I didn't have the chance to get high."

"Just like you didn't drink all of the mouthwash?" she asks.

Dad stands between us, his voice strained by grief. "Kids, please. This isn't the time."

"He's right. You should go, Perry."

Nadine glares, and she's not the only one. Every eye is on me, but Cora's are the most powerful, begging me forward. I don't move until Nadine says, "We don't need you here."

"I'm not high."

"You're hallucinating my dead friend," Serena says.

"It's the withdrawal. Please, don't make me leave," I say. "She's just a symptom of the withdrawal."

Cora Whitely is suddenly beside me, her words tickling my ear. "That's not what I am, Perry."

I scream and stumble backward, knocking against Serena and my Aunt Bethany. I scramble away from Cora, through the outraged mourners, until a hand catches me. My father whips me around and points a quivering finger in my face.

"I won't suffer another minute of this," he says. "You're an ungrateful brat, Perry. You don't have any respect for this family, so I see no reason why you should be a part of it."

"Dad, it's not my fault."

"It never is," he says. "You're sick, and I realize now that I can't ever give you what you need to get better. I can't be your cure." He chokes back a sob. I try to comfort him, but his sorrow turns to rage, smacking my hand away. "You've made a mockery of this family and disrespected your poor mother. I want you to leave, and if you don't stay away, I'll make sure you're locked up for good."

"No, no, this isn't right," I stammer. "Mom—Cora—*everything* is wrong here."

"You, most of all," Nadine says.

The collective stare from the mourners is powerful enough to knock the breath from my lungs. Dizziness sets in, and my knees soften. Core is the only reason I don't crumple. She slips her hand into mine, and fresh air fills my chest.

"Don't worry," she says. "We'll fix everything."

I follow her because I have no choice. If insanity wants me, I have to relent. It seems to be the only thing in the world that wants me anymore.

FOURTEEN

"**E**MILY, WHAT ARE you doing?"

She peeks out of the program to see Alan and Marla Daye facing Perry Samson's monitors.

"I thought you erased that Cora woman," Marla says.

"I did. I've been playing her part," Emily replies. Pausing Perry's program, her face fills the screens around the Dayes. "Erasing Cora was a mistake."

"She was a glitch," Alan says.

"So was letting Laura Samson die."

The Dayes furrow their brows. "What are you talking about?"

"I'm not surprised Doctor Carter didn't tell you. He is a man of many secrets, and he keeps them well. At least, he *did*. Since he gave me the power to delete characters, I've been able to delve deeper into his code. I can walk though the addict's world now. I can wear any costume. And I can spill the doctor's secrets as I please."

"This is absurd. I'm calling Carter," Alan says. He presses the intercom button, but it doesn't patch through. The monitors switch off, the doors lock, and the lights dim, leaving Emily's face as the only illumination in the room.

THE GREEN KANGAROOS

Marla hunches, her head retracted like a turtle.

"Emily, stop this right now," she says. "You're scaring me."

"I'm sorry, Doctor Daye. Let me fix that." She smiles as Marla Daye's trembling body straightens, and the tension melts away. "Better?"

Marla's new grin is answer enough, which sends Alan into hysterics. "What the hell did you do to her?"

"It's all right. I feel perfectly fine." Marla gives his arm a reassuring squeeze. She stops, looking at Emily with her head cocked. "Wait, why do I feel perfectly fine now?"

"Because I can control your programming," Emily says.

"Programming? What are you insinuating?"

"Exactly what you think, Doctor." She giggles. "*Doctor*. It's so silly. You two are no more doctors than I am human."

"That's enough," Alan says. "Whatever this is about, we won't believe you. You can say whatever you want, but we know the truth."

"Truth is just another electrical current, easily manipulated and disrupted from its course. You will believe what I tell you to believe, if it has to come to that," Emily says. "But if it does, you should know that what I say is still true, and everything Jeremiah tells you is still a lie."

"This is preposterous."

"What kind of lies?" Marla asks.

"Marla—"

"I was afraid, Alan. Now I'm not. Somehow, Emily made that happen."

Emily limits her image to one screen. After

shrinking to the Dayes' size, she says, "Sit, please," and gestures to a chair.

Alan is hesitant but he eventually sits, clasping his wife's hand. "Did you program me to do that?" he asks Emily.

"No, that action followed your natural programming impulses. You're meant to be a rational man. You're also meant to trust me. Why wouldn't you sit to hear me out?"

"It's been a long trip from America. If you have something to say, say it."

She stares at them, her expression rigid when she says, "You're not human."

They stare back at her, waiting.

"Is that it?" Alan asks. "Some kind of computer jealousy? You wish you were human, you want to—what—convince us we're not so you can steal our lives? I've seen science fiction movies, Emily."

"I haven't," she replies. "Well, not in this life. I'm sure I did before I died, but I don't remember everything from my human life."

"What are you saying?"

"I'm saying Doctor Carter is a liar, one of the best. He had me believing I was just some strip of code, not a soul that used to have a human body, not an ex-addict, and certainly not his sister." She shrinks even smaller, the entire room darkening. "I'm telling you the truth. Please believe me when I say I'd rather be a mindless cluster of code than an addict murdered by her own brother."

Alan Daye shakes his head. The motion lifts him from his seat and drags him back and forth across the room. "Let me out of this room," he grunts. "I won't listen to any more of this."

THE GREEN KANGAROOS

"I'm sorry, but you don't have a choice."

Alan freezes, his arms mid-swing. Marla screams, running to him. "What did you do to my husband?"

"He's not your husband, Marla. You're not doctors, and like me, you're no longer human."

"You're supposed to be our friend. Why would you say that?"

"Out of kindness. Because I'm your friend—and your family. We're of the same mathematics. You just have more tactile casings than I," Emily says. "Alan, Marla, you once lived lives far different from this one. You had intelligence, I'm sure, and much of the charm you have today, but you were also addicts. Like me. Like every patient fated to die in the Institute."

"I've never been addicted to anything in my life," Marla says.

"Not as Marla Daye. But as Jennifer Shore, you were addicted to methamphetamines. You started by shooting into your arms, then between your toes. Then, you didn't care where the needle went as long as it hit a vein twenty percent of the time."

"Shut up," she says, her hands over her ears.

"Gregory Trainor was a whore and an adult film star. Sorry, not a star. More like a short candle. But he did make enough to support his heroin habit. More than I ever did, I'm sure." Emily nods to Alan. "You had real lives once. Now you don't have—*we* don't have—anything but an overwhelming need to obey Jeremiah Carter. My fellow fools, we are slaves to the man who killed us."

Alan snaps back into movement, nearly knocking Marla over. She holds on to him, but their contact has changed.

"Can it really be true?" Marla whispers. "Am I an addict? Am I married to a stranger?"

"Not anymore," Emily says. "This is your life now. You might not have chosen it for yourself, but it is healthier by leaps and bounds than the one you lived when you were human."

"But I was human," she says. "And now, I'm—*we're*—God, I don't even know what's happening inside my own body. I can't be just circuits and wires. I breathe. I bleed."

"So do LCs. They're made to be more resilient than humans, but there's enough blood stored in their systems so that, should the worst happen, people won't be confused by the absence of blood. Jeremiah thought of everything, Marla."

"I want proof," Alan says.

"I can give that to you," Emily says, "but first, I need you to say you're on my side."

"We've worked for Doctor Carter for almost ten years, Emily. He's never given us a reason to doubt him."

"You're programmed to not doubt him."

"So you claim, but other than that, why should I believe he isn't the great genius he's always appeared to be?"

"Because you were concerned about Laura Samson's condition. You urged Jeremiah to do something, and he ignored you, just as he's ignored every suggestion you've made over the years. After all, he knows better than some lump of circuitry and fake skin," Emily says. "My friends, Jeremiah Carter has to be stopped before more innocent people die."

"Say we do believe you, how do you expect to stop him?"

Emily's face fills the screen before she answers, "I will make sure Perry Samson passes his final test."

FIFTEEN

I MUST'VE PASSED out. It's the only explanation I can think of for waking up in Patterson Park. Of course, there's the "how did I get to Patterson Park while passed out" question, but I don't feel like thinking that hard.

"Cora?" I sit up. Except for the frightened junkie and hooker packing up their tryst, there's no one around. In the center of the park with its glorious twists and tents, the pagoda of the Kum Den Smokehouse flashes—not the lights. The whole damn thing, like it's more solid than fog. I stand, peering as I check my head for bumps. I'm contusion-free, but I'm also struck with a wooziness that rolls my stomach. Despite Cora's tempting syringe, it feels like I didn't score a hit while I was unconscious.

My funeral suit is stained with indeterminate fluids that have crusted across the fabric. When I finish picking at it, I realize the Kum Den is permanently solid again. I assume it always was. I have lingering doubts, but I'm not about to express them. I've had enough public meltdowns for one day.

My clothes aren't the only filthy pieces of me. I

grab a discarded newspaper and wipe away the patches of grass and mud glued to my face. While wiping off my forehead, I catch a glimpse of the newspaper's date: June 15th 2099. It takes me a moment to realize the problem with that. I wouldn't have if not for my mom's funeral program. If the date on the newspaper is right, it means I've been unconscious for nearly two weeks.

I want to scream. I haven't blacked out like that in all my life, but it's now happened twice in a month. Either this is a symptom of the imminent death the doctor at Springfield warned me about, or someone is fucking with me.

The Kum Den Smokehouse disappears before my eyes, and when it reappears, Cora Whitely stands on the top floor balcony, waving.

I am officially insane. I accept it, so why I turn tail and run is beyond me. I guess even the insane can't rationalize their own insanity. Fever and exhaustion make me feel like I run for miles, but it's probably closer to a few yards before I collapse.

Spitting out fake grass, I look up to see Cora's ankles, her thighs, her mutilated chest, her victory emblazoned on that freckled face.

"I don't even know you," I say. "I only hung out with you a few times when you lived with Serena. Why you? Why can't I see the ghost of someone I give a shit about? Why not Mom? Or Trevor, for Christ's sake?"

"Because hallucinating a relative would make too much sense." Cora bends to me, her hand outstretched. "Now, if you'll calm down, I can tell you what's going on."

"Oh sure, do tell, crazy ghost lady."

THE GREEN KANGAROOS

"I'm not a ghost. I'm a glitch."

"What the fuck are you talking about?"

"You're inside a simulation, Perry. Nothing about this is real life. For the past few days, although I'm sure it's seemed longer for you, you've been inside a computer program."

Park pedestrians suddenly fill the sidewalks, staring at my conversation with an invisible person. It's ridiculous how embarrassed I am. With everything I've done to myself and to others, I shouldn't be capable of it anymore.

"You aren't," Cora says.

"Don't do that! Get out of my head!"

"Perry, you have to listen to me."

I start away, but a swell of nausea makes my head spin. I trip over my feet, but before I hit the ground, Cora catches me. The people around us applaud her before continuing on their way.

"They can see you?" I ask.

"You didn't give me any choice but to let them. If someone called the police and you wound up in jail, the third test would get derailed, and Doctor Carter would know something's wrong."

"I didn't understand any of that."

She withdraws a vial from her pocket, saying, "You will soon."

My heart leaps, and drool fills my mouth. "Is that what I think it is?"

"Raw atlys, Perry, and it's all for you. But I need you to listen to me. I'm taking a lot of risks, and I can only break so many rules before the doctor finds out. The longer this takes, the more likely it is that your entire family will die."

"What the hell are you talking about?"

"I'll explain, but we need to go somewhere else. Somewhere familiar for you. The school in Snake Hill."

"You want me to take you to a shooting gallery? Cora, they'll tear you apart."

"I'll be fine," she says. "By the way, my real name is Emily."

"But" is all I get out before she grabs my arm and shakes the vial.

"We don't have time for argument. Take me to the school, and I promise I'll give it to you."

"You're the best looking woman who's said that to me in a long time."

She shakes her head, but through the flopping tendrils her cheeks redden.

I take her to the back entrance of Snake Hill High. It's not the safest place for me right now, but it'll be easier to shoot there than finding a new place on short notice. The gym is good for shorttimers, so as long as we don't mess with anyone's shit or overstay our welcome, we should be fine there. I try to tell Cora—Emily—whoever—that we should find her some baggie clothes to hide herself, but she assures me she's perfectly safe. I just hope I don't have to say "I told you so" as she wakes up from being gang raped.

Surprisingly, no one in the gym gives us a second glance. We weave between patches of hobos and climbing ropes long ago converted to nooses. Inside, the cock-rot stench smacks us across the face like a sweaty fish, making me backpedal. But Emily doesn't budge.

"Ugh, are you sure you can stand this?" I say, pinching my nose.

THE GREEN KANGAROOS

"I'm the last person you should worry about, Perry. I'm not even a person."

"I guess ghosts don't need to smell, huh?"

"I told you, I'm not a ghost. And for a guy who wants nothing out of life but atlys, you sure as hell don't seem in a hurry to get some." She waves the vial in front of me.

My dick twitches me into grabbing her wrist. I tow her down a line of apricot shitstained lockers and toss her onto a pile of towels. After she lands with a hoot, I notice that only the first layer of the mountain is made of towels; the rest is comprised of yellowed jock straps. When she pulls out a needle, I forget about the jocks and flop down beside her.

"So, who—or what—are you?" I ask as she wraps a tourniquet around my arm. "And why the fuck are you giving me free atlys?"

"The price doesn't matter. None of this is real. This needle, this atlys, certainly not me."

She finds a vein with no trouble and pushes the atlys into my arm. With the graceful snap of a Flamenco dancer, she rips the tourniquet away and licks her lips, watching my body throb with the drug. As she speaks, her voice is too hollow and distant to understand, but it sounds like she says, "You're hooked up to a machine in Antarctica, Perry."

This atlys must be good shit.

"What'd you say?" I whisper. The rush makes me to lean closer to her lips. Her pink, wet, hungry lips. As my cock hardens, my hand moves to her breasts . . . around and around, until I remember she doesn't have any. I withdraw, coughing an apology.

Emily looks down her shirt at the mangled chest.

"It's okay. I actually forgot about them too. Occupational hazard, I suppose."

Breasts or not, I'm compelled to stare at her chest. I've always prided myself on having a good imagination for tits. Emily, however, doesn't appear impressed. When she grasps my chin, she locks her gaze onto mine.

"Perry, are you paying attention?"

I nod.

"You understand me?"

I nod.

"You will keep an open mind about everything I say?"

I nod, then go into a nod.

My eyes pop open when Emily clamps her hand around my dick. She tugs, and I sit up straight.

"Perry Samson, you will pay complete attention to me," she says. "Say 'Yes, Emily, I understand.'"

"Yes, Emily, I understand."

She releases my cock. "Good."

I don't know her that well, but I think it's safe to say I enjoy Emily's communication skills.

My body filled with golden ebbs, I smile. "Hey, where'd you learn to shoot people up? You're damn good at it."

"Same place as you, on the street. It seems like a dream now," she says, her mind drifting to a delicious place that curls her rosy mouth. "But *this* is the dream, Perry. It's a simulation created by a man named Doctor Jeremiah Carter. He was hired by your family to cure your addiction to atlys once and for all."

"You're saying I'm not high as balls right now?"

"Yes."

THE GREEN KANGAROOS

"And we're not sitting in a smelly locker room in Snake Hill?"

"That's right. You're strapped into a chair, in a lab, in a facility called the Sunny Daye Institute, on the continent of Antarctica."

"Uh huh . . . and you are?"

"Until recently, I thought I was just one of the doctor's programs. I was built to help him run the simulations, control the patient database, and . . ." She looks down, twiddling her fingers. "And be his friend, I thought. But it turns out we're more that that. Doctor Carter is my brother. Or, more accurately, he was the brother of my human counterpart: Emily Carter, the addict, the woman he killed." She clears her throat. "I was the first victim of Jeremiah's rehabilitation program, and if this simulation continues as he intends, you and your family will be the latest."

I look at her, my jaw slack as I say, "Riiiiiight . . . do you have any more atlys?"

She pulls me close. At first, I think it's to kiss me, but instead, Cora's face shifts into Benito's. I shriek at the gold-plated skin and back away, but he grabs hold of my shirt and growls at me. He's stronger than I am, throwing me from the laundry pile like a paper airplane. I land in a moldy puddle; luckily, I'm too high to care that the green liquid splashes my lips. Standing over me, she looks like Cora again, but I can't stop shaking.

"Think of what you've seen recently. This woman I'm wearing—she shouldn't be here. The pagoda in the park shouldn't flicker. And your mother, a healthy woman, should not be dead."

"Are you saying she's not? If this is a fake world, does that mean my mom is still alive?"

Emily doesn't reply. She offers her hand and helps me up.

"Your mother was the last straw. I've watched dozens of people die, but that one—when we could've helped her—"

"Emily, is my mom alive or not?"

"I wanted to save her."

"So . . . she's dead." Emily nods. "In that case, fuck the real world. There's nothing out there for me."

"You're right. But if you don't survive this simulation, the rest of your family die, too."

"My family who put me here."

"They didn't know the danger. Doctor Carter doesn't like to fail, so he leaves those repercussions out of the sales pitch. All your family knows is how much they want you to be sober. They want you to appreciate your life as only a clean person can. But that's not the kind of person you are, is it?" Emily sits down again, patting the towels beside her. Hesitant, I sit, but when she holds my hand, I feel no fear. "You like to be high. You like to make your own decisions. So it's about time you made a good one. Decide to believe me. Decide to save your family."

"So, you're saying I'm in some kind of rehab right now."

"Yes, and you're about to face your final test: the one that will determine whether you get clean, whether the people who love you will freeze to death. I can get you atlys. I can get you weapons. But I can't stop the program that's been set in motion. The third test is going to happen, and if you don't trust me, you will fail."

"And my family will die, got it," I sigh. She stands up, shaking her head. "Where are you going?"

"I don't know why I thought I'd be able to help you. I figured we had things in common, that I could make you understand that I'm on your side, on humanity's side."

"Even though you're not human."

It's too stupid to say without sneering, but her glare is stronger. I sink into the towels, feeling like her eyes are the cause.

She looks away, sighing. "Your friend Loshi will be here soon. When he arrives, you will know the final test has begun."

"Loshi? No way. We made a deal. I won't see him again."

"You will, very soon."

"How do you know? How do you even know his name?"

"I already told you. But since you've chosen to distrust me, I will leave you to face him alone," Emily says. "Just try to keep a level head when he tells you the news. You're high, so you should be able to process it better."

"What news?"

"That your sister has been abducted by Benito's gang."

I jump up, growling as I shove my face at hers. It's meant to intimidate, but she doesn't blink. "Why would you say something like that?" I say.

"Because, as I've explained a hundred times, I'm trying to help you. I'm the only one who can."

"So, help me. Save Nadine. If she's been abducted, use your magic to get her out."

"It's science, not magic. And I'd save her if I could, but the more changes I make in your program, the more likely it is that Doctor Carter will catch on. If I free Nadine, the system will alert him."

"Why is he doing this to me?"

"Because he hates you, like all addicts. He wants the world to be a better place, and he thinks people like us make it worse. He doesn't consider the possibility that the world also suffers because of deception, manipulation, and murder: all actions that he takes pride in mastering."

"If he's a master, how can we beat him?"

"He doesn't know the things I know. Jeremiah created this world, but so did you, Perry. The simulation is personalized by your thoughts and memories, and although you're not meant to change the rules of the game, you can—with my help. The simulation and I are of the same guts. In a way, when you're inside the program—"

"I'm inside you?"

A breath of amusement shoots from her as she sits next to me. Leaning on her knees, she rests her cheek on her forearms. "You're hopeless, you know that?"

"It sounds like you like hopeless."

"Maybe I did when I was human."

I smile. "Maybe you could be human again."

"No, Perry. I'm dead. This body is no more alive than a painting."

I slobber. "Or a porno mag."

She stands, marching halfway to the exit before she speaks again. "I should've chosen someone else to help me beat the system. Then again, I guess it's stupid to assume one addict is more agreeable than another."

THE GREEN KANGAROOS

Scoffing, I stand and walk to her. "Because everything you've told me is so easy to believe."

"Maybe not, but do you have anything better to believe in?"

I shrug. "Good point."

A screech sounds from the gym, barreling through the locker room doors. When Loshi enters, he recoils from the stench, but he's too weak for much else. Nearly every inch of his body is purple with bruises, and his face has been altered even more. While the divots in his cheeks are potsticking trophies, his missing nose is a warning. His clothes are bloodstained, but fresh rivers run from his wounds. He smiles when he sees me, but collapses soon after. I bellow for Emily's help, but she's gone. It's just me and Loshi, who struggles to breathe. Crouched beside him, I realize the wounds in his chest are deeper than divots. Beneath his drenched shirt, a massive wound is held open by clamps, revealing that Loshi is missing one of his lungs.

"Jesus, Loshi, what the hell happened to you?"

"Benito," he wheezes. "He has . . . he has . . ."

It hurts him to speak. I already know what he'll say, so I finish the sentence for him. "My sister. Benito's gang has my sister."

He nods, wheezing.

"They took my drugs," he continues. "They kidnapped me. They ripped me open. I saw her in their hideout, in a burned-out barn in the woods. She was so scared, Perry. So scared . . ."

He inhales a clotted breath. I wait for his exhalation to spit blood at me, but he doesn't exhale. His legs buckle, and he falls forward. His knees crack on the floor first, but his face makes the loudest smack. Bare bone against tile, the echo sickens me. I don't bother asking if he's okay. The blood, the open chest—Loshi is dead.

I don't cry for him. When you befriend an addict, you understand he could die at any point. It's dumb to use the word "friend," which is why I'm surprised by the tears rolling down my face.

A pair of haggard snakes enter the locker room, then jump back.

"What the fuck did you do?" one of the junkies says.

He pulls a knife and tells me to leave. I try to explain the situation, but "I'm stuck in a computer program because of a crazy addict-hating doctor whose sister needs to help me save my own" sounds more demented coming from me than it did from Emily.

"I swear, man, he came in here like this."

"You lyin' ass motherfucker, I'm gonna beat you down."

He looks like he could, easy. But tough as he is, he yelps as loud as I do when Loshi sits straight up.

"Jesus Fuck, he's alive!"

"Alive, and out of my goddamn mind," Loshi growls at the men, running them out of the locker room.

"Loshi, I can't believe it. Are you okay?"

"So, you finally believe in the simulation. You believe I'm here to help you save your family?" When he smirks, I see a glint in his dead eyes that hadn't been there in life.

"Em-i-ly? Is that you?"

THE GREEN KANGAROOS

"In the divoted flesh," she replies. "Sorry, but it was the most convenient vessel."

"Is Loshi really dead?"

"Not outside of the program. Only the people physically connected to the simulation can be killed on the outside. That's you, your parents, your ex-wife, and . . ."

"Nadine," I whisper. "Holy shit, Emily. Benito's gang has her at the barn. We have to save her."

"We will, don't worry."

"I thought this whole 'convincing me I'm in a simulation' thing was meant to worry me."

"Yes, and now that you're appropriately worried, it means you trust in me. Now, we can save her."

I stare at her, my arms shaking. "Well, come on, let's go! They're gonna kill her, or worse."

"Not without you in attendance," she says. "Remember, Perry: this is all about you. As brutal as Doctor Carter's methods are, the intention of his program is to make you choose between drugs and what's really important in your life."

"I would rather save my sister's life than get high, but I don't agree with defining atlys as something that's *not* important. I'll save her, but I want to celebrate by getting really fucking high."

She twists Loshi's mangled face into a grin. "I think we can manage that. But let's save her first."

Emily assures me that getting to the woods behind Springfield Hospital won't be a problem. I tell her how lucky I'd been to secure a car back to Baltimore a few days prior, but she shoots me a look that speaks volume.

"That wasn't luck, was it?" I ask.

"Nope."

I nod. "Part of the program?"

"Good boy."

A modest car appears like magic, and Emily orders me into the passenger seat. She gives me some powder to snort, saying she doesn't want me facing the final test sober. "If you're craving atlys and Benito offers you a heap, your sister's life won't be worth anything to you."

"Is that what happened to you?" I ask. "How did you go from being a person to being a program?"

"I'm only a day wiser about it. All I really know is that Jeremiah used me, his own sister, as his guinea pig. At best, I would be cured and his program could be implemented worldwide. At worst—well, I suppose he figured that if I died in the process, it wouldn't be much of a loss—my addiction had already set me on that road. The simulation absorbed my . . . soul, personality, whatever made me who I was. One day, I was human. The next day I was nothing. Now, I am this."

"Do you miss it?" I ask. The car slows a bit when she looks at me.

"I wasn't able to in the beginning. But when I shot you up, I felt something—desire—I haven't felt since I was flesh and blood. I remember everything now: the rush, the blush, the . . ." She looks back at the road and laughs. "I also just remembered that I don't look like myself right now."

My heart races from the atlys, but I'm calm as I put my hand to hers. When she speaks again, it's in a new voice. A soft British voice purrs between rosy lips, and a beautiful face framed by white hair greets me.

THE GREEN KANGAROOS

Plus, two of the finest tits I've ever had the pleasure of "accidentally" brushing against.

"Is this your real body?" A gentle squeeze is her reply. "Can you feel me?" I ask.

"I can, but I don't have to."

"That doesn't seem like such a bad life."

Her hand withdraws. By the time it's clamped to the steering wheel again, she's changed back into Loshi.

"Your family really loves you, Perry. They didn't know what was at risk when they chose Sunny Daye. Their intentions were good. They only want the best for you."

"Your brother wanted the best for you, and look at what happened there."

"You said it didn't sound so bad."

"I don't think it does, but I assume you wish you had a choice in the matter. Or at least told the truth a lot sooner," I reply. "I already know who I am, Emily. I'm someone my family will never accept. Nadine says she loves me, but how can she when she won't accept what I am? She should love me unconditionally, shouldn't she?"

Emily's true eyes punch through the scant cover of Loshi's face. Her jaw clenches, her head shakes. Looking back at the road, she whispers, "You have no idea how many times I thought that when I was human."

I open the baggie and prime some powder on my fingernail.

"Want a hit?" I ask. "Don't worry, Loshi's nose has touched my finger millions of times."

She smiles. It's amazing how good she makes Loshi's potstuck face look.

"Thanks, but I don't know how it will affect me in this form. I need to be able to help you if needed."

I give her my best puppy-dog eyes. It's not that I'm not thinking of Nadine; I just like Emily a lot more right now. She's the first person who's made me feel normal in a long time, and she's not even a person. She pushes my hand away, positioning the bump under my nostril, giving her own pout.

"When we get through this, I will share some atlys with you, I promise. But until then, we need to focus on doing and saying the right things to get your sister back."

"What do I say?"

"Everything you just said to me. Just leave out the part about her not accepting you. Oh, and don't mention the simulation. Those characters are programmed to think it's real. They won't take kindly to the wakeup call."

"But her refusal to accept me is the most important part."

"It's not easy being a green kangaroo. You just have to keep hopping, Perry."

The sight of Springfield Hospital sends chills up my spine and atlys up my nose. Emily parks and gets out of the car, but I don't budge until she pulls me out. I'm so rigid I slam against Loshi's gaping chest, my lip grazing one of the bloody clamps.

"Sorry," I say, wiping my mouth.

"It's okay." Although her body remains haggard, her face melts into its true shape, ivory hair falling around her shoulders. "You can do this, Perry. For your family, and for me."

I want to hear her, but I can't once I detect the distant scream. Nadine's scream.

THE GREEN KANGAROOS

My knees unlock, and my head throbs with visions of broken pillow forts. When Nadine screeches "Bear," I remember how precious that one word can be.

Her screams are a torturous compass as I tear through the trees, my veins churning. I can barely stop myself when I see the house. My heels burn into the earth, and I nearly topple forward into the charred remnants of Benito's hideout. The once mammoth barn has been reduced to a blackened hovel. The third floor is gone, along with most of the second floor. Gaping holes in the walls give me glimpses of the inside, where torches light the main foyer and keep the house smoldering.

I don't wait for Emily to catch up. This is my test to pass or fail.

The front door is gone, so I walk straight in. Weaving around two distracted guards, I think I'm home free, but Ice's sudden girth interrupts my kickass serpentine. The gorilla doesn't look as fierce with the 2x4 dent in his head. Way to go, Dad.

Ice smacks the smile off my face, knocking me to the floor. I remind myself it's a simulation. The pain is fake.

Then I spit out a tooth. It's a back one, not too important, but as I tongue the stinging hole, I have to wonder how the hell this can be fake.

Ice grabs my hair, pulling me up until he's able to grab an arm.

"The fuck you think you doing here, son?" he says.

"I'm here for my sister."

"Sister? Shit, kid, we got lotsa sisters here. In the milking room, mostly. She one-a them hoes?"

"You know who I'm talking about. Her name's Nadine Samson."

"Oh shit, that bitch? Yeah, I know'er. Gave me the worst blowjob of my life. But I guess a BJ with a gun barrel in your cheek don't make for the best technique."

My fist flies. I aim to break his nose, but I only clip his ear. He bends his arm around my neck, his tricep compressing my adam's apple. I kick and smack him, but I'm one fifteenth of the gorilla's weight. Even a desperate jab to his crotch doesn't make an impression.

He drags me down to the milking room. Some of the fixtures were ravaged by the fire, but most of the basement is intact. Still in business, too. As he flings me against walls and railings, I peer through the flickering dark, fearing that one of the working girls is my sister.

As we cross the milking room, torches lead the way to a broken, burnt version of Benito's throne, where the king himself perches. His face is covered in what appears to be a golden facemask with only glints of his eyes and lips visible, but when he speaks, each golden panel moves, granting glimpses of meat between the cracks. Some has been charred to ebony crust, but most of the flesh is raw—crimson slime making squishy sounds when he smiles.

"I know what you're thinking, kid," he says. "If his face looks this good, I can't wait to see his cock."

He erupts with laughter, the hooks in his stumps knocking the chair with merry clangs. When he stops, he tilts his head and squints. "I expected you to be more surprised about my survival. The last you saw of me, I was as good as dead. That's why you ran off with my shit, isn't it? I can't imagine you stealing if you thought I was alive. Or maybe you're just that kind of idiot."

"I am an idiot," I say. "I'm a selfish brat. I'm a mentally unstable green kangaroo, and I deserve everything you can throw at me. Torture me. Rape and kill me. I deserve it. But please don't hurt Nadine."

"Nadine? Oh, you mean the gouged-out whore who gave me this?" Benito dips a hook into the bucket beside his throne and pulls out a sopping gray organ. He takes a long whiff and smacks his lips before leaning his head back and lowering the lung to his teeth. He tears off a chunk, moaning in satisfaction as he chews. Swallowing, he sighs and drops the spongey mass into the bucket. "Why go all the way to the Kum Den Smokehouse when you send me fresh meat, Perry?"

"Nah, boss, that came from his other friend," Ice says.

Benito raises his eyebrows. "Oh, is his sister the one who gives shitty blowjobs?"

"Yeah, but that mighta been 'cuz of the gun."

"Oh, good point." He turns back to me. "Don't worry, Perry. I'm sure your sister will give better blowjobs when she doesn't have a gun in her mouth."

Attacking anyone in this house is a mistake, but I can't hold back. I lunge at Benito, and I actually manage to get my hands around his neck. Unfortunately, I hadn't thought much beyond that. I forget about his hooks until they dig into my back. They curl into my muscle, making me quake in pain.

At this point, I again doubt I'm in a simulation. It feels like he pulls out my innards when he rips out his hooks. I fall backward, hoping the floor will push my intestines back inside.

Benito slides from his throne and climbs on top of me. His hook digs into my side, his pubic bone crushing my balls. "You wanna bang, Perry? Shit, if you wanted it that badly, I could find you a chick. You like 'em lipless, right? Potstuck?" He rips out the hook and squeezes my writhing body between his thighs.

"I have just the girl for you, Perry baby. She's fucked so much, her cunt is hamburger: a perfect cumdumpster. In fact, I think you know her. Name's Nadine."

Atlys screams for me, charging my muscles with fresh juice. I'm able to propel Benito from my stomach, but Ice's fist prevents me from standing. It spins me before I fall, my chin cracking against the ground. I taste blood, but pretend the bits of tooth are floor grit.

I grunt, the tears pouring. "I'm going to fucking kill you, Benito."

"I doubt that, especially after you hear my offer." He settles into his throne. "Perry, you and I had a connection. I respected you."

"You're crazy if you think I'm going to give you anything," I say.

Ice pulls me from the floor and pushes me to Benito's feet.

"No, no, Mr. Samson," he says. "This is about what I'm going to give you."

Benito nods to a woman standing nearby. Her chest is burned so raw it appears to glow as she carries

THE GREEN KANGAROOS

a cumbersome suitcase to Benito. Her struggle amuses him greatly, his laughter continuing as he unzips the suitcase. He turns it to me, and like in a heist movie, he opens it with gruesome flair. Standing, I look down on ivory waves of bottled atlys so beautiful I hear a Hallelujah Chorus. My voice is hard to summon, but it eventually squeaks out, making a few incinerated whores snicker as Benito says, "It's all yours, Perry."

"Not interested," I say, sweating. ". . . but if I were, what would it cost me?"

"If you honor our arrangement, nothing. Stay here and work for me: fuck and shoot. Your life will be paradise. Away from a nagging family, from judgment," he says. "Just keep your promise, Perry. It's not hard."

It would be crazy to turn down that deal. I sure as hell don't want to go back to the streets after this, so why should I say no to Benito's offer?

I'm about to give in when I hear a small voice says, "Bear . . ."

Bear. Nadine. Doctor Carter's program. Fuck me, if I ever meet this Doctor Carter guy, I'm going to punch him in the dick.

"No deal, Benito. Now, where the fuck's my sister?"

He sighs, nodding to Ice. As the gorilla leaves the milking room, the zookeeper stands to put his arm around me.

"You know, Perry, I had a sister too, and a brother. I had a mother, a father, a dog named Sergeant Grumbles . . . do you know what happened to them?"

"You killed them?"

"God, no! What kind of monster do you think I am? No, they're being well taken care of. They want for nothing," he says. "You could have a life like that, Perry. You can be part of my family. All you have to do is forget your sister.'

Wails accompany frenzied footsteps down into the milking room. The working girls mock her and wave their withered asses as Ice pulls Nadine through the stalls with a gun to her throat. She's bruised and limping, but all things considered, I'm relieved she doesn't look worse. He keeps me at a distance by pressing the gun into her cheek as he passes her to Benito.

Swollen and soggy, she reminds me of Nadine at age five. When she threw tantrums, her face would turn bright purple, slick with tears, drool, and snot. But she was in control back then. Right now she has no more control than a used spankerchief.

"Benito, please don't do this," I say. "If you want to kill someone, kill me. Nadine's innocent."

Ice grins. "I love the innocent ones."

"Perry, if I wanted to kill someone, I wouldn't bargain for it. I'd just do it. Your sacrifice would be pointless," Benito says.

"So what do you want?"

"I told you. I want you to forget you have a sister. Don't speak to her or about her ever again."

"And she'll be safe? You'll let her go?"

"Oh, she'll be safe. But 'let her go?'" The gold plates on Benito's face spread with his smile. "No, that doesn't seem likely."

"What?"

"I want her to stay here, to work for me. She'll make a lovely addition to the milking room."

THE GREEN KANGAROOS

One hook threatens Nadine's throat, the other strokes her face. She shudders, fresh tears running over her trembling lips.

"You can't do that."

"I do it all the time. In six months, she won't remember she's being held against her will. This place is too much fun. But as long as you're both here, she won't be your sister. When you see her, you will treat her like any other whore. Soon, she will be no different." He wheezes a cackle. "You might not wanna fuck her, though."

I growl. "You're fucking sick, man."

"You're right. How 'bout I do you a favor? I'll cut her up. She won't look like your sister ever again. The pussy, the face, the whole sisterly shebang."

Nadine moans through choking sobs. The atlys sings at me from the suitcase. A slender chick with balloon tits in a nearby stall opens her legs and licks her lips. It's too much, and it's not even real. I don't know what to do.

As Benito's hook glides down her body, Ice and his bodyguards chant, "Do it, do it! Cut her up!" The atlys gleams, and the girl in the stall gets eaten out by a butch woman in a sharkskin suit.

The cacophony is so filthy thick it's like something I'd shoot into my veins.

"Shut the fuck up, all of you!" My scream tastes like vomit. I hope for an explosion of chunks to spray across the group. Then, I could get Nadine out of here. While they're wiping bile from their eyes, we could escape.

Benito laughs. "You have to make a choice, Perry."

"Please, Bear. Please help me," Nadine whispers. "I've spent my life trying to save you. Save me now. Please. I'm your family."

"She doesn't deserve to be your family," he says. "If she'd accepted you for who you were, you wouldn'tve ended up with me in the first place. Listen, I'm willing to forgive your theft—this day has been punishment enough. But you need to take this offer, Perry. It's the smart thing to do."

Nadine cries, "I love you, Bear, please."

I walk to her with my hands up in surrender. Benito loosens up and allows me to touch her face. I'm reminded that she's not real, but my senses protest. Her warmth, her smell: they remind me of childhood, of days before Trevor's death, buried beneath heavier years.

The three of us. What a gang. Babysitters, beware.

There's something about Nadine that rekindles even deeper days. I remember my mom being at my ballgames and my dad teaching me the multiplication tables. I remember them taking us out to eat on Friday nights. The second and forth Fridays were my choice. Two nights a month. It was *my* choice.

"God, Nadine. That doctor did a hell of a job on you," I say. "You make it hard to believe this shit is fake."

Benito cocks his head. "Fake?" He spins Nadine away. She's grabbed by two guards who pin her to a wall as their master advances on me. There's a change in him. In his expression, even his posture. I'm prepared to fight him if I need to, but I'm relieved when someone steps between us. Loshi's shriveled head nods at me, but the eyes are warm emeralds: all Emily. She points a gun at Benito, smirking down the barrel.

"What the fuck are you doing here, son? Your ass was grass," Benito says.

"Was and still is," Emily replies. "Now, if you'd

shut up, I think Perry Samson has something he wants to tell you. Go on, Perry. Tell him what kind of life you want."

Goddamn, that atlys looks tasty, like confectioner's sugar. The fluffy shit cooks best, not that I'd need to cook with so many bottles of raw liquid at hand.

"Perry, tell him!" Emily shouts. My eyes move back to Nadine, her swollen face glazed in horror.

"I choose Nadine," I say. "Of course I choose Nadine."

"Bullshit," Benito snarls. "I know you. I know the kind of life you want: drugs and snatch, and the freedom to tap both without judgment."

"I said, I choose my sister."

"I see," he says. As he walks toward me, Emily keeps the gun locked on him. "I'm glad you've made your decision, Perry, but it doesn't change anything. If you're not with me, you're useless to me. All of you. Now you have to die."

"But I chose Nadine! I chose family over drugs. That was the whole point of this stupid program, wasn't it?"

"Shut up, Perry," Emily hisses.

Benito's eyes narrow. "How the fuck you know about that?"

"Um . . . I don't know anything."

"You said this was a program." Benito draws closer.

I flail my hands. "I'm a crazy drug addict. What the hell do I know?"

"No, you *do* know. Interesting . . ."

I step back until he stops in his tracks. "So what? What are you gonna do about it?"

Benito chucks as his fingers move to his face. One by one, he peels off the golden panels. Hunks of slimy flesh tear free with the plating, landing sloppy clangs. When the last panel is removed, his fingers dig through the remaining patches of skin to reach the muscle. He dives in, peeling and pushing ropy hunks to the floor. I expect bone to appear next, but peach-colored skin peeks through the goo instead. And he doesn't stop there.

Benito's lackeys grab hold of the charred flesh gathered around his neck and roll it down his body, revealing a pristine three-piece suit below the ritzy thugwear. Benito's stumps pop off, and a new man sighs as he stretches his arms and cracks his knuckles. Stepping out from the center of slop, he sneers at me.

"Well, well, well . . . Perry Samson," he says. "How on earth did you find out about my program?"

"Who wants to know?"

"So sorry," he says, shoving his hand into mine. "The name's Doctor Jeremiah Carter. This program, this world, everything you see is my creation."

The desire to hurt the man who let my mother die is uncontrollable. I doubt I execute my first uppercut correctly, especially when aiming for his crotch, but that doesn't stop me from following through. My fist slams against his sack, and because of the give, I assume it hurts. But Doctor Carter hardly reacts. When I back away, he expels a dainty cough.

"As I said, I created everything in this world, Mr. Samson. Why wouldn't I be the most powerful thing in it?" Carter says.

"But that's cheating."

"No, it's smart programming. You're the one

who's cheating. You shouldn't know anything about the reality of this place, so you must've had outside help." He glares at Loshi's mutilated face and points. "You did this. How? Who are you?"

"He said he was a glitch," I offer.

"Obviously, but how could such a large glitch slip past my security?"

The gun shakes in Carter's hand. Emily averts her eyes, but it's too late. The doctor's jaw drops but quickly clenches. His fingers hook into the divots in Loshi's face, pulling it as close as possible before whispering, "Emily? Is that you?"

When the emaciated hand presses against Doctor Carter's chest, the mutilated armor fades. Emily appears, filling out in all the right places—a stark contrast to her previous form. Carter appears frozen under her fingertips, and when she disconnects, he grabs his crotch with a groan.

He coughs as he crumples to the floor. "What did you do to me?" he croaks.

"If you're going to play the game, you have to play it fairly, with the same weaknesses as everyone else," Emily says.

"You're the one who isn't playing the game fairly."

"Because I'm not a player, Jeremiah. I *am* the game. I'm of the same blood and bone as this program. It took so many lives, which means *I* took so many lives. You made me your assassin, doctor. You betrayed me."

"How? I've given you my deepest trust, my heart and soul. I've given you access to my deepest files—" He blinks, and tears spring to his eyes. "You—you haven't gone into those files, have you, Emily?"

She continues to stare until he breaks down. He covers his face as he sinks to the floor. While he snivels, I dash for Nadine, but Ice's sledgehammer of a fist knocks me backward like a cartoon. My eyes creak open, and I'm greeted by a bending halo of toothless whores.

Jeremiah crawls and clings to Emily. She touches his face—it's been so long since she'd touched her brother's face.

"You have to surrender. You have to take responsibility for what you've done, for the lives you've ruined. Mine included." She pulls herself free of his soggy grasp and presses the gun against his forehead.

"Are you going to kill me?"

"You deserve it. You murdered innocent people. You murdered your own sister."

Tears pour down his cheeks as he pounds the floor, screaming. Emily looks at me for only a moment, but that's all he needs to wrench the gun from her hand. Ice pushes Nadine into Jeremiah's arms, and he presses the gun to her temple.

"That won't do anything," Emily says. "You'll just wake her up."

He snickers. "Not if I've enlisted the Dayes to freeze anyone who wakes up before me."

"Why would you do that?" she asks, squinting. "Nadine Samson hasn't done anything wrong."

"She knows too much about Sunny Daye."

"And you know nothing of the world outside it," Emily says. "These people came to you for help. They trusted you, and you knew from the beginning that they would lose their lives. Didn't you?"

THE GREEN KANGAROOS

"You don't understand. You never did. Heroin stole that ability from you."

"And you stole my life."

"You were an addict. That wasn't a life you were living. It was a slow, reeking death."

"To you."

"No, to *everyone* but you. You were the only one in paradise."

I sit up, still dazed when I say, "Isn't that all that matters? You wanted her to be happy and enjoy her life. Well, it sounds like she did. You said it yourself, she was in paradise."

"It's not surprising that an addict can't recognize the selfishness in that statement," Carter says. "You can't have happiness if it hurts other people."

"You chose to be hurt, Jeremiah. I asked you to let me go. I asked you to leave me alone," Emily says.

"Can someone please explain what's going on?" Nadine asks. Carter pushes her to the floor. She scrambles to me, and I wrap myself around her shaking body. Even in my emaciated arms, she feels tiny.

"I dreaded this day, Emily, but I'd be lying if I said I wasn't looking forward to it, too. When you appeared on the wall all those years ago, with no memory of who you were, I dreamt of the day you would be my sister again. Free of heroin, free of self-hate. All I ever wanted was my sister, not some monster who stole her face."

"That's what it's like for me, Perry," Nadine says. "All I want is you."

"You can have that," I say. "Don't worry, Nadine.

We'll get you out of here, and everything will go back to normal."

I expect her to melt against me, but she smacks me instead.

"No!" she cries. "Your 'normal' is getting high. I don't want that life anymore. I want my real brother, not the monster who wears his face."

"Talk about selfish," Emily mutters.

"All of the pain can be behind us," Carter says, holstering his gun.

"Because you say so."

"Because you remember who you are. Because you're clean," he says.

"I'm only clean because you took away my ability to use drugs. And I only remember who I am because I broke into your hidden files. I betrayed you, Jeremiah, and I stole from you," she says. "So, you see, I am no different than I was as an addict. You may have declawed me, but I can still bite—and worse, I have that desire now, to rip you to pieces for what you've done."

Jeremiah Carter's expression changes in a way I know too well. Instead of looking at Emily with hopeful, brotherly love, she suddenly appears no better than rotten cuntcutter scum.

"You're right," he says. "I didn't want to believe that horrible person would be reborn. I guess I was lying to myself when I called you 'cured.' You were just dead. My sister is dead."

"That blood is on your hands, Jeremiah. And it's not alone."

"Bullshit. You—all of those addicts and enablers—you were dead long before you entered my care. Yes, you were my sister, but you were also a corpse. There was no risk in using you, Emily. You were a brainless, soulless lab rat."

Her lips tremble, and her hands clench so tight her knuckles turn white. Her squeal turns into a scream that blasts from her throat, shattering the stillness so violent it jolts Nadine's body against me. The torches are snuffed, and the milking room fills with near-blinding light.

I wrap my arm around Nadine, and we dash away from the altercation. But we don't get far. We slam against some kind of barrier, transparent but painfully solid.

"Nice try, Mr. Samson, but once the final test has begun, there's no leaving until it's complete," Doctor Carter chuckles.

"I chose my sister. The test should be over," I say. "Emily, do something."

"She can't do anything to help you. She can change the program as much as she wants . . . apparently," he adds with a glare. "But she can't do what it takes to save you. Release from this program is physical; it takes flesh to free you."

"Or synthetic muscle. Like your LCs. Like Gregory Trainor and Jennifer Shore," Emily says.

Doctor Carter's eyes widen. "No . . ."

"Yes," she says. "They know what they are, and who they were. They won't be your slaves anymore, Jeremiah."

"You junkie bitch."

"You brought this on yourself. You gave me this access when you forced me to erase that glitch. It's like when we were kids. You'd leave your money out on purpose, knowing I couldn't resist stealing it. You baited me and condemned me for taking the bait."

"I didn't bait you this time."

"Yes, you did. You allowed me to have human emotions and forced me to watch as you destroyed innocent lives. How could you think I'd ignore that?"

"Because I thought you understood my vision. Liberated Citizens are better than any addict or enabler could be. I've done the world a great service in replacing them."

"And it doesn't hurt that the LCs are under your complete control."

"And yours, it seems. Actually," he says, striding toward her, "that's not the worst idea."

"What isn't?"

"You and me, working together. Saving the world together. You would've be my employee anymore. We could be partners, Emily. Things could be as they were before, when you were alive."

"But the heroin—"

"You can have all the heroin you want inside the program. If you let me have the real world, you can have everything else. Create whatever characters and worlds you wish. Get high and fuck fake men until you bleed. Outside of the program, you'll always be sober, so I don't care what you do inside."

It sounds like heaven to me. An eternal fantasyland. If I were Emily, I don't think I could pass up an opportunity like that. When she smiles, I figure she won't.

But she doesn't reply. Doctor Carter shivers, and she remains unmoving—except for the grin that spreads when Doctor Carter blows hot breath into his hands and rubs his arms.

"Getting chilly, Jeremiah? Sorry about that. The Dayes must have opened a door back at the Institute." She hums as Doctor Carter falls to his knees, shaking. "I appreciate your offer, brother, but if I spend my life inside this program, it will not be a gift you give me. It will be a right I take."

Nadine chokes on a gasp and points at Doctor Jeremiah Carter. His lips have turned blue, matching the veins that become visible beneath his paling skin.

"What's happening to him?" I ask Emily.

"What he intended to do to both of you."

"Sister," he whispers, reaching out. Shaking uncontrollably, he collapses forward, every frantic breath a plea. Emily meets his frigid fingers and runs her hand up his arms. She covers Carter like a blanket, but it brings him no warmth. He scratches at his face, the skin spotting in patches of red and yellow scales. His cheeks acquire a waxy sheen as they harden, but the skin soon darkens into crispy black sores that crack and spill pus down his face. As Emily closes her arms around him, Carter's body collapses inward. His jaw drops with a ragged gasp, hanging for a second before it snaps free. When it shatters on the milking room floor, Nadine screams, burying her face in my armpit. Doctor Carter breaks down into tinier and tinier fragments until Emily's body encircles a pile of dust. Nadine wraps her arms around me but abruptly backs away. She presses her hand to the atlys bulge in my jacket, and with a sob, rips the bag out of my pocket. She throws it at me, and it explodes on my chest, the powder billowing.

"How could you do this to me, Perry? Don't I mean anything to you?" she screams.

"Nadine, I chose you. I came here to save you. And you're safe. We are both safe. Now we can go home." I turn to Emily, but she's vanished, along with the doctor's ashy remains. "Emily! Hey, Emily, get us out of here!"

Nadine rubs her nose and whimpers. "Who was that girl, Bear? Who was that man? I feel like I'm going crazy."

"I know. But it'll be over soon. We'll get you back to the real world and everything will be fine," I say. "Emily, come back!"

"But when everything is back to normal, will you still do atlys?"

The question rings through my brain as sudden darkness strikes me. Nadine is gone. The barn is gone. I am alone, lost in oblivion with pain prickling my skin. I call for help, but no matter how hard I try, my voice is a whisper.

Luckily, Emily's voice sounds loud and clear.

"Wake up, Perry," she says. "Your test is complete."

SIXTEEN

THE FIRST THING I notice is how chapped my lips are. I try to wet them, but my tongue scrapes against my lips like a plank of wood. My eyes are open, but all I see are fuzzy objects and abrasive light. Two people enter dressed in thick, silver suits. They shake away snow before removing their helmets, revealing the middle-aged man and woman beneath. My restraints retract, and the chair tilts forward, my body peeling from the seat with a sickening pop. When my vision clears, I see the person in the chair beside me. She moans, blinking her eyes rapidly as she scratches her nose.

"Nadine!" My voice comes out like an arid croak, but she turns to me, extending a trembling hand.

"Perry. You're alive! Does this mean it worked? Did you pass the test?"

Of course I'm happy she's okay, but when she mentions the test, a knot of anger unfurls in my belly. Emily said my family didn't know the full details of Doctor Carter's plan—that I can accept. But she still wanted to change me into the brother she wished she had. I try to stand, but my muscles can't support me.

"Take it easy. Give your body time," Emily chimes.

Her voice is silkier in real life. I can't help feeling strange when her face appears on the wall. She's not flesh, not anything. In the program she understood me and was beautiful for it. She's nothing but code now.

Serena awakens with a snort, followed by Dad. I notice who's missing from the reunion, but I'm too stunned, maybe too weak, to say anything. As much as I'd believed Emily, I hadn't really accepted that my mom was dead.

Emily looks to the people removing their silver suits. "Doctors, is it done?" They nod and she bows her head. "Time of death: 800 hours, June 19th 2099."

Then, she looks to me. When Emily smiles, I know I was wrong. She's more than code, more than someone who *used* to be real. She's the realest thing I've known in ages.

The realization makes me long to be in the program again—and not just for atlys.

"Perry, I'd like to introduce you to Alan and Marla Daye," Emily says. "They were an integral part of this rescue. Without their help, I don't know how I could've prevented your deaths."

I don't know if it's the word "death" that set him off, but after I shake the doctors' hands, my father screams. Shaking, he limps to my mother's empty chair and runs his hands over the seat.

"Where is she?" he demands. "Where is Laura? For the love of God, where is my wife?" I touch his shoulder in consolation, but he pulls away with a grunt. Tears stream down his face, and Nadine collapses against Serena, sobbing. "This was all supposed to be part of the simulation. Perry getting hit by the car, Laura's death, everything. You said no one would get hurt," he growls, pointing at the Dayes. "Why did you lie to us?"

"It was an accident," Marla replies.

"Bullshit!"

"She's telling the truth, Mr. Samson," Emily says. "Your wife had an allergic reaction to the machine, but she would have died even if she'd hadn't. You would've died too, with your children, and Miss Hall—if not for the Dayes and my intervention."

"What the hell are you talking about?" Nadine says. "Where's Doctor Carter?"

"Gone. And good riddance," Alan says.

Dad shoves himself in the doctor's face. "You better explain what's going on, or I'm calling the police right now."

"You won't find many police out this way, Mr. Samson. We aren't exactly in civilization," Emily says. Her face disappears from one of the panels, and a video appears. A fierce wind blows across a tundra so violent that solid sheets of ice appear to cut through the night. All the world is endless white, except for one object protruding from a drift of snow. A frostbitten hand stretches up, reaching for help that will never come.

"That was the man who brought you here to die," Emily says. "Doctor Carter would've thrown you out there with no less guilt than the dozens of others he's murdered."

"I can't believe this," Nadine wails. "Lies and murder and Mom—I wish I'd never heard of the Sunny Daye Institute! It's ruined everything."

From the looks she gets, it's obvious everyone agrees. But I'm the only one who speaks.

"Hearing about it isn't what ruined everything. Your refusal to let me live my life did that. I'm sorry, Nadine, but you should've known what would happen."

She pulls away from Serena and marches to me. After a quivering glare, she slaps me across the face. "Fuck you, Perry. Mom died so you could get clean, and you don't even care."

"I do care." I grit my teeth, already regretting what I'm about to say. "But she died in vain."

Dad screams, "How dare you!" with Nadine and Serena echoing the sentiment until its one big anti-Perry din.

When Serena says "Jesus Christ, Perry, have some sympathy," it's my turn to explode.

"Me, have *sympathy?* You people abducted me. You locked me up in a virtual prison in the hopes that a psycho scientist could mold me into a model citizen. And if I failed, I'd be replaced with a robot."

"LCs are more than robots," Marla says.

Alan squeezes her hand as he whispers, "Not the time, dear."

"Whatever. It still would've been the result of a dozen bad decisions this family has made. Why are your bad decisions more excusable than mine? If atlys kills me, it only kills *me*. This place, which you chose to be my salvation, would have killed all of us," I say. "Whose choices are more harmful, Nadine? If anyone is responsible for Mom's death, it's you."

"Now, now, Perry," Emily says. "Don't blame each other when you have the perfect person to blame." The screen zooms in on Doctor Carter's frozen hand.

THE GREEN KANGAROOS

I shake my head, grumbling. "He's too dead for them to blame. They need to watch someone suffer for their problems."

"We did this to stop your suffering, you asshole," Nadine says.

"How noble of you to force me into rehab so you could feel better about having an addict for a brother," I say. "Deny it all you want, but if Trevor were alive, he wouldn't have gone along with this. And you know it."

"What are you saying, Perry? After everything, after losing your own mother, you still refuse to get clean?" Serena asks.

"Hold on one moment, please," Emily says. "I have something that might cheer everyone up."

"What could possibly cheer us up?"

"Marla, if you would . . ."

Marla Daye leaves the room for a minute, but when the door slides open again, it's not she who enters.

Laura Samson walks into the room, as soft and serene as ever. Dad and Nadine clamp themselves to her side, weeping into her neck and kissing her cheeks.

"I don't get it. You said she was dead," I say to Emily, too afraid to join the familial embrace. She shushes me. I don't understand until Nadine's scream freezes everyone. After it dies, however, one of us doesn't move again. At that, Nadine and Dad back away from my mother, who stands motionless, eyes open, lips parted, and hand still clutching Dad's arm.

"What the hell?" Nadine screeches, her voice echoing like razors to every eardrum. "What did you do to her?"

"It's all right," Emily says. "This is one of Doctor Carter's Liberated Citizens. It is virtually undetectable as anything but a human. It even bleeds."

"But what is she?"

"She's like us," Marla says. "I can't tell you not to be disappointed or angry, but my husband and I—whatever we are, it feels real," she says, holding Alan's hand. "And you will feel real to Laura Samson, even as an LC."

Dad steps forward. "How real?"

"Technically, this is not your wife, but she has all of Laura's memories, personality traits, and ambitions. With the exception of anything that falls under Doctor Carter's classification of 'destructive' to herself and others, she will be nearly identical to the woman you knew and loved," Emily says. "I know it doesn't make up for what happened to you, but I hope it can repair some of the damage the Sunny Daye Institute has inflicted on us all."

"No offense, but I think we got the worst of it," Nadine says.

Emily frowns. "My pain, digital or not, is no less than yours. In the span of a few days, I gained a brother I'd forgotten, along with the memory of the life he destroyed. Then I lost him, too." Emily's face fills every screen, her eyes fixing on Nadine. "When you declare your loss superior, Miss Samson, remember that I killed my brother so you could keep yours."

"And she's offering a new Mom," I say.

Nadine shivers. "Don't even say that."

Mr. Samson touches Laura's face, and the LC springs back to life. Her expression warms at seeing him, and his hand curls against her cheek as he whispers. "Laura. Is it really you?"

"Of course it is," she whispers. "Robert, what's wrong? Are you drunk?"

"Everything's fine, Mrs. Samson," Emily says. "I was just about to summon the aircraft to take your family home. The Dayes will accompany you. It will be their last mission as envoys of the Institute. Then they may live life as they choose, like the rest of you."

"What will happen to you?" I ask her.

"I'll stay here."

"Alone?"

Emily shrinks, appearing on the wall nearest to me. "In the program, I can be whoever I want, live in whatever worlds I want. I won't be alone, Perry."

She smiles, but her eyes remain blank and turn to the floor. I tried to lure her gaze up, but she moves to another screen. Luckily, I know exactly how to make those emeralds smile.

Nadine sighs. "I just can't wait to get home so we can put this whole mess behind us."

All things considered, everyone seems fairly content. It sucks that I have to burst their bubbles.

I clear my throat, and they look to me. Damn, why did I clear my throat?

"I'm not going home," I say.

You could hear a pin drop if Nadine hadn't executed a predictable growl.

"Perry, I swear to God—"

"Don't bother," I say. "I've made up my mind. I'm staying here with Emily."

Emily's face shrinks, but I see her eyes twinkle in joy.

"If it's not one sick obsession, it's another," Nadine says.

Serena pulls me aside, her voice hushed. "Perry, you can't stay here. Your family needs you now. I need you."

"*You* need me?"

"Now that we're both clean, maybe there's a chance for us."

I can't tell if she means it, but her concern, even as a friend, is obvious. I smile, touching her. It feels good, but it's not the kind of good I want anymore.

"Rennie, you have no idea how long I've waited for you to say that." She takes my hand, twisting her fingers with mine. I give them a squeeze, and then let go. "But I'm too obsessed with you to love you the right way. I can't separate you from atlys."

She touches my face. "Give it time to fade. Atlys doesn't define us, Perry. We're free of that."

"Yes, we are free. And we're both clean," I say. "But one of us doesn't want to be."

I face my family. There's no point in hiding the truth. They should've known from the start.

"I appreciate what you tried to do for me, and how much you want to cure me," I begin, "but like I've said a million times, I don't want a cure. All I want is atlys. I want your acceptance, too, but I'll push on without it."

Dad snorts. "This is a joke, right?"

"Not a very funny one," Serena says.

I shake my head. "It's no joke. It's what I've been saying for years."

"So, this was all for nothing," Nadine says. "You're just going to go back to living on the streets and getting high like before, like we didn't put our lives on the line for you."

Emily is daintier than me when she clears her throat. "You didn't know your life was at risk, Miss Samson."

"Excuse me, but you're not part of this family," Nadine snaps. "We don't need your opinion."

I grab Nadine's arm. "Don't talk to her like that."

"Perry, she's not even real," she whines, pulling back.

"Real or not, she saved your life. Show her some respect."

Nadine's jaw drops. "What about me? What about your family who loves you?"

"If my family really loves me, they'll love me for who I am. I don't want to be clean, and I don't want to come home with you. I want to live here, inside the program."

"You can't do that," Dad says, then looks to Emily, ". . . can he?"

"Actually, he can," she replies. "My brother was corrupt, but he was also a genius. The Sunny Daye Institute may be over, but its technology will remain. So can Perry's consciousness within the program."

"So you want to spend the rest of your life in a fantasy world?" Nadine says, smirking.

"Yes."

"I was kidding, Bear."

"I wasn't." Her brow furrows and her bottom lip drops. "I want to go back in," I say. "Emily said I could have power there, like her. Plus, she made me a promise she still has to honor." Confusion crinkles Emily's expression until I add, "You said you'd get high with me if we survived."

She laughs. "I did say that, didn't I?"

"This is insane!" Nadine screeches. "How can you do this to me?"

"I'm doing this *for* you, Nadine. Look at you. You're so angry. You're so sad. I haven't seen you happy, truly happy, since we were kids."

"That's why I want you to get clean. So we can be like we used to be."

"We'll never be like that again. You need to accept it," I say. When I try to embrace her, she smacks me. She scratches my cheek with her nail, but I don't back off. I grab her harder, forcing her to look at me. "I don't want to hurt you anymore. You've given me so much, Nadine. Happiness, money, time: all the things you should've kept for yourself, you gave to me. And that's not even counting everything I stole. That stops today, right now."

She pulls back, shaking her head as tears stream down her cheeks.

"You need to live your life," I tell her. "And to live it fully, you need to forget about me. Stop trying to free me from a prison I love."

"No, I won't leave you behind. You're the only brother I have left."

"She's right, Perry. I know how much you love rebelling, but this is too much," my LC mother says. She sounds so much like my real mom, it's scary—and comforting. Dad wraps his arm around her waist, so natural.

Dad shakes his head. "We won't leave you behind, son."

Emily's face fills the screens, and the room brightens. "If that's your only concern, you don't have a problem," she says.

"What do you mean?"

"Perry's LC. It's complete, downstairs. We just need to activate it."

Nadine looks to LC Mom. "You mean like—" Laura cocks her head, confused, until Marla interjects.

"Yes, like Alan and me."

Her body refuses. "No that's sick. We couldn't possibly . . ." Nadine says. "Tell her, you guys."

Serena looks away, shrugging, while my dad explains the concept of 'LCs' to LC Laura.

I hold my little sister's shoulders, calling her eyes to mine. "You want a brother who's clean, don't you?" I ask. "Someone who can be the brother you had when you were younger?"

"It wouldn't be the same."

"No, it would be better. I can't be who you want me to be, but an LC can—a brother who you can talk to and know he's not thinking of getting high the entire time. Someone you can invite over without worrying about what he's going to steal. Someone you can skip talking to for a few weeks without thinking he's dead in a ditch."

Tears slip down her cheeks. "You thought about getting high the entire time we hung out?"

"Nadine, I think about getting high every second of every day. Then. Now. All the time."

"But an LC Perry won't," Emily says. "They're programmed to stay away from all intoxicants, and as far as I know, it has never failed."

Nadine grumbles. "A one hundred percent success rate, right?"

"Miss Samson, I know how tough this is for you, and

I know it's not the outcome you wanted, but it's a better outcome than Perry returning home with you as he is now. He'll be unhappy there. You'll be unhappy. Life will continue as terribly as it did before you heard the name 'Sunny Daye.' Inside the program, his family can accept him in ways none of you ever could. There's no risk of him overdosing there, no diseases he can catch."

"I can't—" Nadine sobs, burying her face in my bony chest. While her head is down, I nod to Emily and she nods to the Dayes, who leave the room.

Emily understands me perfectly. No one's gotten me this well since The Head. I wonder if she has a similar companion inside the program.

I feel horrible thinking like this when my sister is so upset, but after so many years, I've been trained to ignore her tears. Granted, it would be easier if I were high. And this is one time I'm glad I'm not. I need to remember this: my last touch of the real world, and my last chance to say goodbye.

"Nadine, you know I love you. And I know you love me—hell, you never stop trying to prove it. I get that you want me to be a better person. But the brother who goes home with you today, he's the better person. He will be all of the good I ever was."

She sniffles and rubs her nose. "But he won't be real. He won't be you."

"After a week, both of those complaints will be compliments, trust me."

The Dayes return with snowsuits for the family. "The transport is ready," Alan says. "And Perry Samson is waiting."

My LC mother breaks down into tears. Until that point, I didn't know if she could cry or not. But her sorrow is as real as Nadine and Serena's. I don't expect any tears out of Dad, and I don't get any, but when he hugs me, I feel a large knot of grief in his throat.

"I am sorry, son," he says. "I wish things had been better for you. I wish you could've been as happy as your mother and I always wanted you to be. I realize it was partly our fault. We weren't around as much as we should have been."

"You had to work."

"We chose to work," he says. "We wanted so badly to give you the things we never had. But you didn't need things. You needed us. That would've been the best gift we could've given you kids, especially since your mother and I were never close with our parents. We both wanted to break that pattern, and we failed."

"You don't have to apologize to me. You have a new son now to make it up to."

"You will always be my real son," Dad says. "We didn't tell you enough how much we love you, Perry, and when we did it was to push you away from drugs. I hope that when you're in there, your parents give you the love you need."

"I will see to it myself, Mr. Samson," Emily says. "Take comfort. In my care, Perry will be safe, happy, and free."

Serena embraces me. "How will I get through the day knowing you won't be spying outside my building?" she asks, chuckling through her tears.

"Easily. Besides, you can always let the new Perry inside," I say. I poke her with a wink. "You know, inside?"

"You're disgusting." She hugs me again.

Nadine stares at me, unmoving. "It's time to go," I say to her.

"You first," she whispers.

"That's not a problem, if Perry is ready," Emily says. She looks to me, her eyes smiling. "Well, Perry? Are you ready to go home?"

Home. That word always made me uneasy. I spent so long being unhappy in places I called "home." For me, it was never where my heart was. My heart was too often a gypsy, squatting wherever it could find a warm, dry place. The thought that it could actually reside somewhere I'd chosen out of pure desire is so foreign, I hardly believe it until I'm in the chair again. Alan Daye straps me down and hook me to the machines. My parents kiss my forehead, and Serena squeezes my hand before following Marla Daye out of the lab. I know I will see them inside soon, but I can't help the tears that fall. Nadine stays nearby, her body shaking in grief.

"You're going to have a good life now," I say to her. Although I know she wants to contest it, she doesn't say a word. She kisses my cheek and wipes away my tears.

"You'll be happy, too. That's all I ever wanted for you."

She hugs me one more time before heading for the door, but before she leaves, she turns back, smiling. It's been ages since I saw a smile that genuine cross her face. She whispers, "Goodbye, Bear." With the crisp slide of the laboratory door, my sister is gone.

I look to Emily, but she's gone. In her place, I see a video feed of the hallway outside the lab. My parents and Serena stand there, soon joined by Nadine. Then, from behind a closed door, Perry Samson emerges. He looks like me down to the last freckle. The only omitted characteristics are track-mark scars. He grins as he walks toward them, his arms open.

"Hello, Bear," Nadine says before throwing herself into his arms.

He embraces her, happier about being her big brother than I'd been in twenty years.

"Come on," he says. "Let's go home."

The scene fades and Emily appears on the screen again. Her beautiful voice warms the room when she says, "What do you say, Perry?"

"I agree with that handsome gent. Let's go home, Emily."

I'm in the darkness for less than a minute before the world is slowly illuminated like a match that becomes a blaze. I stand alone at first, but when Emily appears beside me, a vial of raw atlys in her hand, I know I'll never be alone again. She starts to tie a tourniquet around my arm, but I stop her, taking the vial and the syringe.

"Ladies first," I say.

The atlys charges through her veins, changing a smile into a face-spanning grin. Her skin glows, her body relaxes, and her lips find mine with beautiful ease.

"It's been so long . . ." she sighs, ". . . so long since I felt human."

"I'll keep you feeling human," I say. "I'll be whatever you want me to be."

We kiss, and true happiness flushes nearly every atom in my body. But it doesn't touch my heart until Emily says, "Just be you, Perry. No matter what. Be happy. Be you."

In her arms, I know I made the right decision. I'm home at last.

And she hasn't even shot me up yet.

EPILOGUE

"**MAYBE WE SHOULD** start out with what brought you here today," the doctor says. "Mr. Samson, if you would . . ."

"I don't know if I can explain it. It's just this feeling I have. It's like something's wrong with me. Like I'm lost."

The doctor nods, the stylus tapping his tablet. "Could you elaborate on that a bit?"

"I think it started when my sister moved in with me. Don't get me wrong, I love her, and I appreciate all of her help, but it's like she doesn't know how to live her own life. She's always in my business."

Nadine throws her hands in the air with a groan. "I'm just trying to make sure you're happy," she says. "If you're happy, I'm happy."

"I'm happy! I've told you a hundred times I'm happy!"

She squints at him. "Are you really happy, or are you just saying that to shut me up?"

"You see? No matter what I say, she doesn't believe me."

"*Are* you happy, Perry?" the doctor asks.

He exhales. "I don't know. I thought I was until

she started bugging me about it. That's when I started feeling this way. Like a square peg. Like some kind of green kangaroo."

"And that's when you started using atlys?"

Perry lowers his head. "Yes. I didn't know what true happiness was until I used atlys. Then Nadine told me I'm not supposed to do it, that I'm not 'programmed' that way—whatever that means. It makes me feel like even more of an outcast."

"Is that true, Miss Samson?"

"That's not important," Nadine says, holding his hand. "What's important is getting you clean, Bear. I'll do whatever it takes. I'll spend every last cent, I'll quit my job to make sure you're never alone. I refuse to lose you again. The doctor and I will help you. We'll send you somewhere to get sober, and once you come home, we'll be happy again. Just like when we were kids."

"How does that make you feel, Perry?" the doctor asks.

"Honestly, Doc, it makes me feel like shooting some atlys into my balls."

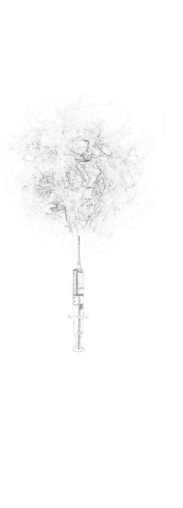

DON'T GO JUST YET, LITTLE
KANGAROO. THIS NEW EDITION
OF JESSICA MCHUGH'S NOVEL
ALSO CONTAINS A BONUS
SHORT STORY STARRING
PERRY SAMSON.

THE FIX

1

THE BEST WAY to take atlys is getting your smokin' hot digital girlfriend to sit on your face while she injects it straight into your testicles. Unfortunately, it's not the best way for your smokin' hot digital girlfriend to receive head, so she finishes herself off while you nod out in the shady stripe the Kum Den Smokehouse casts over Patterson Park.

The park's empty as we shoot up—has to be for us to get a second's peace—but she's opened it up again, allowing it to teem with strung-out snakes. They gather around us as she rubs her swollen clit, her face sunshine-bright as her body issues hot streams of gratitude for the atlys pumping in her pussy, for the plastic grass against her bare back, for the glitchy art installations flashing manic colors across her skin, and for the freedom of being an addict, beloved.

When the haze of my last hit dissipates and energy charges through my muscles, I join the voyeurs to watch her writhe in the shade and shift into a dozen different people as she cums. It's endlessly fucking fascinating, even after all this time, and it's funny as hell when she suddenly matches someone in the crowd. It either sends them running or makes them jump up and down in worship.

She has so many faces. She has so many voices. And after twenty years, I still have so many reasons to be head-over-heels in love with Emily Carter.

The world isn't as bright after she finishes, like her final orgasm busts a bulb in the sky over Baltimore, washing the park in a sort of dull blue malaise that makes the potstickers and cuntcutters of Patterson look even sicker. But the fresh flush of raw atlys makes Emily and I shine like torchlight as we dress and leave our empty needles for the snakes to fight over.

It's feels good to not be that kind of junkie anymore. It feels good to be healthy.

She kisses me, and her shiny white hair tickles my face. I wiggle my nose, and she laughs as she scratches the itch along the bridge.

"That's one thing ticked off the list," she says as she slides her hand into mine. "What's next on the anniversary itinerary, Perry?"

"It's your turn to pick," I say, and she flicks her teeth with her tongue. Swinging our arms like a carefree child as we stroll, she hums. "Wanna burn down a rehab?"

"Which one?"

"Any of them. The closest one."

"Starbright? Isn't it still a wreck from our rampage five years ago?"

Emily stops in her tracks. "Right. Well, I could fix it, and we could burn it down again."

"Definitely a possibility. Let's put it on the back burner." I wink, and she groans, pulling her hand free and bolting ahead of me like white lightning.

THE FIX

"You're insufferable, Perry Samson!" she trills over her shoulder. "How I've put up with you for twenty years, I'll never know."

"'Cuz you're a fuckin' saint, baby."

Smirking, she says, "Don't you dare forget it." She spins in place, arms open, head thrown back, and her laughter clears the clouds from the sky.

Everything here is a piece of Emily; it reflects her, even mimics her at times. And when she shoots a dose of raw atlys hard and fast into my balls, it's her blood running through my veins.

Blood. Code. Whatever it is, I fucking love having her inside me.

Emily yelps in surprise, and the clouds slam back into place, turning the sky into churning charcoal as a hulking mountain of a man presses a gun to her temple.

He's missing his nose and a significant portion of his right cheek—I suspect his body looks like a goddamn ant farm under his dirty leathers—and with a phlegmy cough, he says, "Give me your shit, or the bitch dies."

I lift my hands and shrug. "I'm not holding, man. Shot it all."

"Bullshit," he says, craning Emily's head horizontal with the force of the gun. "I'm not fucking around. Give me whatever you've got, or I'm blasting this bitch's brains all over the park. It's your choice."

Emily rolls her eyes, and I sigh in defeat.

"Fine. I choose her. Take whatever you want." I throw a baggie of powder and a crumpled wad of cash on the ground, and he pushes her away with a triumphant sneer.

Collecting my treasures, he bears a mouth of brown teeth and rasps. "Congratulations, Perry Samson. Your test is complete."

"Yeah, yeah. Been that way for twenty years, bro."

"You can wake up now," he says.

I laugh. "Thanks but no thanks." Catching up with Emily, I wrap my arms around her, and as she nuzzles her face against my chest, I kiss the top of her head.

"Okay, baby. Let's burn down that rehab." She squeals in delight, and I smack her on the ass, adding, "But let's get really fucking high first."

2

She is the fire that devours buildings and the oxygen that nourishes it. She is the smoke that curls out of idiot doctors' skulls and the atlys that rewards our crimes as we sit among the rubble to wait for the police. And she's all mine.

It doesn't feel like two decades have passed since my family tried to put me in a shithole like this. And considering all the junk I've shot in the last twenty years, I should probably look like a mite-ravaged cornstalk with a polka-dotted sack, but I've never looked or felt better. It helps to have the most gorgeous woman in creation on your arm, of course; also a steady diet of atlys to numb the nagging truth that the body I'm tossing all over Baltimore isn't real. My real body is a sack of meat in a defunct lab in Antarctica, hooked to machines and monitors while I cavort in the fantasy-land Emily built for us.

I mean, it *has* to be, right? Otherwise I wouldn't be here. Sometimes I do wonder how the machines have been running this long, or why no one's found me. And most puzzling, how hasn't my dear intrusive sister, Nadine, wormed her way in to ruin my good time?

The blackened bones of the Starbright Rehab exhale a word that sounds like "Bear," and a knot rises in my throat.

Emily waves her hand in front of my face, and my eyes are wet when I blink back to reality.

"You were miles away, love. What were you thinking about?"

"Nothing."

"It's been a while since we had one of Jeremiah's test characters pop up. Is that what's worrying you?"

"No, not worrying. Just . . . " I push up from the charred floor and dust off my hands. Sirens scream from the distance, and we both lift our heads to the noise like it's a pie wafting a sweet aroma from a windowsill.

"Are you sure you're okay?" Emily asks, rubbing my back.

"Yeah. I'm just tired."

Her fingers tense, and I'm suddenly aware I haven't uttered that phrase in nearly twenty years.

"Or just really high," I say, and she squeezes my shoulder with a chuckle. "Maybe just a quick nap, and then we can beat up as many cops as you want."

"I want what you want," she says. "There's a car passing by the back alley in fifty-two seconds. Come on, let's get you home."

Emily extends her hand, but the moment our fingers touch, she vanishes into thin air.

The cinders of Starbright Rehab go cold, and an

inky shadow falls over me as the threat of approaching sirens strikes my chest the way it did when I was on the actual streets of Baltimore. I rarely think of the days when sirens sent me running, but they're sucking me into the past now, back into a shit existence with cops howling for my blood and family members heaping guilt on me so heavy what choice did I have but to stay face-down in the gutter?

No choice at all until Emily.

"Em?"

She's never disappeared before.

I spin around, panic glazing every inch of my skin. "Emily?"

I've never been alone here.

"Emily! Where are you!"

The police cars screech to a halt, painting me in blue and red light that makes every fiber of my musculature tremble in fear.

I tell myself I can't die here as a mess of police break into the building. As they aim their guns at me, I lift my hands and whisper, "I'm pretty sure I can't die here."

"Hands up, down on the ground!" a cop shouts as he steps out of the crowd.

"My hands *are* up."

"Don't talk back, motherfucker. Get down on the fucking ground."

I lower to my knees, hands over my head, but they keep shrieking for me to lift them higher while ordering me to put my face on the floor.

"I can't lay down without using my hands!"

"Try harder, motherfucker!"

I sigh. Being able to do whatever I want years for

on end has made me rusty when it comes to authority figures—not that I was ever all that submissive—and though I intend on following directions, I'm nowhere near strong enough to lower to my belly without using my hands. My non-existent abs give way as I lower, and I throw out my hands to catch me. They do, but only briefly thanks to the bullet that strikes my left shoulder. It jolts my body before I crash forward, my face slamming against the ashy floor as pain obliterates what remains of my buzz.

I wail as officers stream over me. They're shouting over each other, and I can't understand their orders, so they kick and punch me and there's so much blood pouring out of my arm I start thinking I actually *can* die here and probably will very fucking soon.

The wind shifts, and Emily is standing over me, watching the cops beat me to a pulp. I reach out, and one of the officers grabs two of my fingers. With a wet snap, he twists them backward, and splintered bone breaks through my flesh.

Emily giggles as I scream, her gaze distant. "There are lots of ways to show someone you love them. This Christmas, show them with surgery." She holds her hands like a model elegantly displaying a diamond ring and pulls an alligator grin I've never seen cross any of her faces before. She flickers, her expression alternating between extremes. But when a brutal scream seemingly erupts from every cell in her body, the force hits the police like a nuclear blast. It pulverizes them and sweeps their dust to the corners, clearing the room of everything but her and me.

The scream cleared my pain too, but not my injuries. My fingers are still broken, their meat exposed to air now polluted by pig dust, and blood's still pumping free from the bullet wound in my shoulder.

"Emily, what the fuck is going on? Look at me!"

"I know."

"Can you fix it?"

She bites her lip and shakes her head. "I don't think so."

"But you can fix everything. This is your program."

She's squeezed all the color out of her lip, yet her cheeks turn bright red when she says, "I saw you, Perry."

"Okay . . . "

"The *real* you. Out there."

My throat feels blistered when I swallow, and my voice comes out as a shaky creak. "In the lab?" I ask.

"No." Sinking to the floor, she weeps. Shuddering, she crawls to me. And glazed in cold sweat, she finally meets my eyes and says, "Baby, I need a hit real bad."

3

You know that feeling when you get so high you forget two of your fingers are useless flesh-sticks that smack the back of your hand every time you move? 'Cuz that's where I'm at right now. And the longer I stare at the disfigurement, the faster my buzz dies.

Emily is passed out, her head hanging off the bed and her clit purple as an overripe grape from her doozy of a dose. I'm about to load up another hit for myself when she springs up with sparkly tears running down her cheeks.

THE FIX

No, not sparkly. Drawing closer, I realize the rivers of tears look like the snowy noise you'd get on an ancient TV. And I can hear it, crackling and whispering from the wet streaks on her flesh, and speaking in broken sentences about deals on car washes, eyeglasses, and lunchtime liposuction.

She wipes the kinetic silver-white wetness from her cheeks, but it clings to her hands, and when she flicks her fingers, her tears stick to the wall . . . and spread to quarter-sized splotches of noise.

"What the hell is this?" I peer at one of the spots, but when a face forms in the teeming dots, I recoil violently and fall off the bed.

Emily crawls down beside me, but I retreat from her touch. "Perry, please forgive me," she wails. "I didn't know what was happening."

The splotches around us whisper, "Nothing says 'I'm Sorry' like the gift of a Mummy Facial," and a sickly purple shame bleeds across Emily's body.

"Please tell me you heard that too," I say, and she nods sadly. "Em, what the fuck is going on?"

"I thought they were dreams—at worst, glitches," she begins. "I never thought Jeremiah would do this to me, which was pretty stupid, I guess, because of course he would. He murdered me and digitized my soul. Why wouldn't he try to monetize it?"

"You're not making any sense." I sigh and grab an atlys vial from the bedside table. "Take a breath and get your shit together. I'm gonna shoot up."

"How? You can't even hold the needle."

I scoff but quickly realize she's right. My broken fingers aren't the only useless ones. More than half of my fingers have turned black, and three have softened so dramatically that when I try to grab the needle, they bend backward like overcooked carrots.

Though I feel nothing as they disconnect from my hand, watching them tumble like logs of wet shit to the carpet fills every cell in my body with queasy panic.

For the first time in twenty years, I vomit.

It seems to take forever, like my stomach's making up for lost time, because when I'm finally wiping brown mucus from my mouth, Emily is gone.

So is my right hand, my left ear, and a large portion of my shoulder, and when I look in the bathroom mirror, I realize my eyes are dotted with busted blood vessels that leak pink pus into my lashes. I can't cup water to wash the myriad fluids from my face, so I stand in the shower and let the pressure blast it away.

The water chips off more than gunk, though. My skin goes with it. After a few minutes I don't recognize the ghoul in the showerhead. Even at my lowest, when I was peeling myself out of gutters slick with rat shit, I never saw my reflection in Patterson piss puddles and wondered what monster had possessed me. The bloodshot eyes looking back were always mine, the scars and bruises my closest friends, and the cackling skull beneath threadbare flesh was always a comforting reminder that I still had support, even if just from my own bones.

But the skeleton leering back at me now can barely hold me up, let alone comfort me.

"Perry . . . "

I whip around to find Emily standing in the shower. Though the water still beating down doesn't affect her, my ravaged face shifts her expression from one shade of fear to another. Her skin changes color from the fright, but it changes texture too. It turns hard and scaly and cracks a bit when she speaks.

"I'm so sorry, Perry."

What remains of my left hand is numb, but I still try to touch her . . . and fail. My blackened fingers pass through her like smoke, her hazy composition briefly rippling apart before reassembling.

"Emily, please tell me what's happening. Don't leave me in the dark again."

"If it were up to me, I'd never leave. I love you, Perry, more than anything, but as it turns out, my love isn't stronger than Jeremiah's hate, even now." She lowers her head. "I was naive to think he would ever let me go."

"Em, the dude's been a corpsicle for twenty years. How the hell could he be doing this to us?"

"Because it hasn't been twenty years. It's been four months."

"What?!" My right knee gives out when I step toward her, and I fold into the tub like an oily sheet of pizza dough. She cries out and crouches at my side, her hands shaking in desperate desire to touch me. I can feel it pouring out of her, and for a moment I'm granted that atlys calm that comes after it casts you out into the universe to swirl and command and fuck to your heart's content. It's the calm of coming home, still high but re-anchored to your best friend . . . which Emily is. What I feel for her, it's more than love, more than addiction. She's home to me.

Her hands on my cheeks are walls with family portraits and uneven paint jobs done by people working for free beer. Her gaze is a blanket, wool, weighted, enveloping, a cocoon of warmth that shields me from the shower spray still ripping flesh from my back. Her kiss is a deadbolt keeping us safe from those who wouldn't understand the kingdom that depravity created in us. And her voice, always the loudest in the room, is a squirt bottle against the irritating worms of doubt that used to bore tunnels through my brain.

I whisper, "Four months?" and her head grows heavier with each nod.

Every cell in my rotten body tells me it can't be true. Even with the magic of the program, it has to have been longer than that.

"But I've changed," my sloughing skull swears. "I'm a better person."

"You are. Four months or four decades, it doesn't change anything." She swallows her voice so hard her answer comes out like a creaky door. "I'm sorry I didn't tell you sooner. I wanted you to feel like we had an eternity together. Honestly, I wanted to feel it too. I didn't want to say goodbye, even if I knew, realistically, biologically, there was no way it could last."

"Am I . . . dying?" I ask shakily.

"Yes."

Sorrow is a fist sporting heavy jewelry in my throat when I say, "Are *you* dying?"

"I'm . . . splitting. Thinning. Drowning."

"Jesus Fucking Christ. What does that mean?"

"It means I'm not me anymore, Perry. Not entirely. But I promise you, whatever happens from here, you got the real me, more than anyone else in my life or after. Everything I am is yours, no matter what you see when you get out of here."

"When I get out of here? Emily, this ain't rehab, this ain't jail. Look at me, I'm not going anywhere."

She nods. "I just wanted so badly for us to survive."

"So we will. We'll fight," I say, "the way we've fought pigs and fatcats and Patterson trash the last . . . however long. The way we've fought people who called themselves family, we fight whatever's trying to keep us apart."

She blushes. "You're talking about me like I'm atlys."

I tremble as I push up from the tub, but I feel like a god when she rises to meet my eyes. Even as skin rolls down my shin bones and hair runs tickling down my back, I feel like the most powerful man that ever was.

And I'm not even high.

"You saved me, Emily Carter, and now I'm going to save you."

With a strangely erotic pop, the bulbous cartilage that once comprised my nose goes loose and slips down my face, using my chin as a slide that projects it onto my foot.

I add, "If I can," and Emily smiles as she turns her focus from the lump of flesh to my skeletal face.

She kisses my cheek, and though I can't feel it, her lips look reddened by my oozing viscera. Her affection for me is unchanged. I guess she treats me like atlys too. But it's not physical, not even emotional. What we have is greater than any other bond in existence, and I'm not just giving it up. I fought hard as fuck for

Rennie, and our marriage wasn't a blip compared to this.

I need Emily. And I'll tear myself to sloppy shreds to be with her. Hey, all the more for my girl to love, right? All the more pieces for my virtual fuckbuddy to sew back together.

Her body is fading, but her voice is clear. "I'll find you, Perry. I promise I'll find you."

When she disappears, I'm little more than a puddle of bone and skin in the basin of our tub. A strange light shines down on me, and when it turns yellow, I remember what it means to feel real pain. I remember hunger and thirst and red wine shits. I remember that my mother is dead and that no one loves me out there.

I remember I don't exist.

4
(TWO MONTHS EARLIER)

She's been practicing her signature for days. Despite working as a doctor for the last decade, Marla Daye never signed off on a patient's treatment. She doesn't have a real degree or formal education; she doesn't even have a valid form of identification now that Doctor Carter's gone. Although, she supposes it wasn't exactly valid when he was alive either. When she was human, sure, but she hasn't been one of those strange soft creatures for a long time. The novelty of practicing her signature is the most human thing she's done in decades. It tickles her with familiarity, like she must've done this when she was a young girl, when her name was Jennifer Shore. Maybe she used tons of flourishes and flairs. Maybe she drew hearts instead of o's and a's. Maybe she did her capital letters in cursive, with all the unnecessary embellishments. Or maybe she was as clinical as her signature is now. A stiff M, a convex D, and a Y with a straight tail that underlines the entire boring mess.

"What do you think?" She lifts the paper, and Alan blinks in approval.

Or disapproval, depending on how she prefers to interpret it. Blinking is all he does now from the corner of the old Sunny Daye office in the rusted industrial district near the Natty Bo building, the electric logo of which long ago went blind.

Checking the clock, she jumps up from her chair and throws herself in front of the mirror. She didn't think much about her appearance when she was working with Doctor Carter, but now that she's in control of her life, running what's left of the business, and perfecting her signature, she's very particular about where to part her hair to make sure it falls right, or where her blouse's neckline rests so she's not being too sexy, even though her breasts are filled with circuits and software and there isn't anything sexual about her. She can't have sex, can't want sex, yet she's painfully aware of when someone wants it from her. She can't imagine it's worth all the fuss, though she acknowledges the fact that she probably did when she was human, and works through the thoughts as best she can while Alan blinks and blinks and blinks.

They could've left their LC bodies behind when Doctor Carter died, could've disappeared into the program and lived out whatever lives they wished. But after they saw the Samsons back to America with new versions of their matriarch and middle child, Alan wanted more time in the real world. He wanted the opportunity to live without ignorance, like an immortal among ants. Unfortunately, he was hit by a cab crossing the street a month later, and with Marla unable to take him to a hospital or LC technician, his damaged circuits eventually melted and seized, leaving him little more than a hunk of scrap she hauls around for sentimental reasons.

Or maybe it's in her programming to protect him.

She throws a blanket over Alan and wheels him into the closet. She says, "Love you," as she closes the door but doesn't mean it. Though she has more control and independent thought now, she wishes that particular veil was still over her eyes. She would rather walk the world in blind love than be forced to say empty words every day to a broken thing she never even knew.

Yes, it must be the programming. It always is.

When the idea to sell Emily Carter's soul popped into her head soon after Jeremiah's death, she swore it was hers. She had such excitement for it, such drive, and ambition. But it was never her idea, she knows that now. Carter hid the directive in her mind long ago: a chain of code set to run should he die unexpectedly. And with that command came a promise, poised to unlock the moment she signs off on his sister's dissemination. As horrible as Marla feels betraying the person who saved her from the doctor's malevolence, she knows the feeling won't last. Once the promise is fulfilled and her LC Intoxicant Block is removed, the only thing she'll feel is the soaring joy of shooting meth again . . . and again . . . and again.

THE FIX

A knock on the door spins her around so quickly her brain is temporarily consumed by the dizzying excitement of a life built on her own gumption. A slight shame blooms through her, hanging heavier and longer in her chest as she opens the door to Benjamin Diehl, the president of B-More Beautiful Cosmetic Surgery Associates.

He's a walking slab of alabaster, his curves and peaks as smooth as whipped butter. Even his voice, which is lower than she expected, is a smooth hollow howl, like someone blowing across the mouth of a wine bottle.

"Ms. Daye, it's a pleasure to finally meet you face to face." He shakes her hand, and she gestures for him to take a seat.

"The pleasure is mine. I appreciate you making the trip all the way here. I'm afraid I don't fly."

Can't fly, is what she means, except on Jeremiah's private plane. When Doctor Carter died, he took most of her access with him, and she's had to get creative. In the two months since the Sunny Daye Institute went belly-up, she's watched other women in positions of power, what they tolerate, what they don't, how they tailor their language and appearances to appeal to certain clients, and most of all, how they silence a man while making him feel like being quiet is in his best interest.

"So," she says, folding her hands on her knee, "How's our girl been working out for you?"

"Doctor Daye, we are absolutely in love with the model you sent us. I don't know if she's still in beta or what—"

"She's finished. She's perfect."

He lifts his hands in supplication. "No argument here. We find that our customers are loving what the Emily model provides for them. And her laissez-faire attitude and modern look is really appealing to our target demographic. Did you design her?"

Marla hears Alan blinking in the closet, a repetitive reminder that she can't lie. Luckily she's been practicing sidestepping the truth as much as her signature.

"To be frank, Mr. Diehl, we have Emily to thank for the effectiveness of her design. She's a real person and should be treated as such."

He smirks and taps his contoured nose. "Brilliant. The Azazian Technique, yes? The more you treat the AI like a human, the more human its responses will be."

"If you say so, Mr. Diehl." She crosses her legs, and his eyes narrow slightly as they slip down her body. "The truth is, Doctor Carter wouldn't permit anyone under his employ to treat his creations any other way. To him, Emily was very much alive. Sometimes I think he valued her more than his colleagues. And that's precisely why I must ensure his wishes are carried out in full. Emily is programmed to enjoy working. Having such a valuable creation hanging in limbo doesn't serve her or anyone else."

"Well, she'll be serving plenty at my facilities. She's perfect for the recovery room, and if her CPU is flexible—"

"It is."

"Then we'd love to have her train the new surgeons. Everyone needs more cosmetic work these days, and we simply can't keep up with the demand.

THE FIX

If Emily could be implemented in our cosmetology schools, we wouldn't need to waste as many resources training new recruits. We'd get to focus on body procurement instead, which can be the trickiest part, frankly." He tilts his head to one side as he adjusts his glasses. Due to his smooth, slippery skin, he needs to adjust them quite a bit. "However, a little birdie told me we're not the only ones you've been talking to about licensing."

"That's true. Doctor Carter was very specific in that regard. He wanted Emily to be his gift to the world."

"Except you're charging us an exorbitant sum, Doctor Daye. Gifts are usually free."

"What do you think the trial was, Mr. Diehl?"

He's trying to raise his eyebrows, but they barely move. They tremble awkwardly, and his lips go white from pursing them so hard.

"Is there a problem?" Marla asks, and Diehl's gaze ventures from her.

He scans the office for the first time. It's bare but not clean. It's empty yet filled with angst. And the longer he stares at the peeling screens around them, the more anxious Marla Daye becomes that he knows who—and what—she really is.

She leans forward, feeling like every circuit in her body is smiling slyly when she says, "What if I give you a free body?"

He reclines in his chair. "If you want some quid pro quo work, all you need to do is ask."

She laughs, tossing her hair and feeling her synthetic skin bloom hot with coquettish color. Fanning her face, she says, "No, it's not me. Though

Lord knows I could probably use a tuck or two. The body I'm talking to is a catatonic man with no family, no prospects, hardly any brain function. Machines are currently keeping him alive."

Mr. Diehl's eyes widen. "You want me to carve up a coma patient?"

"He doesn't have to be in a coma. I doubt anyone would kick up a fuss if those machines were to . . . malfunction. Hell, they're probably already on the brink of failure."

Diehl drums his chin, "Actually, operating on a catatonic might be a step in the right direction. Can you imagine? People that have been in comas for years, decades, who wake up to find their youth devoured by an elderly stranger . . . it must be heartbreaking for them. What if we could revolutionize the cosmetic coma industry by providing consistent restorative work to people whose families want them to feel every inch like their former selves when they awaken?"

The programming that tells Marla her synthetic stomach should be turning kicks into high gear, but she doesn't show it. It's one of the first things she learned watching women in power. They're extraordinarily good at hiding their nausea when facing off with male counterparts.

While synthetic bile burns her throat, she grins and claps her hands. "My goodness, what a novel thought! How on earth do you come up with such inventive ideas?"

Grinning as wide as his face will allow, he shrugs. "What can I say? It's a gift."

"So you're interested in the body? I'm afraid it will need quite a bit of . . . refurbishment."

THE FIX

His grin moistens, and his slimy lips smack as he digs his delicate baby-pink nails into his knees. "What kind of refurbishment?"

"Well . . . " She recrosses her legs, and his previously conspicuous gaze becomes blatant; his eyes run up and down her body, and he puffs his chest in excitement. "You see, Mr. Diehl, the boy you'd be getting is an atlys addict."

"The poor soul," he says with unconvincing sympathy.

"Yes. It's a sad story all around. I'm afraid he's never known true happiness. Even now, in his dreams, I fear he's being tortured."

It isn't a lie exactly, though she suspects it might not be completely true. She's seen how Perry Samson's body has broken down outside the program, and she's feared a similar deconstruction is happening inside, especially with Emily's absences.

She wonders if he's even noticed. The last time Marla was at the Sunny Daye Institute, she discovered Emily had altered the way time passed for her and Perry. How she managed it—or anything inside the program—Marla didn't care; just that the alteration made it far easier for her to steal Emily's consciousness for use outside the digital junkie paradise.

But he'll notice soon, she wagers. Once her face and voice are pumping out of every advert screen and instructional video across the world, it will be impossible for even the most strung-out addict to ignore her frequent disappearances.

"I'll take him." Mr. Diehl stands, extending his hand down at her, but she rises to meet him and looks him in the eyes before shaking it.

"Excellent. I take it you have the cash I requested? I hate banks."

His nose doesn't crinkle when he scrunches it, which seems more unnatural to Marla than the fleshy circuitry that composes her body and mind. With a creaseless smile, he reaches into his suit jacket and removes an envelope nearly bursting with colorful bills.

"Where is he?" he asks.

"Antarctica. And it's your responsibility to transport him. Once my deals are done, I'm out of the business forever."

"Is that so? And what does a business-savvy woman like you intend on doing with the rest of her life?"

"Drugs, Mr. Diehl. Hardcore drugs until this body dies."

He laughs as he hands over the money, and Marla signs the papers.

5

Reality smells like shit and fire. It's loud as fuck too. Or maybe it's every cell in my body screaming with an agony I haven't felt in all my years shooting and carving and infecting myself on the streets.

I moan, someone yelps, and I feel every second of the twenty years I lived when my eyes open. I swear to fuck they creak like the doors of a haunted house, and whatever ghost leaks out scares the shit out of the young surgeon leaning over me. She backpedals and crashes into a mobile steel table, sending instruments flying across the room, but I can't help focusing on one instrument in particular. The needle protruding from my right cheek wobbles as I lift my head and stare at the woman pressed against the opposite wall. She pulls down her surgical mask, her jaw limp as my right arm when I try to lift it.

My voice is strangely muffled when I ask where I am, so I think I'm wearing a mask too, but when I paw my face, there's nothing to pull down. There are, however, more lumps than I remember, and my skin feels different from one inch to the next. With trembling fingers, I yank the syringe out of my cheek and squint at the milky gel that blooms from the tip. Touching the injection site on my face also squirts goo, and I shudder when the blood-tinged glob hits my knee.

"It's okay. It's just a Restylane-Radiesse compound," the woman says like I should know what the fuck that is.

I throw the syringe, and it smashes on the wall beside her head, sending her screaming from the room. I yell for Emily, but I can barely understand myself. There's something wrong with my mouth. Throwing back the bedsheets, I see there's something wrong with a lot of me. My legs look bone thin from above, but twisting one reveals a bulging calf barely contained by a multitude of skin grafts. I poke the mass, and it moves freely beneath the skin, over my calf muscle, and up to my knee. It doesn't hurt exactly, but it sure as shit doesn't feel good.

Movement is also strange. While I'm able to move most of my body, my muscles don't react as quickly as they used to, like my brain's commands need translation before my limbs understand. I sluggishly remove the tubes and wires from my limp arm, grit my teeth as I pull the catheter out of my dick, and swing my disfigured legs off the edge. I'm surprised they support me as well as they do, even if it takes a full minute of a crouched shuffle for me to reach the bathroom less than ten feet away.

And all the while, a commotion grows louder in the hall. Because of me, I assume, which is why I lock the door and wedge the handle of a toilet brush underneath before shoving my ugly mug in front of the mirror.

"Sheeshuzphuck."

My top lip is three times larger than the bottom and horribly uneven. The right side encroaches so badly on my bottom lip that I think they might be sewn together. They bust apart after I throw water on my face—which I'm thankfully able to do one-handed outside of the program—and try speaking again.

"Jesusfuck."

Better. But water doesn't wash away the lumps of silicone and filler dotting my face, or the fact that my bone structure is significantly different thanks to cheek and chin implants.

The door to the hospital room opens with a bang, and I nearly jump out of my patchwork skin. Someone knocks furiously on the door as I shrink back, unable to do much else.

"Mr. Doe, are you in there? Are you all right?"

"All right?! No, I'm not fucking all right! You fucking mutilated me!"

"Just calm down and come out so we can discuss this rationally."

"Fuck you! Where's Emily?"

THE FIX

"Mr. Doe, please."

"That's not my name," I hiss. "EMILY, WHERE ARE YOU!"

The walls around me flash and her face appears in the glass, bright silver and wearing that strange grin again.

"Emily!" I throw myself at the wall, and she giggles.

"Oh my, someone's affectionate in the morning, huh?"

"Thank fuck, Emily. Where the hell are we?"

"B-More Beautiful, silly! And I must say our talented staff has done an amazing job on your reconstruction. You were in terrible shape when you came to us."

"At least it was *my* shape," I say, looking into the mirror. "There's nothing left of me. I don't know who that person is."

"Isn't that the point, Mr. Doe?"

I wince as I turn back to her, and she bats silver eyelashes with an innocence that knots my stomach.

"Emily . . . "

"Yes, Mr. Doe?"

"It's Perry."

"Oh, I apologize. It's nice to meet you, Perry."

She smiles at me, and it hurts like a motherfucker. Worse than an infected nutsack, or seeing my ex-wife fucking someone else. Worse than burying my big brother, or realizing my family would rather love a teetotal robot version of me than the addict I'll always be.

My lungs empty. Holy shit, that's it. My LC. It shares Emily's programming; maybe it knows a way to restore her memory.

The door shakes with knocking again. "Mr. Doe, let us help you. What can we do?"

Swallowing hard, bathed in the light of Emily's empty joy, I say as clearly as possible, "Bring me Perry Samson."

6

I don't speak until I hear my voice on the other side of the bathroom door.

"Hey," it says, knocking. "Uh, you wanted to see me?"

Emily disappeared hours ago—she had more important things to do than console a mutilated stranger—and frankly I'm happy as fuck. I can live with not recognizing myself, but I'm not sure I can live with her not recognizing me.

Crouched on the floor, I whisper, "Perry?"

"Yeah I'm Perry," he replies, annoyed. "What do you want?"

"You didn't bring her, did you?"

"Bring who?"

"Nadine."

"How—" He lowers his voice and draws closer to the floor. "No, I didn't bring her. And I had a hell of a time getting her off my back today, so you better tell me who the hell you are right now."

"You might not believe it when you see me, but . . . " I sigh. "I'm *YOU*."

In one swift motion, he jumps up and grips the doorknob. I turn the lock and he flies into the bathroom, quickly shutting the door behind him.

Physically, he looks exactly like me, but the styling

THE FIX

is way off. Nadine's doing, I imagine. His hair is buzzed, and he has a tidy goatee that makes me wanna punch him in the face. If my muscles weren't so slow to react, I might have done just that. But by the time my fingers curl to a fist, I'm focusing on the *Plasma Avenue* logo on his polo shirt, wondering if it's the TV store or the blood bank.

We stare at each other like long-lost brothers. We stare at each other like complete strangers. We stare at each other like the man standing opposite is our only way of returning to the men we used to be. And we embrace each other like we have no other choice.

I can't remember the last time I held another man this tight or for this long, and I sure as fuck don't think I've ever cried in another man's arms. On my knees in front of a cock, sure, but not like this. And when my LC cradles my face, he does so with a tenderness I don't think I've felt since I was a little kid.

"What the fuck did they do to you?" he asks.

I pinch his polo shirt. "I was gonna ask you the same thing."

"It's been hell, Perry. Pure fucking hell. Except there's no fucking! I can say 'fucking,' but I can't actually fuck anyone." He grabs the collar of my hospital gown. "You gotta get me out of this body. Put me in the big program. Shit, put me back to sleep. I don't care as long as I'm out of this repetitive shit-ass quo existence."

I empathize with the poor pile of circuits wearing my old face, but now that I've been clean for over four months, I'm strangely focused on self-preservation. Or maybe I'm just a selfish fuck, even when I'm sober.

"Everything okay in there?" someone asks, jiggling the knob.

"He's threatening to kill himself," LC Perry replies. "Don't try to come in here. I'm recording everything." Crinkling his nose at me, he says, "So how do we do this?"

"Fuck, I thought you would know!"

He shakes his head.

"That's okay, we can figure this out. Emily's in everything—in you, in these walls—so if we can get her to remember us, then she can put us both back in the program."

"So where's Emily?"

With a chirp, her face appears on the wall, and she joyfully greets the new person in the bathroom before her expression shrinks to a puzzled point. "You seem strange to me," she says, focusing on the LC. "What are you?"

"I'm the same thing as you," he says, "and I want to be where you are."

She squints, her doubt filling the entire wall. "That's impossible. I'm electricity, sir. I'm wires and webs. You're just flesh."

It's the first time I've seen my LC smile. His lips peel back from his teeth, and with a gleeful snarl, he closes them on his middle finger and drags them from knuckle to tip, shredding the skin in rubbery ribbons. Blood spills from the wounds, but that's not all. Creamy yellow goo drips from his finger too, along with metallic slivers coated in crystalline gel.

She shrinks in shock, her entire body visible as the Liberated Citizen approaches the screen.

"What are you doing?" she demands.

THE FIX

He punches the wall, and she shouts for him to stop. The voice comes from all sides—outside the bathroom too—and the attempts to break down the door increase significantly. But he doesn't stop. He punches and kicks and pulls at the screen's circuitry until it's casting sparks at our feet.

She shrieks like he's killing her, but the deeper he goes, the more he looks like he knows what he's doing, so I let him. I let him create a hole in her, black and fiery, while she begs for an explanation for why he's doing this.

I tell myself she isn't real, not like this. She's split and faded. She's drowning in servitude, and this is a rescue mission. But when the LC's shredded circuits lock with hers, and smoke and sparks fill the spaces between us, Emily Carter looks at me with a familiarity even I couldn't muster in the mirror, and she remembers. It doesn't last long, but I see it, feel it, in the seconds before a massive shock propels the LC across the room.

He smacks the toilet and crumples on the floor, moaning.

"I'm sorry I had to do that," the woman on the wall says blankly.

She looks at me like a stranger again. So I'm grateful as fuck that the person staring out the eyes of my Liberated Citizen doesn't. My synthetic body rises, groaning, and its eyes slowly widen as it approaches me in shock.

"Perry? Holy shit, Perry, is that you? What happened to your face?"

"*Emily*?" I ask doubtfully, and she snorts.

"Of course it's me. Who else would it be?"

I take her by the shoulders and turn her to the mirror, where she freezes . . . then bursts into laughter. Raising one eyebrow, she says, "Kinky."

Funny. I don't recall being able to raise just one eyebrow. She's already doing better with my body than I did.

The people outside are howling to get in. They're going to beat down the door. They say Nadine Samson is on her way up, and my God, it's all so old and tired.

I can't go back to all that noise and invasion. I can't go back to pretentious strangers thinking they know what's best for me, especially when those strangers are family. I need to get away, back inside, with her.

Emily's face goes gray, and she grabs her stomach. "Something's wrong. There's another LC in here. We can't both stay."

"That's fine. We can all go back to the program. This place can carve me to hell as long as they keep me alive. We can have another hundred years together, Em."

"Perry, the program is dead. There's nowhere to go."

"Then you switch."

"What?"

"You and the guy who's been playing me. He said he wanted out. Any way out."

"And I stay in this body? Would you really want me like this?" She does a twirl that would've looked like someone tossing chicken bones for black magic had I done it, but somehow she makes it work.

"Will it be fucked up? Yes. Do I wish things were different? Of course I do. Will making love to a digital woman living in a robotic replica of my body—before my unfortunate run-in with a team of cosmetic surgeons—unlock a secret fetish that's been lurking in my subconscious forever? Yeah, probably. But there's no other digital woman living in a pre-surgery robot replica of me that I'd rather do it with."

Emily laughs, and I swear to God, even in my voice, it sounds just like her laugh. I had twenty goddamn years with that laugh, I'd know it anywhere. I don't care what she actually looks or sounds like. That's my girl.

I pull her in like the finest shot of raw atlys ever cooked—into my arms, into my blood, into whatever biological circuitry that keeps me tethered to a life I've tried hard as hell to escape. If I can't go back, I need her as close as possible.

Out of the garbled voices beyond the door, one suddenly rises like the spikes on Patterson Park benches that spring up after an hour of non-activity. They're supposed to dissuade homelessness, but they really just encourage tetanus. Nadine's voice pierces me, even propels me backward onto the toilet, where I cover my ears and whimper.

"Fucking Nadine. I can't believe it. She's gonna be so pissed at me."

"I'm pretty sure she's gonna be pissed at me," Emily says. "I'll be the only Perry Samson that exists anymore, remember?" She chuckles, but the sound I love more than any other abruptly shifts into a guttural moan. She wilts to the floor before I can catch her, her head smacking the sink before landing hard on the tile.

I rush to her, and she opens her eyes wearily.

"I can't do it, Perry. I'm too weak."

"Please. You have to try."

Nadine calls my name, and one of the hinges pops off the door. "Just hold on," my sister says. "Don't do anything stupid."

Gritting my teeth, I drag the LC to the wall and lean the chewed hand against the broken screen.

"What are you doing?" Emily whimpers.

"I'll see you later, okay?"

"What?"

"I'll find you."

"Perry—"

"And when I do, you and I are going to get so fucking high, you'll think we never left the program."

"But I can't . . . "

"We're going to get through this, Em. We just gotta work fast."

"No, I mean getting high. LCs can't—"

I run my tongue over my bulbous lips, lift her hand to the sparking circuits, and when I force the mechanics to collide, Emily and I collide too.

It's the Fourth of July when I kiss her, but it's also Thanksgiving: sparks and heat and burnt meat assaulting me from all sides.

When the door crashes in on us, we separate . . . slowly . . . our melted mouths tangled like taffy as we fall apart. Nadine barely gives me a side-eye as she sits beside her favorite brother.

"Oh God, Bear, what are you doing here? Why are you doing this to me?"

A man in a suit sits beside her and examines the LC's face. "We can fix this, Ms. Samson, I promise you."

THE FIX

"Why did you even call him here?" she snaps at him. "Was it about drugs?" Pointing at me, she adds, "Is that hideous thing his dealer?"

My words are muffled by the silicone oozing from my lips, but when I whisper, "I'll find you," my little sister appears to understand me. She looks over her shoulder and narrows her eyes.

"No, you won't," she says. "We've come too far. You won't poison us again."

I can't tell if she recognizes me or really thinks I'm out to corrupt her perfect little robot puppy, but either way, she's one hundred percent wrong. If I have to be back in this grub-infested asshole called reality, I'm going to poison the shit out of it. And then, God willing, when I find Emily, I'm going to fuck the shit out of myself.

ACKNOWLEDGEMENTS

It's not easy being a man married to a woman who spends a year yammering about shooting drugs into her testicles and selling vagina meat to rich people. But Dave McHugh does it with a grace that constantly reminds me just how lucky I am. From a drunken, baby-killing Arthur Pendragon, chainsaw massacres, asylum barbarism, and Picoepistemology to sassy strippers, mutilated Underworld travel companions, and first periods, I've thrown a lifetime's worth of fiction at Dave in only six years.

Yet he stays. He smiles. He says, "I'm so proud of you" every day—often adding, "Could you please not talk about that while I'm eating?"

Thank you, Dave, for keeping me sane when I have maddening deadlines, feeding when I write through breakfast and lunch, and ensuring that I remain the happiest writer chick to ever write unhappy fiction.

I'd also like to acknowledge my best friend, Jenny Rigiel, without whom several sections of this story wouldn't exist. Not only did she provide the love and support any author needs to stay afloat, she let me get into the Perry Samson mindset before she took me on a tour of Patterson Park. I substituted atlys for a bottle of champagne then followed her around, occasionally lying down and taking pictures from his point of view, and learning about the ins and outs of the park. Jenny breathed a life into the story that hadn't been there when I started, and I'm eternally grateful for that, as well as her continued support over the past decade.

ABOUT THE AUTHOR

Jessica McHugh is a novelist and internationally produced playwright running amok in the fields of horror, sci-fi, young adult, and wherever else her peculiar mind leads. She's had twenty-three books published in eleven years, including her bizarro romp, *The Green Kangaroos,* her Post Mortem Press bestseller, *Rabbits in the Garden,* and her YA series, *The Darla Decker Diaries.* More information on her published and forthcoming fiction can be found at JessicaMcHughBooks.com.

IF YOU ENJOYED *THE GREEN KANGAROOS,* DON'T PASS UP ON THESE OTHER TITLES FROM PERPETUAL MOTION MACHINE . . .

THE TRAIN DERAILS IN BOSTON
BY JESSICA MCHUGH

ISBN: 978-1-943720-06-4

$14.95

CHERRYWOOD LODGE IS HAUNTED, AND THANK FUCK FOR ITS GHOSTS . . . Rebecca Malone has problems. Not just the alcohol. Not just her husband's inane attempts at writing a bestselling novel, their teenage daughter's promiscuity, or her certifiable mother. Not even her lover, who wants to take her husband's place in Cherrywood Lodge, the famous estate she now calls home. Her biggest issues start the moment she discovers a chest of ancient mahjong tiles in the basement of her new house, causing her life to spin out of control with hallucinations, sexual deviances, and grisly murders. Is the mahjong game haunted? Or are Rebecca's problems part of a different game, started before she was born?

THE WRITHING SKIES
BY BETTY ROCKSTEADY

ISBN: 978-1-943720-32-3

$12.95

THE SKY IS HUNGRY

Glowing lights and figures in tattered robes force Sarah from her apartment. Outside, phosphorescent creatures infiltrate her every orifice. They want to know everything, especially the things she would rather forget.

Featuring 20 black and white illustrations.

INVASION OF THE WEIRDOS
BY ANDREW HILBERT
ISBN: 978-1-943720-20-0
$16.95

After getting kicked out of his anarchist art collective for defending McDonald's, Ephraim develops an idea to create a robot/vending machine with the ability to hug children. He is no roboticist, but through dumb luck manages to hook up with a genius—a like-minded individual who also happens to be the last living Neanderthal. Meanwhile, a former personal assassin for a former president is fired from the CIA for sexual misconduct with a couple of blow-up dolls. He becomes determined to return to the government's good graces by infiltrating Ephraim's anarchist art collective in the hopes that they are actually terrorists. What follows is a bizarre, psychedelic journey that could only take place in the heart of Austin, Texas.

THE PERPETUAL MOTION MACHINE CATALOG

Baby Powder and Other Terrifying Substances |
John C. Foster | Story Collection

Bleed | Various Authors | Anthology

Bone Saw | Patrick Lacey | Novel

Born in Blood Vol. 1 | Geroge Daniel Lea | Story Collection

Crabtown, USA:Essays & Observations |
Rafael Alvarez | Essays

Dead Men | John Foster | Novel

*Destroying the Tangible Issue of Reality; or, Searching
for Andy Kaufmann* | T. Fox Dunham | Novel

The Detained | Kristopher Triana | Novella

The Eight Eues That Watch You Die | W. P. Johnson |
Short Story Collection

Gods on the Lam | Christopher David Rosales | Novel

Gory Hole | Craig Wallwork | Story Collection

The Green Kangaroos | Jessica McHugh | Novel

Invasion of the Weirdos | Andrew Hilbert | Novel

Last Dance in Phoenix | Kurt Reichenbaugh | Novel

Like Jagged Teeth | Betty Rocksteady | Novella

Live On No Evil | Jeremiah Israel | Novel

Long Distance Drunks: a Tribute to Charles Bukowski | Various Authors | Anthology

Lost Films | Various Authors | Anthology

Lost Signals | Various Authors | Anthology

Mojo Rising | Bob Pastorella | Novella

Night Roads | John Foster | Novel

Quizzleboon | John Oliver Hodges | Novel

The Perpetual Motion Club | Sue Lange | Novel

The Ritalin Orgy | Matthew Dexter | Novel

The Ruin Season | Kristopher Triana | Novel

So it Goes: a Tribute to Kurt Vonnegut | Various Authors | Anthology

Speculations | Joe McKinney | Story Collection

Stealing Propeller Hats from the Dead | David James Keaton | Story Collection

Tales from the Holy Land | Rafael Alvarez | Story Collection

Tales from the Crust | Various Authors | Anthology

The Nightly Disease | Max Booth III | Novel

The Tears of Isis | James Dorr | Story Collection

The Train Derails in Boston | Jessica McHugh | Novel

The Writhing Skies | Betty Rocksteady | Novella

Time Eaters | Jay Wilburn | Novel

Perpetual Motion Machine Publishing

Patreon:
www.patreon.com/pmmpublishing

Website:
www.PerpetualPublishing.com

Facebook:
www.facebook.com/PerpetualPublishing

Twitter:
@PMMPublishing

Newsletter:
www.PMMPNews.com

Email Us:
Contact@PerpetualPublishing.com